FRACTURED

Living on the Edge, Book 2

Alan Van Ormer

Winged Publications

ISBN: 978-1-956654-31-8

Charity

Hopefully you'll enjoy this book.

It was wonderful working on it.

Alan VanDine

Chapter 1

Myles Cason cuddled his wife, Willow, in his arms. An explosion a few minutes earlier had rocked their wedding ceremony, and not in a good way. He could smell the smoke, and his eyes were watering from the burning sensation. In addition, his ears were still ringing. At the least, at the best, she was still alive, but where were the others?

He frantically surveyed the building. "Brielle, where are you?" Please, Lord, let her be okay. I just met my daughter.

"Right here, Dad. I'm okay. I'm searching for Olivia." The seventeen-year-old had only been living with him since November. The other seventeen-year-old, Olivia, was Willow's sister and had been living with them since October.

"I'm taking Willow to a medic, but I'll return to help you find her." Myles gently carried Willow out of what had been an old railroad depot along the Missouri River in the River Valley community in South Dakota. People screamed through the smoke, crying for their loved ones after two separate blasts had rocked the historical building.

He turned toward Willow's shaky voice. "Myles, there is something I need to tell you."

"Shh. Keep your strength. I'm taking you somewhere to make sure you're okay."

The two headed in the direction of sirens, arriving at a bench where the injured waited for EMT crews to arrive. The sheriff's department and other emergency personnel, along with community members sifted through the rubble searching for survivors.

Myles gazed down at Willow. “What is it, Baby?”

“It was supposed to be good news. I may be pregnant with our baby. I’ll know in a week or so for sure.”

“Wow, that’s wonderful.”

“You’re not mad that I didn’t tell you about it sooner?”

“No. What happened?”

Willow rolled her eyes and offered a weak smile. “You know what happened. It was our first night in the snow along the campfire. My gut reaction is it happened that night. But I wanted to talk to Brielle first before I told you.”

“Brielle?”

“It was important to me that she was okay with her father having another child in his life. She missed the first sixteen years of life with you. It isn’t fair that she would have to share another child with you. Brielle told me it was okay because you loved me.”

“I do love you.” Myles did his best to wipe blood away from her lips. “Hang on. We have our whole life ahead of us. You’re a strong woman.”

The EMTs finally arrived. One ran over to Willow. “I’m not sure what’s wrong with her. She just spit up some blood.”

“Don’t worry, we’ll take care of her. We’ll take her to the hospital.”

Brielle raced over to Myles with tears in her eyes. “I can’t find Olivia anywhere.”

“Okay, you go with Willow. I’ll search for her.”

Brielle climbed into the back of the ambulance. The ambulance’s siren screeched as it sped toward the hospital ten minutes along the Missouri River. Myles ran into The Depot. The first person he saw was Jacie Tuthill, the wife of the River Valley School District principal. She tried to lift her body off the ground but struggled. Myles bent down and grabbed underneath her arms.

“Where’s that no-good husband of mine? Right before the first boom and right as the final marriage vows were uttered, he raced out of the building saying he had to use the bathroom.”

Both turned at Tuthill’s voice. “Dear, here let me help you. I’ll take it from here, Myles. Thank you.”

Myles dashed toward the front of the building where Olivia had been the last time he saw her. He heard moaning. Walter

Crocket, his good friend, was under a slab that had fallen from the walls. "Here I got you, Walter."

He smiled weakly. "I was fortunate."

Myles and another man removed the slab that pinned him. "Hey, you're a cancer survivor. We'll find you some help," the other man said. Walter peered up at Myles. "Olivia's over there in that corner holding a boy."

"Thank you," Myles said hurrying that way. He finally found Olivia. She stared straight ahead. The principal's son, Joshua Tuthill, was in her arms. Myles squatted to check his pulse. The boy was dead. He reached over for Olivia. "Come on, we have to get you out of here."

She studied him. "Is Willow okay? Is my sister okay?"

"Willow's going to be fine. She's at the hospital now with Brielle." Myles scooped Olivia up off the ground.

She shivered. "Please hold me. I'm so cold."

"Wrap your arms around my neck."

Olivia buried her head on his chest. He walked slowly out of the building. "Olivia, keep talking to me."

"Willow is lucky. She's found someone who loves her, and I thought I had too. I just bring problems to everyone. The first time I saw you, you probably know what I wanted. That's what my mother and father taught me, and they taught Willow the same thing. We need to sleep with men to get what we want." She glanced up at him. "That's screwed up, right?"

"We'll take care of you. You're going to be okay. You just saw something horrific."

"It wasn't horrible. Trevor didn't suffer. He shielded me from the piece of slab that fell and killed him instantly. I moved it and held him."

Myles wouldn't tell her it wasn't Trevor she supported because he was still missing. She held the principal's son.

Tears streamed down her face. "I tried so hard to save him, but I couldn't. Just like I couldn't save myself from the boys who slept with me. It was an awful feeling having a boy I didn't like all over me. It's what I deserve because I'm a Konnor. You know Willow felt that way for the longest time until she met you. She has not even considered another guy since she first saw your blue eyes. Willow loves you that much. And I'm glad. At least one of us will be happy." Olivia closed her eyes.

"No, Olivia, you have to stay awake." Myles shook her. The EMT hurried toward him. "She's in shock."

"We'll take her. Is she your daughter?"

"My wife's sister."

"We'll get her to the hospital."

Myles crawled into the back of the ambulance, and it raced toward the hospital. Myles found Brielle sitting on a chair in the waiting room. She ran over to him and put her arms around him. "Is Olivia okay?"

"I don't know, sweetheart. She's in shock. She saw Joshua Tuthill die in front of her."

"Oh my. Has anyone found Trevor? Devin?"

"I don't know. How's Willow?"

"They haven't said. Just told me to wait out here."

Myles took a seat next to her peered at his daughter. "This isn't what I quite expected for my wedding."

"Who would do something like this? Kill all those innocent people and possibly the two people we love most in the world?"

"They'll be okay."

"How do you know? How could you possibly know that, Dad?" Brielle started shaking. Myles reached over and held her tight. "The two women are strong. Look at what you've all gone through." He wiped away Brielle's tears. "Willow thinks she is going to have a child. Our child."

The comment brought a smile to Brielle. "Willow was so worried about it because of me. She didn't want to put another child before me because you missed the first sixteen years of my life. Right there I knew she was the woman for you. She cares about others before herself. No one in my world, other than you, has done that. Willow wants so badly to have your child, but she put me first. I know she became a mother when you two spent all night in the snow on your engagement night."

Myles laughed. "Okay, how do you know that?"

"Simple, Father. Willow told me she planned to go out and try to get rid of your heartache. At seventeen, I know what that means."

Myles blushed. "Embarrassing."

"She loves you."

Myles glanced toward the emergency room. "I remember that Saturday morning I saw her walk into the volleyball gym before your match. Our eyes met and didn't drop for what seemed like forever but was only a second or two. I knew that woman with those sparkling hazel eyes and dark mascara on her eyelids and her beautiful dress would be who I wanted to spend the rest of my life with. My next thought was that would never happen because of who I was."

Brielle grabbed her father's hands. "When she waited to walk down the aisle to marry you, I asked her if she was nervous. She said no, she had waited for you her whole life. Her issue was whether to take all the makeup off because then you might not find her attractive. I added those words. I told her you loved her no matter what."

"You're correct. All that goop was never about her. It was all about young girls like yourself who tried to be someone they weren't just to impress a boy or to be part of a group. I could never understand why you didn't fit into that crowd."

"Why? I saw my birth mother wear it all the time. It didn't make her a better person. I do like to wear it but only for special occasions like yesterday. There will be other times."

"Got that right."

Both turned when the doctor came out of the examination room and jumped up. "Doctor?" Myles started.

The doctor lifted his hand. "Calm down. Your wife is going to be just fine."

"And Olivia?"

"She's physically okay. But mentally, she'll take time. It was a major trauma seeing a boy die like she did. They both should stay here overnight. You two need to get some rest. I'll let you know if anything changes."

"Can we see them?"

"Let them both rest. It's been tough on them. With sleep, Willow will be fine. Now Olivia could be another story. It may take more time."

"Thanks, Doctor."

The doctor glanced at Myles. "Myles, your wife said something about your baby. Fortunately, she isn't pregnant."

"How is that fortunate?"

"The trauma would have killed the baby." He hurried away.

Myles turned toward his daughter and blew out a breath. "Let's have some breakfast and head to school. It'll keep us occupied."

"Dad, school is out for Christmas break."

"Yeah, right. I do have to check on some things, though."

She took his hand. "Are you okay about Willow not having a baby?"

Myles smiled. "I'm glad she's okay. If we have a child, it'll be great. And I'll always have you."

The two headed into the school to Myles's classroom. He grabbed his textbooks to make some lesson plans along with notes for upcoming basketball practices and games. Then he sent out announcements that practices would be halted until next week because of what happened. The next game wasn't until January tenth.

Miss Roberts knocked on the door and approached. "May I?" she said, lifting her arms.

"Please do," Myles said.

She hugged him tight. "I'm so sorry. I had planned to attend the wedding, but Isaac suggested I not go. I'm glad I didn't."

"Isaac?" Myles questioned.

"Isaac Reynolds. He and I have been dating for the past several weeks. And wow, is he worth it." She smiled widely and hurried out of his room.

Myles and Brielle eyed each other. "She's a piece of work," Myles said.

Brielle laughed. "Dad, you told us to be kind to people. And she's one of your coworkers. But yep, I agree. A piece of work."

~

All practices were called off for the week because of the tragedy. Several students had died in the explosion. Along with Joshua Tuthill was one of Joshua's best friends, Robert Simpson. Three other students—Devin Bush, Brody Davis, and Trevor Reynolds were still missing. There was so much debris scattered everywhere making it hard to account for everyone.

Myles, several teachers, and students joined emergency crews digging through the rubble. On Sunday, one of the boys founds Devin. He was unconscious but fortunate because a falling wall barely missed his head. Debris had hit him knocking him out.

After Myles and others moved the cement wall away, emergency crews pulled Brody out of the debris. He was alive and no broken bones. Gavin and Lydia Tuthill were not as fortunate. Both had been crushed by the debris. Brody sat down next to Lydia, tears rolling down his eyes.

Myles helped him up.

"She's dead. The first girl who ever liked me."

"I know, son. You need to be checked over."

After accounting for everyone who attended, thirteen people were dead and twenty-seven wounded. The F.B.I. had been called in immediately, and in collaboration with the local sheriff's department, they began the investigation of what happened. Still no Trevor Reynolds.

Myles answered his cell phone.

"Dad, Mom is awake. She's okay and can talk. Olivia is much better but seems depressed. I just wanted to give you an update."

"How about you, Bri? How are you doing?"

"I'm hanging in there. Yourself?"

"I'm okay. We found Devin and he's fine. It's surprising that a wall fell down and missed him."

"Wow."

"He's on his way to the hospital. Brody is alive also. Freaked out because he saw Lydia die. No Trevor Reynolds yet. Sad news—both Gavin and Lydia Tuthill weren't so fortunate. They didn't make it. Please keep that to yourself until their parents are notified."

"Will do. I'll see you soon. And I love you."

"Love you, too, Bri." Myles had just clicked off his cell phone when he heard his name called. "Yes, right here."

"Myles, I'm Lynus Throckmorton with the F.B.I." He stuck out his hand. Myles grabbed it and shook it.

"What can I do for you, Mr. Throckmorton?"

"Please call me Lynus. Your secret contact has asked that you help us with this investigation."

Myles stared at him. "Secret contact? I have no idea what you're talking about."

Lynus smiled. He dialed a number and handed his phone to Myles.

"Myles Cason, code name Wolf. The president is tired of you balking. He wants you to solve this case and return to Washington, D.C. In addition, your wife will be managing all legalities in this case. You're in charge of the case."

"I have no idea who you're talking about." He handed the phone back to Throckmorton who smiled at him.

"I'm glad you're with us, Wolf."

"It's Myles. Like I told the man on the phone, I have no idea who you're talking about." Myles hurried away to help others in The Depot.

~

Lynus peered at Sheriff Jack Watkins who shrugged.

The sheriff took a deep breath. "Mr. Throckmorton, who do you have with you?"

"A computer expert and two field operatives."

"Okay, we'll meet in ten minutes at the River Valley Bar and Grill. It's a couple blocks down on Main Street."

He sighed. "I thought for sure Myles Cason was the person the U.S. Government calls the Wolf."

The sheriff shrugged. "I wouldn't know anything about the man. He's new to the River Valley area." He frowned at the man. "Mr. Throckmorton, I understand you work with the F.B.I., but let's make one thing clear. This is my county. I know these people and you'll need their help to solve this case."

"I understand that, Sheriff. It's just that the Wolf is authentic. And no one knows who he is."

The sheriff surveyed The Depot. "What's so important about this so-called 'Wolf'?"

"Well, sir, he's gone into places that no one else would dream about and come back out alive. And he's the president's so-called go-to man when things get tough. Sort of an enigma."

"Then it couldn't be Myles Cason. He's just a social studies teacher and coach."

"Sheriff, we had better head over to the bar and grill."

Ten minutes later everyone involved in the investigation was there, including five people from the sheriff's department and several firefighters.

Throckmorton stepped to the front of the crowd. "My name is Lynus Throckmorton and work with the F.B.I. I've been assigned to find out what has happened here. And we will find out what happened. That's a guarantee." He did a quick scan of the room. "We'll be talking to several people. If you know of anything, please come talk to us."

A man raised his hand. "Do you have any theories on what happened here?"

Throckmorton exhaled. "I have my theories about what has happened, but we'll do a solid investigation before we release any information. Sheriff, can you have a couple of men ask all of those who have any connection to the victims in the blasts meet at the school gym tonight at seven? Help them with anything they need, within reason?"

"Yes, sir."

"My men will do a thorough sweep of the facility. Have the computer expert find out what she can. Let's get started. I want to have some information to provide those who are grieving."

~

Myles waited until everyone left the room. "Sheriff, can I talk to you?" He nodded. Myles continued. "I'll help out as much as I can, but it'll have to be behind the scenes. No one can know I'm helping you. No one."

"Understood."

Myles surveyed the area "Is there anyone you can trust in the county who is an expert on computers? I mean, really trust that will keep their mouth shut."

"Yes. Viola Ingram has assisted in some of our investigations."

"Okay. Please call her and have her come as quick as possible." Myles took a deep breath. "Jack, this is your county. The president has asked the F.B.I. to take over this investigation. I hate the idea because you and I have been good friends."

"Whoa, Myles. No worries. I'll make sure Throckmorton doesn't get out of hand."

"Are you sure?"

The sheriff nodded. "Never knew you as the Wolf." He smiled at Myles.

"Yeah. Jack, I'm trying to get out of that racket. I want to enjoy my life. And I have someone to finally enjoy it with."

"I can understand that. No worries. No one will know who you are from me."

Myles sighed. "Okay, don't trust anyone other than Willow and me. That includes those from the F.B.I."

"That serious?"

"Yes, the F.B.I. has tracked stolen pieces of dynamite for at least two years if not longer. Rosewood officials are connected in some way as well as River Valley officials. My theory is it involves a group from Rosewood that includes Ronald Halter and his wife, Cadence, Randolph and Samantha Konnor, and George Jackson. And here in River Valley, Jeremiah and Isaac Reynolds, Principal Jordan Tuthill, County Attorney Reginald McKenzie, and Judge Wade Garner. And who knows who else? Keep your eyes on everything. You and I will communicate behind the scenes."

"Okay. You realize Throckmorton is going to call you in to talk."

"Willow will oversee all legal aspects of the case. She has a disk that will break this case wide open. That's why I need someone to help her. Much easier for two of them to work together. Hopefully, Willow will be coherent enough to work with Viola. If not, I'm counting on Miss Ingram to manage that end of it." Myles hesitated. "There was dynamite confiscated outside of Fairview, but suddenly it disappeared. I hope the disk will shed some light. I'm almost one hundred percent sure the dynamite used here came from that stash. And I don't think this is the only target."

Sheriff Watkins pondered what Myles had said. "What's your theory about this one?"

"I'm not even going to hazard a guess."

Chapter 2

Myles and the sheriff drove to the school auditorium together. When they walked in, the place was packed with those who had lost loved ones and other concerned citizens. Throckmorton strode to the front. He scanned the audience before he spoke.

"There was a tragedy on Saturday. No other words to describe it. My name is F.B.I. Special Agent Lynus Throckmorton. I've been assigned to handle the investigation into this tragedy. Know that I've been trained in counter-terrorism and chasing down criminals—all who would harm this country for the past twenty-five years." He sighed. "The sheriff and I want to offer any help we can for those who have suffered loss of loved ones. Anything. Please come to us. We'll figure out how to help." He checked the list he brought. "We've found everyone except Trevor Reynolds. If anyone knows anything about him, please let the sheriff or me know. There have been thirteen deaths and twenty-seven injuries. Our condolences to everyone who has lost a loved one."

Throckmorton took another breath. "We don't have much to tell you now. We do know that two explosions occurred almost immediately after each other, or at least within twenty to thirty seconds of each other. There has been a complete sweep of the building and the surrounding area. I can assure you there are no more bombs or explosive materials in the area. We believe those two were it.

"The school board president, Mr. Swanson, has cancelled all activities until Monday. More word on that if needed. We also have opened an aid station at the high school gym. It offers food, water, and counseling to help those who are struggling with this tragedy. No questions asked. I have asked the F.B.I to send psychologists and other specialists to help with those who need it. They'll be here tomorrow. So please don't hesitate to take advantage of any of the resources being offered."

Throckmorton scanned the room once more. "This was a targeted event, and we're just not sure who or what was targeted. We'll find out what happened and who did this, but we can almost guarantee that this was a one-time bombing. I'll take any questions."

A reporter raised her hand. "Mr. Throckmorton?"

"Please call me Lynus."

"Lynus, how do you know for sure this was a one-time event?"

"We found two explosion areas in the building. They were specifically set at those locations. In our experience, the two were set for a specific purpose to go off at a specific time. It would appear that it was targeted for the wedding."

"Why would you say targeted for the wedding?" the reporter asked.

"Ma'am, the wedding has been planned for a couple of weeks. And everyone knew that Myles and Willow Cason were to be married. They also knew there would be many people in one spot. Terrorists concentrate on large crowds to send a message to."

"Is it a possibility Myles or Willow or both could have been the targets?"

"A possibility, but I can't comment on that until we dig deeper into the details. Be rest assured this was a one-time event and you're safe."

Another question popped up. "Why would bombs be detonated in a small town like River Valley?"

"That's what we're going to find out."

Another hand lifted from the back.

"Who is Wolf?"

Throckmorton didn't blink. "A wolf is a wild animal. I don't know what that would have to do with this."

"No sir. It was said that the 'Wolf' has arrived."

"I still don't know what you're talking about. May I have your name, sir, and I'll find out?"

"Merrill Glasgow. I'm with the *Washington Tribune*. Been assigned to cover this tragedy."

"Mister Glasgow, I understand you have a job to do also. But please take into consideration what has happened here and the feelings of the people who have lost loved ones. Any other questions?"

No one raised their hand.

"On Saturday at eleven thirty a.m., we'll have another town meeting to update everyone on what we've found." Throckmorton stepped down off the podium and walked toward the sheriff and Myles.

"Good job, Mr. Throckmorton."

He smiled. "Done this many times."

"Can tell. Aren't you concerned about the code name?"

"Nope. As soon as the man said the word Wolf, he was toast."

"What? How?"

Throckmorton pointed over to people who had been recording the event. "With the government. They monitor everything that happens to us. Especially when it comes to The Wolf. My contact already knows and will have men talking to Mr. Glasgow immediately."

~

After the town meeting, Myles strode to the front desk of the hospital. "Myles Cason. Looking for Willow Cason."

"She's in Room 101 with your daughter right now."

"Thanks. What about Olivia Konnor?"

"Olivia Konnor. Oh, you mean Cason?"

Myles frowned at her not sure what was happening. "Yes?"

"Room 111 down the hall a bit further."

"Thanks again." Myles hurried down to Room 111 and peeked in. Olivia was staring out the window. He knocked on the door. She spun toward him and smiled. "Myles, I'm glad you're okay."

He strolled into the room, grabbed a chair, and sat down by her. "You seem a little better."

"Yeah, the doctor said I'm not that crazy." She smiled.

"You never were. Don't you dare worry about a thing."

Tears rolled down her eyes. "I'm so sorry your wedding was ruined. Willow looked so beautiful."

"It wasn't ruined. Just a minor setback." He grinned.

Olivia laughed. "Ouch, it hurts to laugh."

"What is this about Olivia Cason?"

"I didn't want anyone to know I was a Konnor. They were involved with the bombing. It was safer."

"I see. There is no evidence they're involved."

"Yeah, right. I'm not stupid. You and I both know they had a hand in it as well as the Halters, Jacksons—you name it."

Myles sighed. "The only thing you need to worry about is healing. How are you dealing with Trevor? His body still hasn't been found."

Olivia stared over at the window once more. "One of the characteristics our family ingrained in us was not to feel sorry for others. I've always been able to distance myself from boys and others. It hurt at first, but I have you, Willow, and Brielle in my life." She paused. "Is it wrong not to feel worse than I do?"

Myles took the young girl's hand. "Each of us deals with a tragedy in separate ways. I do know that people have seen your strength, seen the way you've grown over the last few months. You're going to be fine. You'll have a wonderful life."

Olivia smiled at him. "First, it was Willow who helped me be a better person. Or I should say she tried. She had issues of her own. But you came into our lives, and you've showed us there is another way. Willow always knew that you had a tough road yourself. That's why she changed who she was so it would make it easier for you to fulfill your destiny. You don't realize how much my sister loves you. I saw it in her eyes when I pointed you out in the gym. She was totally in love."

"And as a seventeen-year-old, you know this how?"

"My big sister always told me there would be that special man out there for us. She found her special man. I will too."

"I know you will."

She dropped his hand. "Go see that lovely wife of yours. I'm sure she misses you. Thanks for always being there for me."

He reached over and kissed her on the cheek. "I am. You're the sister of the woman I love." Myles headed to Willow's room, then stood in the doorway as Willow and Brielle were talking about what they were going to name the baby. "Do I get a vote?"

They both whipped around. Willow's hazel eyes held that same sparkle he saw the first time they had met.

"What?" Willow blushed.

"Oh, nothing. Just peering into those same amazing eyes I saw when you were walking into the gym the first time we met."

Her face pinkened even more.

Brielle went over to her father and hugged him. "I'm glad you're here. I'm going to check on Olivia."

"I was just in there. She seems to be doing better." Once she left, Myles grabbed a chair and sat beside Willow. "You doing okay?"

"Yeah, I'm feeling much better. I was so worried we lost our baby."

Myles changed the subject. "You're a strong woman. You'll be fine. We're going to be fine."

"I'm glad you feel that way. Brielle told me about Trevor and the three Tuthills. Losing all your children. How devastating! Thirteen deaths, sweetheart. Who would do such a thing?"

"Hey," he said grabbing her hand. "Don't you worry about it. Your job is to get better."

"How can I just lie here and do nothing?"

"Because I'm asking you to. I need to know the woman I love is safe."

Willow frowned at him. "What are you up to?"

Myles sighed. "They asked me to oversee the case."

She smiled at him. "So, you are more than a schoolteacher and a basketball coach?"

"You always knew there was something different about me."

"Yes, sweetheart. First, you always protect the ones you love. Second you finish the job you start."

What? He threw her a quizzical look. She smiled at him. "You landed in Newton Hills State Park to bring my family and others to justice for the crimes they've committed. This bombing is one more crime."

His eyebrows raised. "As a county prosecuting attorney, you can't make assumptions without facts."

"You'll find them. And I'll help you."

"You will, will you?"

"Of course, I will. You and I are in this together. And we will be for the rest of our lives. Once this is finished, our family is moving to D.C. That's where you belong."

"I declined it."

"Why?" She tried to sit up.

"Whoa, Willow. Take it easy. I'm through with that life. Now I have you and the girls. That's who I want to be with." Myles gazed deeply into her eyes once more.

She gently pushed him away. "Stop."

"You'll always be the best thing that happened to me." Myles reached down and kissed her gently on the lips. He stood to leave but turned at her voice.

"The doctor said I'll be released tomorrow. And Myles, I'm going to help you solve this case."

He held up his palm. "I'm not that person anymore." Myles was leaving the hospital when his cell phone rang. "Hello."

"Myles, can we talk?"

"Cadence?" Why was she calling him? Brielle's mother, and his first girlfriend, but that was ancient history.

"Please meet me in Mitchell at the Corn Palace Gift Shop? Seven p.m. tonight."

The phone clicked on the other end.

Myles headed to his car wondering what the woman was up to. She had not talked to him for several months, or seventeen years for that matter. It sounded like a scared woman. He would pass it onto the sheriff about meeting her in Mitchell. He drove to The Depot and exited his car. The sheriff was waiting for him, his face long.

"Myles, sadness all the way around. All the Tuthill children gone. Trevor Reynolds still missing. He's the only one missing. Jacie Tuthill hasn't said much to her husband at all."

"Could be she lost her whole family."

"That's part of it. But I have a feeling, and it's just a feeling. She believes her husband had something to do with it or knew something was going to happen."

Myles pondered the sheriff's comment. "She did say something about her husband skipping out right before the explosion. Did you talk to her? Find anything on the site itself?"

"Not yet. The F.B.I. continues to sift through the debris. I have a couple of my trusted deputies working on it also."

Myles understood the 'trusted' connotation. "I'm glad you did. I've worked with many of the F.B.I. agents. Most are trustworthy, but all have an agenda of sorts. Who knows what their agenda is today?"

"I hope it's the same as ours. Find out who did this."

"I'm with you. My suggestion would be to bring in Miss Roberts, the English teacher, and question her. Keep her away from the F.B.I. for now. She mentioned something about Isaac Reynolds telling her not to go to the wedding. And what's weird is Cadence called me a bit ago and wants me to meet her in Mitchell. I can tell she's scared."

The sheriff sighed. "You suggested Rosewood families may have had something to do with this."

"Yep. My gut tells me this isn't going to be the only bombing. I just don't know what to think. Why don't you have Willow and your tech expert go over that disk thoroughly and quickly? Willow will be out of the hospital tomorrow."

Myles' cell phone beeped. "Yes, Willow."

"I just received a call from Halter's first wife, Cynthia. She heard about the bombing and said she has information that may help us. Won't talk to anyone but you or me. Cynthia's afraid even to talk to her husband about it. She wants to meet in person."

Myles took a deep breath. "Cadence wants me to meet her tonight in Mitchell. She also has some information she wants to pass on."

"What do you think?"

"Weird. Both Halter's love interests have something to say to us? Cadence sounded scared on the phone. I don't know what's happening. I'll let the sheriff know about both calls."

"No, Myles. It has to be you."

Myles sighed. "For some reason, I can never say no to you. I'll drive to Mitchell tonight and catch a flight to Minneapolis as soon as I can. Don't worry about the girls. Crocket will watch over them. I just can't figure out what happened to Trevor."

She sighed audibly. "Do you believe he played you like the Reynolds do everyone?"

"I really don't know what to think. My gut reaction is no, but where is he? I'll worry about Trevor later. Right now, I'm going to talk to the two Halter women. Please, take care of yourself. And if you're able, Viola Ingram will meet you to decipher the disk. Any information only goes to the sheriff."

"Understood."

"Love you, Willow."

"That's sweet."

"What?"

"That's sweet you told me you love me before I said it to you. I do love you, sweetheart. Be safe. And I'll see you as soon as possible."

Myles clicked off his cell phone and started toward the sheriff. "Willow asked me to drive to Mitchell and then on to Minneapolis to talk to Halter's women."

The sheriff laughed. "It doesn't surprise me Cadence would turn and run when she found out something was about to happen."

Myles frowned.

"That's what happened seventeen years ago when things had gone down with you. When that kid was hit by the car and died later. She turned to Halter because you were in trouble. Now she figures her current husband is in trouble. And as for Halter's first wife, she may have valuable information for us. Halter played her. And from what I've heard from colleagues around Sioux Falls, she knows more than she's let on."

"Okay. Hopefully, this will give us some information. I talked to Willow and she's going to help Viola tomorrow. She knows to provide the information to you. I'll reiterate, Sheriff. Don't trust the F.B.I. And don't say anything to Throckmorton about where I'm going."

"Will do. Go enjoy your night with the Halter women." He waggled his eyebrows.

"Ugh."

~

It was just over an hour's drive to Mitchell. After gathering tape-recording gear, Myles drove north to connect with Chamberlain at I-90. He arrived at the Corn Palace around six-thirty. Upon entering the massive building, he scanned the area. There were a few people near the entrance.

Myles headed back toward the gift shop where several people milled around. From what he remembered, the Corn Palace was a huge attraction for out-of-state visitors, as well as for locals. Again, once in the gift shop area, he surveyed what was around him.

He recalled the balcony on the second floor. The gift shop opened into a basketball gym that he had played in once when he was a senior in high school. The Corn Palace was always loud. Myles found a place to sit where he would make an easy escape if something should go haywire.

Moments later Cadence walked in and peered around. When she spotted him, she hurried toward him and plopped down. "Wow, you did show up."

Myles eyed her. "Why wouldn't I? Despite everything we've gone through, I've always cared about you."

Cadence nodded. "Yeah, it has been tough on both of us." The pause that ensued became awkward. "How's Brielle?"

"She's doing fine. Cadence, what is it? You're not here for chit-chat."

"I'm sorry. I thought maybe you would still want to talk about us."

"No. You decided you wanted nothing to do with me. So, what is it you want?"

Cadence glanced around the room. "I'm scared. Big-time screw-up. I should have gone with you when you asked me to. There's a book that Ronald and the others are searching for. Do you have it?"

"I don't know anything about a book. What's in it?"

Cadence sighed. "Information that coincides with the disk that we gave Valentine. Did you know he died in a car wreck?"

"Heard about it. Too much to drink."

"I don't think so. Myles, you know we never saw Valentine have a drink in high school."

"That doesn't mean he didn't start drinking."

"You're right. So you don't know anything about a book?"

"I said I didn't. Cadence, I've never lied to you—no matter what you believe or have heard about me. It's not just about a book, is it?"

Cadence took a deep breath. "No, it's not. I want to be with you and Brielle. That's the way it should have always been. I made a huge mistake with Ronald. It hurt me when you wanted to leave. I've changed or I will change because I want to be with you."

Myles sighed. "It'll never happen. You told me to stay away."

"Is there another woman?"

"If there is, that would be none of your business."

"So, you are shacking up with Willow Konnor. It wouldn't

surprise me. She always had a way with men. Uses them and dumps them. You're just another in the extensive line of men whom she supposedly fell in love with and wanted to marry. And she always gets what she wants. True Konnor."

"Cadence, go home and live your life with your husband and children. Or are you scared because you know his world is about to fall apart? Just like you did when ours fell apart."

She huffed. "I was pregnant with Brielle, and you were going to jail. I had to do something to protect my child."

"Yeah, right. You could have told the truth. And the truth was I had nothing to do with that hit-and-run accident. An accident I spent a year in prison for. Ronald did it and you know it. Just like he's been involved in many other criminal activities."

"It was never Ronald. It was the Konnors who killed the boy. Willow knows that and so do you."

"And how would she know that?"

Cadence looked around once more. "She was there when it happened."

Myles followed her line of vision. "What do you keep looking for?"

"I'm just nervous."

"Yeah, right. You set me up, didn't you?"

"I would never do that."

Myles caught two men walking in out of the corner of his eye. "Thanks for this pleasant discussion. You've turned into a good liar. And why not? You've been married to one for the past sixteen plus years."

He sprang out of his chair and headed toward the balcony. The two men finally spotted him when he reached the top. Myles hurried down the back balcony and out the door of the Corn Palace, then raced toward his car. He should have known Cadence wanted something from him. Now he knew. It was all about a book.

Chapter 3

It was eight p.m. when Willow called.

"How'd it go?"

"Just about like I expected. She was looking for information. A book."

"Myles, don't say anymore. I'll call you back later. Love you."

Just like that his phone went dead.

Myles arrived at the Sioux Falls Regional Airport two hours later and headed to the ticket counter.

The woman at the counter checked his driver's license. "Myles Cason? A ticket has already been purchased for you. Also, here's a gift from you wife."

The ticket lady handed him a cell phone.

"Okay. Thanks."

He went to find a place to sit for the hour before he boarded. His phone rang, but he didn't recognize the number.

His wife's cheery voice was honey to his ears. "Hey, sweetheart. This is better for us to talk on. Are you okay?"

"Yeah, just kind of confused about this so-called book."

"Yeah. Guess what? Brielle has a book that the Halters have searched for. She showed it to me the night you and I had our little spat and talked it out at the gym. Brielle didn't know what to do with it."

"I can understand that. Cadence was scared tonight. The book has something to do with the disk."

"I'll work tomorrow with both and see if I can produce anything. I booked a room for you at the Hampton Inn & Suites near the Target Center. Cynthia Gold, Halter's first wife, will meet you at eight-thirty tomorrow at a small coffee shop near the hotel.

She sounds really worried."

"Okay."

"What happened with Cadence?"

Myles sighed. "She mentioned the book a couple of times. Also, how she screwed up with us and should have not let me get away."

"Do you still feel that way? That you two should be together?"

"Not since the moment I gazed into your beautiful, sparkling hazel eyes."

She laughed. "You have no idea how many times I've heard that I use men to get what I want. I can't disagree with that in the past. That's not me anymore. Myles, I just need you to know I've loved only you since the first day my eyes set upon you. Please believe that. Also, believe I do love you with all my heart. Be safe and see you tomorrow."

"I love you too, Willow."

Myles surveyed around the terminal. There weren't many people he could trust, but one thing he never doubted for a moment—Willow loved him, and he loved her.

~

The next morning Myles waited at the coffee shop that Willow had set up a meeting with Cynthia Gold. Several women walked in. A dark red-headed woman entered, peering at a photo in her hand. She glanced over at Myles and hurried over.

"Myles Cason?"

"Yes, ma'am. Cynthia Gold?'

She smiled. "Cynthia Dawson now. I'm glad we could meet."

"Please have a seat. Would you like a cup of coffee or something?"

"Please. With sugar."

Myles waved to the server, and a young lady walked over. "Coffee with sugar for the lady."

"Yes, sir."

Once she left, Cynthia peered around the room. "You chose a very inconspicuous place," she said.

Myles smiled. "Mrs. Dawson, it's okay."

"Cynthia. Please call me Cynthia. It's not safe for you anywhere, Mr. Cason."

"Call me Myles. And why isn't it safe?"

"Ronald Halter has been hunting for you for sixteen years. He won't stop until he kills you."

"Why would he want to kill me? What did I ever do to him?"

She took a deep breath. "When you were eighteen, you knew about what happened with that young boy at The Diner. He's dead because he wanted to turn state's evidence. The boy never had the chance."

"How do you know about that?"

"Austin was my little brother. He used to run drugs for Halter and Konnor when he was sixteen. They used high school kids for all that stuff. In addition, girls like Willow and Olivia Konnor and Courtney Jackson would always dress inappropriately at functions over the years. Willow took the biggest brunt of it because she's so darn pretty. You hit the jackpot with her. Anyway, Ronald Halter killed my little brother and framed you. Cadence was in on it."

"Cadence?"

"Yes, she slept with my former husband several times while she was in high school. I take it she never said anything to you?"

"Of course not. But how would you know?"

Cynthia smiled. "I know Ronald Halter. He's a scumbag galore. I married him because I thought I loved him. Boy, was I wrong. So, I documented every movement he and his men made in secret. In a book of sorts. That book will send him and his cohorts to jail for a long time. The problem is I put it in code and can't remember how I did it."

"What do you mean?"

She frowned. "Early-stage dementia. So, I don't remember certain things. I wanted to tell someone about this before I forget it all. For sure I want to make sure Ronald Halter gets what he deserves."

"Do you know where the book is?"

Cynthia studied him. "Your daughter has the book. Or did have it."

"My daughter has no book."

The lady frowned for a moment, then continued. "She always knew Ronald wasn't her father. And yes, Myles, Brielle is your daughter. I've known that from the start. Cadence has done everything she could to change Brielle's mind. Never worked. When Brielle was twelve, she wanted to find out more about you.

Her mother kept telling her Ronald was her father so she would drop it. Brielle must be like her father. Stubborn. Because she kept asking more questions."

Cynthia sipped her coffee. "Then she saw you on the trail in Newton Hills State Park when you took them cross-country skiing. Your eyes told her right away you were her father. She went snooping around the house and stumbled on the book. I had thought I'd taken it with me but didn't. It was in her room. Or the room that she took over from Jasmine before she left. She's had nothing to do with the family since she left. And will have nothing to do with the family."

"How do you know any of this?"

Cynthia sighed. "After she met you, she found a phone number on her father's desk and dialed it. Mine. She asked me all kinds of questions. I told her never, under any circumstances, tell anyone about it. Basically, I told her to get rid of the book. She asked me if it had to do with her real father. Like a dummy I said yes. I'm sure that's why she kept it. Someday she was going to help you if she could. That book will do it."

"Do you know anything about dynamite?"

She sighed once more. "Yes."

"How? You haven't communicated with your ex-husband in forever."

"Yes, but he is involved."

"What?"

"You don't know how far this goes. It goes all the way to Washington. Even if you nail Halter, there are still others out there who will continue."

"Continue what?"

"Once Willow told me you were part of a super-secret organization, I figured now would be the best time to come out and help. Realize, if anyone finds out, my life is over. It's for the better. I sure don't want to live with dementia for the rest of my life."

"I know nothing about a super-secret organization. I'm a schoolteacher and a coach."

"Then why are you here?"

"Because Willow asked me to meet you. She had no reason. If there is such a book, explain the importance of the book?"

She took another sip of her coffee. "Believe me, there is such a book. Ronald would write down all the names of any associates he worked with, their information, their liabilities, and other stuff. The three years when we were married was when everything started coming together. He was developing contacts. Halter always stored secret stuff like documents, affidavits, etc. in a wall safe behind a picture of himself being sworn in as mayor in his office at the house. Over the years he has gathered more contacts, including my current husband, Michael Comforti, and a man in Washington, D.C. Don't know his name."

"Comforti?"

"Yes, he's the man who's always had the hots for Willow. He's kind of a go-between—a middleman. And he is very evil. Watch him. My husband is being groomed for a special mission that even I don't know about. I just know it has something to do with the president and those in power."

"You still communicate with Willow?"

"Yes. She's always been nice to me. Once she found out I had dementia, she's worked to find ways to help me."

"That wouldn't surprise me."

Cynthia glanced up at him. "You have no idea how fortunate you are with Willow. She'll be right beside you forever. All she's ever wanted to do is find someone she could love and who would love her back. Sounds like you both have found that."

"Is there anything else you can tell me about all of this?"

"Just be careful. Who knows who's involved? I do know they are desperately searching for that book. I heard they had destroyed some disks when they killed Valentine. Once they have the book, no one will be able to stop them."

"Do the disks and book go together?"

"Yes, they do. But Halter and his gang don't realize that."

"You keep saying Halter and his gang."

"Yes, Ronald Halter is the mastermind. Or I should say, he, Konnor, Comforti, and a fourth person in the hierarchy in D.C. make up the gang. No one has any idea who that is. Not even the president."

They both took a sip of their coffee. "How's your mother doing?" She asked.

"All right, I guess."

"She is a nice woman. Your mother's done all she could to keep you kids away from their father. You know your father was killed in Vietnam on a humanitarian mission?"

"I had heard that."

"He is the president's cousin."

"I had heard that also."

"Son, you and Willow can go far. Please do what's needed to stop this all. These people mean to destroy parts of our society bit by bit. And who knows for what reason. They just enjoy power, I guess."

Myles stood. He needed to think about all she'd said. "It's been nice to meet you."

She laughed. "Yeah, right. We've been talking about death and destruction, and you're telling me it's been a pleasure. Son, I'm glad I could help. Take care of Willow for me. Don't ever let anything happen to that young lady."

"I won't."

"I should go. Since you have that book, you'll figure everything out."

"I don't have a clue what book you're talking about. Nor does my daughter have the book you're speaking of."

She looked out of sorts. Cynthia climbed out of her seat and plodded out the door. Myles paid the bill and started to follow her, but he stopped, then glanced at the bag she'd left.

"Everyone out. Now."

People scattered out of the building. Myles quickly dialed 9-1-1 and told them about a bomb. They told him to get everyone out. Myles rushed toward the back to make sure the staff was out of the building.

The sirens screamed toward the sight. He imagined the bomb crew entered the building and found the bag. Myles had opened it before he left and noticed the sticks of dynamite attached to a detonator. There was five minutes left before it would blow. He also noticed a note in the bag. Myles grabbed the note and left.

Once outside, he read the note. "Cynthia, good girl in getting Myles out to see you. Willow has no clue what's happening. Love always, Ronald."

Myles stared up at the building. "What the hell is going on? Cynthia was in on it also." He quickly dialed Willow.

"Hey, sweetheart. How did it go?"

"I'm still in one piece."

"What are you talking about?"

"A bomb was set in the cafe."

"Are you okay?"

"Yes, but your friend Cynthia is the one who set it."

There was silence on the other end of the phone. "Myles, I do not know Cynthia Gold or Dawson. The first time I heard her name was at the conference in the Twin Cities."

"She's a decent liar."

"What does that mean?"

"I'll tell you when I get home tonight."

"I've really missed you the last couple of nights. Especially last night."

"Everything okay?"

"Yes, it is. Just so many things going on in our lives. I need you to hold me."

"I'll do that tonight."

"Promise."

"All night long."

"See you in a bit. I love you."

"Love you also."

Myles scanned the area. There in the corner was Cynthia Dawson with a younger man. He looked like the man who was in Willow's office. Myles snapped a quick photo with his cell phone. The two turned and walked away.

A police officer came over and talked to Myles. "Do you know who could havc placcd thc bag?"

"I'm not positive. I had a meeting with a Cynthia Dawson, and she left it in a bag."

The police officer frowned at him. "Senator Dawson's wife?"

"I don't know who her husband is."

The police officer studied him. "You met with her? And why?"

Myles took a deep breath and pulled out his badge. The police officer glanced at it and handed it back to him. "Mr. Cason, if we can help, let us know?"

"I know this may be difficult for you. But the first step is to have a conversation with Cynthia Dawson and the senator."

He grimaced. "Now that'll be difficult."

"Why's that?" Myles asked.

"A difficult man to deal with."

Myles smiled. "Well now, how about we both go and pay a visit to one of Minnesota's fine senators."

This time the police officer smiled. "I'd love to fly out to D.C. but don't think my boss would like that."

"Got ya. Let me handle it then."

"Thank you," the police officer said letting out a breath.

Once the police officer left, Myles dialed Willow.

"Twice in thirty minutes? You must really miss me."

"Yes, I do. Feel like taking a trip to D.C. with me?"

"Would love it."

"Book four tickets for D.C. tomorrow. We're going to pay a visit to Senator Dawson, the president, and some others."

"The girls will love it."

"How are they doing?"

"Olivia is much better. Many of the kids from school have visited the hospital. She's hamming it up. They're releasing her this afternoon." Then silence on the other end.

"What is it, Willow?"

"Someone spotted Trevor Reynolds leaving the building right before the bomb went off at The Depot. Still no sign of him."

Myles took a deep breath. "We'll have to consider him part of it. Can you pass that along to the sheriff and have him follow up with his family? I'm sending you a photo of a man our age with Cynthia Dawson. I think it's Comforti."

"Will do. See you tonight."

Myles shut off his cell phone. Everything was getting hotter, he thought to himself. He had one last call to make—to find out where Senator Dawson's mansion was in St. Paul. Renting a vehicle, he took a drive to the home. Big place with guards on the front gate. Myles had planned on knocking on the door to talk to Cynthia Dawson once more but decided against it. He'd deal with her husband instead.

Chapter 4

Myles had barely walked through the front door when the girls ran toward him. "We have everything packed," Olivia said. "Think there'll be dancing? We'll need a dress, won't we?" She spun around and ran back upstairs with Brielle. They both stopped and hurried back to Myles.

"Glad you're home, Dad. We missed you," Brielle said, kissing him on the cheek. Olivia did the same. The two scrambled back up the stairs.

Willow came over and kissed her husband. "They're excited."

"I can tell. Missed you."

"I'm glad because I sure missed you."

Myles took Willow into his arms, and she snuggled into him.

"I've really wanted that. Really needed to feel your strong arms around me."

"What's up?"

She peered up into his eyes. "It's really weird. I've never felt like this about anyone in my life. I'm not needy or anything like that, but I just missed you over the past couple of nights."

Myles smiled at her.

"What?"

"Remember I told you the reason you didn't marry Isaac Reynolds was because you didn't love him? It's safe to say you must be in love with me."

"You wouldn't believe how much. I'll show you how much later. Right now, I just want to talk."

"Okay."

Willow took his hand and led him over to the couch. After bringing a couple of drinks from the kitchen, she slid down next to him. "Perfect."

“What’s this about?”

“This is my perfect world. Our perfect world. I have several things to talk to you about. Viola and I did some work on the disk and I followed up with the book after she left. The disk gives surprisingly good details of Ronald Halter and the people he does business with. Unbelievably detailed. Now after reading a few pages in the book, I was able to piece together a couple of things. For instance, Michael Comforti, the guy who tried to pick me up in Minneapolis recently, is the person the group uses to bring others to the table. For example, Senator Dawson. He’s interested in economic development in Minnesota.”

“Makes sense since he’s from the Minneapolis area.”

“But it’s not the Twin Cities, dear. It’s a small town up north called Liberty. Liberty is on Native American lands. And it’s more about being involved with a casino. As you know casinos on Native American lands are big deals.” Willow took a sip of her lemonade. “I’m glad you hooked me on lemonade. I really love it.”

They both laughed. “I know. You love me for it.”

Willow continued. “Here’s a new name. By new name I mean within the last couple of months. Zachary Hunter."

Myles eyes shot up toward her. “What?”

“Yes, the same guy. Did you know he’s an expert with demolitions?”

“I didn’t. Isn’t he still in prison?”

“I talked to him several days ago. He was in prison then but was released the day after. You made good on your word. But you shouldn’t have, sweetheart. Hunter worked with dynamite in the military—the type of dynamite that was stolen. At least that’s what the book and the disk say.”

“Damn. Are you saying he used me?”

“I don’t know what to think. It is a coincidence the bombs went off after he was out of prison and within a few days’ time. And when you were around. Myles, you’re not listed anywhere on that disk. Nowhere.”

“Why would I be?”

“Cadence is on the disk. But I’m not.”

“Did you show the book to Viola?” He asked.

She grabbed his hand. “I’m not putting our daughter at risk, ever. Only you and I know about that book. Especially after two people you talked to had questions about it. The two of us together will bring the operation down. It's just putting all the pieces together." Willow leaned forward. "I know you said you wanted nothing to do with this. But you really don't have a choice if it involves our daughter."

Myles took a deep breath. "Hopefully, tomorrow we'll fill in another piece of the puzzle."

Willow shifted her body toward her husband. "So, tell me about your fun?"

"Lots of fun. Cadence wants me to be back with her. Said she made a mistake."

Willow took a deep breath. "How do you feel about that?"

"I don't. You're the one I love."

"Good. I was worried that you still had feelings for her."

"Nope. You're the only woman I want to be with."

Willow wiped away a tear.

"What is that about?"

"You'll continue to find out more about my life, and it'll be things you won't want to hear. I can't change my past, although I wish I could. But I hope you always remember that since the day our eyes met, my heart has belonged to you and no one else."

"Like Cyrus Vincent?"

Willow wiped her eyes. "I met him once when I was sixteen. He…he had a sexual encounter with me. A forced sexual encounter."

"Did you do anything about it?"

Willow shrugged. "Nothing I could do about it. My family was behind it. I told you who they are." She could see Myles was livid. "Sweetheart, it's over. Please move forward. It's who I was in the past. I'm not that woman anymore."

He took a deep breath. "Cynthia said something about Comforti being groomed for a special mission that includes the president and others in that realm of power."

Willow nodded. "His name is on the disk. I'll continue scrolling the disk and study the book."

"Maybe think about copying all the information onto a Jump drive and hide it. If they find out we have the book and/or the disk, they'll come searching for it." Myles could tell Willow's mind was racing.

She frowned. "Why would Brielle think about taking the book and not telling anyone about it?"

"She was trying to find out who her father was. That was her only link to me."

"And she stumbled onto something that could destroy much of our world. Or even kill the father she loves? She told me she never told anyone because she had a feeling it was important."

"Boy, was she right."

Willow peered up into Myles' eyes. "You've hugged me. Now I think it's time we do a little more."

He stared deeply into her eyes.

"What is it? You're scaring me."

"Honey, the doctor told me you're not pregnant."

She backed up, furrows forming between her brows. "What do you mean?"

"While you were in the hospital, you mentioned nothing happening to the baby. The doctor checked and said you weren't pregnant. He also said it was fortunate because if you were pregnant, the trauma would have killed the baby."

Willow's shoulders sagged, and she stared at her hands.

"It's okay. Someday we'll have a child."

She finally peered at him. "What if I can never have children?"

"Don't think like that. Even if we don't have children, that's okay. We'll always have each other." Myles climbed off the couch and lifted her up into his arms. He kissed her gently on the lips.

"Thank you for telling me." She snuggled into him. "Oh, by the way, the photo you sent is Comforti."

Myles shook his head.

"What?" she blushed.

"I don't know what you ever saw in that guy."

"He's handsome, dear," she said with a smirk.

"His eyes are slits."

Willow laughed. "You're such a goofball!"

~

The next morning Myles went down to The Depot. The sheriff was talking to one of his deputies. He waited until the two had completed their conversation.

The sheriff smiled at him. "How was your night with the two

Halter women?" When Myles grimaced, he laughed. "That good."

"Yep. Both wanted the same thing. Wanted to know about a book."

"A book? Throckmorton asked about a book just yesterday. Had no clue what he's talking about."

Myles sighed. The sheriff shook his head. "You know about the book?"

"Just found out about it yesterday. Willow used it and the disk to find out some information that may help us. We may have found the bomber."

"What do you mean?"

"Zachary Hunter. He was the reason I went to prison a few years ago—to help him and his family. Now he's out, and I've been almost knocked out twice."

"What are you talking about, Myles?"

"Another bomb was found in Minneapolis. Left by Halter's ex-wife."

"Geez, you are bad luck. Why would anyone want you dead?"

"Lots of reasons. Many I can't tell you about. We've found out what the F.B.I. is up to. They want that book. I'm guessing they already have a copy of the disk. And knowing their intel, they would know the two fit together. No matter what, no one can know we have the book."

"Understood. On another note, I talked personally to the Roberts woman. She sure is a tease. I thought she was going to come over my desk and do a lap dance for me."

Both laughed.

The sheriff continued, "She told me Isaac Reynolds told her not to go to the wedding because something might happen that could harm her. When I continued questioning her, she added that he didn't want her to go because he wanted to spend time with her. She met him at a hotel in Mitchell, and from what she said, the two didn't come up for air for several hours." He shook his head. "She has no clue what is going on. Anyway, she gave him an alibi. I had a deputy call the hotel in Mitchell. The desk manager confirmed the two were there. And it's not unusual for Isaac to be at that hotel during the day. In fact, he's been there several times with another woman when he and Willow were together. Get this. One of them was Samantha Konnor. Willow's own mother."

"What an asshole!" Myles said.

"I will agree with you there. What's even more interesting—Jeremiah Reynolds' wife took off the day of the explosion. Someone thought they saw Trevor with her. We're trying to track down where they might have disappeared to. I know they have a cabin in the Black Hills and also have a place in D.C."

Myles took a deep breath. "Do they have a private jet?"

"No. However, the pilot that flew Willow to Minneapolis several weeks ago flies the rich and famous here to different places. I'll have that checked out. What are you thinking?"

"Holly Reynolds found out about what was going to happen and decided it's time to get her and her grandson out of here. What is the relationship between the two?"

"Solid. Holly's nothing like her husband. She's tried to protect Trevor any way she could. They may have both known about the explosives but were too afraid to say anything. It was her way to escape and help her grandson escape."

"But D.C.? Wouldn't she realize Jeremiah would know that?"

"Possibly. But she also has a brother who's powerful. Maybe Holly felt safer there."

"Could be. Willow, the kids, and I are flying to D.C. later today. Do you know where Holly is? I'll visit her."

"No, but I'll find out easy enough. My wife is one of Holly's friends. Like I said she's a decent woman who just happened to marry into a monster's den."

"Okay, call me once you find out? Anything from Tuthill?"

"He's gone. Can't be found anywhere. Jacie kicked him out of the house right after the bombing, and he hasn't been seen since."

Myles rubbed his jaw. "Where could he have gone? Does she know?"

"All Jacie had to say about it was, 'the guy can go to hell, as far as I'm concerned.'"

Myles grinned. "I'm sorry, but that woman didn't deserve him either. Follow up with her and see what else you can find out. My gut reaction is Tuthill's not that big of a player in the scheme of things, and they may have offed him."

"They could have done that at the wedding," the sheriff said confused.

"Yeah, but he already knew about the bombing. Nothing they

could have done about it then. But after—yep."

"I'll check into it."

"Have the bomb experts figured out the type of bomb, detonation sequence, etc.?"

"Still working on it."

Both turned as Throckmorton rushed over. "Cason, what brings you here?"

"Talking to the sheriff."

Throckmorton smiled at the two of them. "I have some news, Sheriff."

"I'll catch up with you later, Jack."

"You don't have to run," Throckmorton said, "You may want to know that our bomber is someone close to you."

Both glanced at Throckmorton. "Zachary Hunter. The man you befriended in prison. Guess he came back to haunt you, didn't he?" Throckmorton strode away. Myles and the sheriff glanced at each other.

Myles grimaced. "Did they plant a bug on you?"

Chapter 5

Willow booked the family a flight on the twin-engine plane to Minneapolis—a Cessna 402, to be exact. The three ladies were on the runway waiting for takeoff when Myles finally came running out.

"Sorry, I'm late."

Willow smiled. "No worries. Chet provided us a complete description of the plane."

"Yes, Dad. It's cool. It has been a popular choice for many small regional airlines worldwide. The problem is they usually only fly the short routes to hubs where passengers can connect to other airlines. But Willow talked Chet into flying us all the way to D.C."

Chet smiled at Myles. "We'll have to make several stops enroute for fuel. But we should arrive sometime around supper."

"Works for me. I'm ready."

Chet was right. They made at least four stops along the way. Chet landed in a small airport in Winchester, Virginia. "Sorry, this is as close as I can get to D.C. for you."

"We're good," Willow said. "Thanks for everything."

"Always. It's great to finally meet your husband—the man you've been telling everybody about."

Willow blushed. "Yeah, he's kind of awesome."

Myles shook his hand. "Why don't you join us for supper?"

"Thank you. I'll do that. It'll be fun." They loaded their gear into a rental vehicle that Willow had called ahead for, then headed toward a Mexican restaurant—the girls' choice. Tacos and enchiladas were the order of the evening. Myles tried a Tacos al Pastor which had pineapples and pork.

"Wow, Dad," Brielle said. "Exquisite."

Everyone laughed. Myles smiled and turned toward Chet. "How often do you fly out to the D.C. area?"

"Several times a year. Usually bring out Mrs. Reynolds. Her brother lives out here. Just brought her and her grandson a few days ago."

Olivia's eyes darted up. She glanced over at Willow, who shook her head.

Myles frowned. "Trevor was at the wedding. We couldn't find him. You're telling me he's alive and okay?"

"I knew nothing about a bombing until I flew back the day after. The missus and Trevor arrived at the airport between noon and twelve-thirty the day of your wedding."

Willow and Myles stared at each other. That was a half an hour after the wedding started. Trevor had been there at the start, but nobody saw him disappear.

Myles shook his head. "An investigation is underway as to the cause of the bombing. And Trevor disappeared. Presumed dead."

Chet took a deep breath. "I told Holly several times to get the hell out of there, but she stayed for Trevor. He's a good kid. Just happens to have a father and grandfather who are devils."

"What happened to Trevor's mother?"

"She was smart and left. Trevor wouldn't go with her because he was so young and didn't understand what was happening. Thought his father was a wonderful man."

Willow touched Chet's hand. "You love Holly, don't you?"

"Always have. But it's never worked out."

"Chet, please tell us where they are? Myles needs to talk to her."

He sighed once more. "She and Trevor are with her brother who lives on Smith Island on the Eastern Shore of the Chesapeake Bay. Even her husband doesn't know her brother lives there. It's the safest place for her. I know you won't tell anyone, so that's why I told you."

"Why did you fly her here?" Myles asked.

"Because the sheriff had told me to make sure I protected her and Trevor."

"What does the sheriff have to do with it?" Myles asked.

"He's Holly's cousin. Always looked after her. One of the few good guys in River Valley."

Myles eyed Willow and then turned to Chet. "I'll make sure nothing happens to her."

The meals came and the group enjoyed their food. Willow told Chet she had purchased a room for him to stay in until he flew back the next day.

"Thanks for everything, Chet," Willow said the next morning.

"No problem, ma'am. I've always said along with being the prettiest woman in South Dakota, you're also the nicest. You just happened to be born into the wrong family."

She smiled. "Thanks. That's changed for good now. No way will I ever be that woman again. The man walking down those stairs is my knight in shining armor, as they say. I'll love him forever."

"Good for you. I hope you all find what you're searching for."

"We will. Myles will figure it out."

The two hugged each other. Chet grabbed a taxi and headed toward the airport. Willow peered up at Myles who had wrapped his arms around her chest. "Do you think he and Holly will get together?"

"I hope so, if he or she isn't involved."

She turned around. "What do you mean?"

"Sweetheart, the only thing I know about anything is that you and the girls have nothing to do with this. After that, it's anybody's game."

Willow smiled. "Let's go to D.C."

"Nope. We'll start at Smith Island. It's a couple of hours away from here. A honeymoon of sorts for us."

Willow laughed. "With a couple of teenage girls? How about we have our honeymoon after you solve this case? Right now, I'll just enjoy our family time together."

"Sounds like a deal," he said kissing her on the lips. "I'll rent the car. Remember, I'm not involved in this case."

~

She wrapped her arms around her waist. Willow was in love with this man, and she would always be.

Olivia's voice made her turn. "Myles said we had to bring our luggage down. Is that what we're going to be this whole trip? Bell girls?"

"Why not?" Brielle asked. "Could be worse."

"And how's that?" Olivia asked.

"Could be sitting in South Dakota while my parents are whooping it up out east."

"You have a point."

The three hurried toward the car Myles had driven up to the hotel entrance. Once loaded Myles drove toward the Chesapeake Bay.

"Wow," was all the girls could say looking at the sights along the way. Finally, the girls pulled out Brielle's laptop and started doing some research on Smith Island.

"Listen to this," Brielle said. "According to Google, Smith Island is on the border of Maryland's and Virginia's territorial waters in the United States."

Olivia sighed. "This is sad. Most of the islands are eroding because of sea-level rise. Smith Island is also experiencing that threat and is expected to erode by 2100. There are less than three hundred people living there. How can anybody live where there are no people?"

Willow turned toward the girls. "Many people like the solitude of island living. They enjoy escaping the everyday rat race, as some people call it. You'll enjoy it."

"Have you ever been to an island like this, Dad?" Brielle asked.

Myles peered into Willow's eyes. She nodded. He took a deep breath. "I've been to places all over the world."

"What do you mean?" Olivia asked.

"Girls, I've done a lot of traveling in my work with the government."

Brielle asked a question. "What do you do with the government?"

Myles sighed. "I rescued people and brought in terrorists and those on America's wanted list."

Olivia snapped her fingers. "I knew it. I knew your father was some secret-agent type. It all makes sense. He's been after our parents."

"Yes, he has," Willow said taking a deep breath.

"You knew?" Brielle asked.

"Not until the night you asked me to talk to your dad in the gym. He told me everything about his life. And I'm glad he did. I was so scared he was having second thoughts about me because of my past."

Both the girls laughed.

"What's so funny?" Willow asked.

"Big sister, Myles has loved you since he first saw you. Everybody could tell that. Including your fiancé at the time."

Brielle touched her father's shoulder. "Thanks for telling us. No one will ever know who my father is. Other than he's the best dad a girl could have."

"I second that," Olivia said. "And we'll spoil the heck out of your kids. Do you know if you're pregnant or not?"

Willow stared out the window.

"Did I say something wrong?" Olivia asked.

Willow took a deep breath and turned back toward her sister. "No, Olivia. You didn't. I'm not pregnant. I was hoping, but I'm not."

"I'm sorry," Brielle said.

Willow tried to put up a positive face. "It's okay. Someday."

Myles grabbed his wife's hand. "Let's find out more about Smith Island."

"I second that notion," Willow said.

Brielle brought up some more information. "Listen to this, they speak a unique style of English, and most families still make their living off the water. Google also says the restaurants have the best Maryland blue-crab cakes and soft-shelled crabs on the Chesapeake Bay. Wow, I can't wait to try them. And they also have something called a Smith Island cake with fresh strawberries on the side."

Willow said. "I'm game to try that."

"Oh, Oh," Olivia said. "The only way to reach the island is on a ferry from Crisfield, Maryland, or Lookout, Maryland. The island is ten miles from Crisfield and includes three communities. Ewell, Tylerton, and Rhodes Point. This is all on the Maryland portion of the island. The Virginia side is currently uninhabited."

Brielle glanced over at Olivia. "We could also take a boat."

"Yeah, we could."

The girls were both quiet for a moment. Brielle finally broke the silence. "How are you going to deal with seeing Trevor?"

Olivia shrugged. "I'll be okay, Brielle. Willow and I have

been trained not to let a boy interfere with our lives."

Willow turned around. "Olivia, it's okay to have feelings for a boy. Our past is behind us. You don't have to think like that anymore."

"I started feeling that way when I first met Myles. He's helped me through a lot. Willow, I like Trevor, but I have my whole life ahead of me. I'm only seventeen, but I know for sure this boy is not the boy I'll love. He's still out there. Brielle feels the same."

"Yep. We're young, attractive, sexy girls who have our whole lives ahead of us."

"Whoa," Myles interrupted. "Brielle, maybe tone down the sexy talk."

"Why, Dad? You married a gorgeous woman."

They all laughed when Myles' neck reddened. "Yeah, you're right. But I was in my thirties when I said something like that. You're only seventeen."

Willow looked his way. "So, you're telling me if you were eighteen and saw me at sixteen, you wouldn't have thought I was sexy and beautiful?"

Myles stuttered, making the females laugh. "Let's think about Smith Island."

Thirty minutes later Myles drove across a bridge toward the inner city of Annapolis.

"Where we going, Dad?" Brielle asked.

"A history lesson for the two of you with a visit to the U.S. Naval Academy." He parked in a lot, and the group headed toward Commodore John Barry Gate. Willow linked her arms with Myles' arm. A security guard approached them at the gate. Myles handed him an ID.

"Welcome, sir."

After being screened, they walked toward some of the buildings but halted when a group of midshipmen marched by.

"They call that 'College Right,'" Myles said quietly.

Brielle's and Olivia's eyes were glued to the men and women marching in a tight formation. After they watched for a few minutes, they continued around the campus. They came upon the Naval Academy chapel and stopped outside of the facility.

"Amazing," Brielle said. Her and Olivia's eyes were glued to the architecture.

"Myles Cason, is that you?"

They all turned to the voice.

"It sure the hell is. What are you doing here?"

A short man with large, wire-rimmed glasses ran over to them and stuck out his hand. Myles took it and shook it. "Xavier McNulty. Lieutenant commander now."

"Yep, promoted to the rank in part because of what you did."

"Xavier, my wife, Willow, my daughter, Brielle, and my wife's sister, Olivia."

"Wow, what a lovely family. I can't believe you're married. Can't believe anyone would actually want you once they knew all the things you've been up to. What happened to the long hair and beard?"

Myles reddened. Willow took Myles's hand. "He's still sexy without the hair and beard."

"If you say so. Come on, let me show you a couple of places and then we'll get a bite to eat."

The girls jumped in. "We'd love to," Olivia said. "This place is fascinating."

"Okay, let's do it. First, we'll go inside the chapel."

"Oh my gosh, this is just so beautiful," Willow said once they were inside. "Look at the stained-glassed windows. Wow."

McNulty smiled at her. "The two stained-glass windows facing the altar are symbolic. One is Sir Galahad holding a sheathed sword which portrays Naval Service ideals. The other signifies the Commission Invisible, the beacon a new officer must follow. The other four windows are memorials to Lieutenant Commander Theodorus B.M. Mason and admirals David Dixon Porter, David Farragut, and William T. Sampson."

He hesitated for a moment. "Theodorus Mason was the founder and first head of the United States Office of Naval Intelligence with the post of Chief Intelligence Officer. Porter was the second U.S. Navy officer to attain the rank of admiral after his adoptive brother, Farragut. Farragut was the first rear admiral, vice admiral, and admiral in the Navy. He is remembered for his order at the Battle of Mobile Bay when he famously said, 'Damn the torpedoes, full speed ahead.' The final memorial is for Sampson who was a rear admiral known for his victory in the Battle of Santiago de Cuba during the Spanish-American War."

They walked over toward an organ. “The Naval Academy Chapel boasts a 268-rank organ controlled by one of the largest draw knob consoles in the world. Beneath the main chapel is the crypt of John Paul Jones. He is sometimes referred to as the ‘Father of the American Navy.’”

“How cool is all of this?” Brielle asked Olivia.

“Way too cool. We’d never see anything like this in South Dakota.”

McNulty grinned at the girls. “South Dakota, huh? You have some iconic structures in the state. Mount Rushmore for one. It’s extremely popular amongst the Naval Academy cadets. That’s one of the top places they want to visit.” He walked with them down the path. They stopped in front of a building that had a tall clock tower. “This building houses a library and auditorium. The Mahan Building was named for Naval historian Admiral Alfred Thayer Mahan. As you can see, its formal entrance is emphasized by a tall clock tower.”

Everyone took time to look at the building. “Let’s take a walk toward Bancroft Hall. It’s said to be the largest contiguous set of academic dormitories in the United States. You probably saw the midshipmen marching out earlier.”

The girls nodded. They arrived at Bancroft Hall a few minutes later. The commander opened the door for them. They stepped inside and admired the ceramic floor.

“Wow,” Willow said. “This is iconic.”

“It sure is, ma’am,” McNulty said. “Bancroft Hall is home for the entire brigade of four thousand midshipmen, contains seventeen hundred rooms or so, almost five miles of corridors, and thirty-three acres of floor space. It has all the basic facilities that midshipmen need for daily living.” McNulty glanced at his watch. “Wow, if we’re going to grab some lunch, we had better do it now. I have a meeting at one-thirty.”

Myles put up his palm. “If you’re tied up, no problems. We can move onto our next destination.”

“Myles, no way am I letting you leave Annapolis without eating at a local dining landmark. Follow me.”

They all jumped into their vehicles and drove toward historic downtown Annapolis.

“Chick and Ruth’s Delly is a local dining landmark. It’s

family-owned and operated since 1965."

The group walked in and found a place to sit in the crowded diner. The menu included pizzas, burgers, and sandwiches.

The waitress smiled at them. "Everyone loves our legendary piled-high sandwiches. In addition, the hungry ones like to take on Chick & Ruth's Man versus Food Challenge. They have to consume a six-pound milkshake and a colossal one-and-a-half-pound burger or sandwich within one hour to win a t-shirt." The woman gave Myles more than a glance. Then she walked away.

Willow laughed at Myles. "What?"

Brielle rolled her eyes. "Dad, you sure are oblivious to everything. That young girl was eyeing you."

"Maybe she was trying to persuade me to try the challenge?"

Olivia laughed. "No. She was picking you up like Miss Roberts was at school. Maybe if she sat next to you, you may have realized what was happening."

Myles smirked at Willow. "We're going to have boys, okay?"

Everyone laughed.

Willow glanced over at McNulty. "Sir, how do you know Myles?"

"Simple, he saved mine and several dozen men's lives in the Strait of Hormuz. Your husband is not part or has never been part of the military. Truthfully, I have no idea who he is. I just know he showed up when we needed him and saved our lives."

Myles shrugged. "It was nothing."

"What do you mean it was nothing? I was a junior officer at the time, and we went in to pick up a group of Navy Seals who had just completed a mission. A couple of them were wounded. They were sent to arrest a known terrorist in Iran. Came back empty-handed and shot up." He turned to the gals. "For a geography lesson, the Strait of Hormuz is between the Persian Gulf and the Gulf of Oman. It provides the only sea passage from the Persian Gulf to the Arabian Sea and then to the Indian Ocean. On the north coast lies Iran, and on the south the United Arab Emirates and Musandam. It's ninety miles of what some people call hell because of terrorist activities on either side of the strait."

Myles interrupted. "How about we talk about something else?"

"No, Dad. We want to hear about it."

Myles rolled his eyes at Willow. She took his hand. "It's okay," she whispered to him.

McNulty continued the story. "We reached the site and started loading the men onto the boat. The Islamic Revolutionary Guard Corps were chasing them. The Guard is Iran's most powerful security and military organization responsible for the protection and survival of the regime. They were founded after the Iranian Revolution in 1979 by order of Ayatollah Ruhollah Khomeini. There are some in the U.S. Government who consider the Guard terrorists. Others don't."

He took a deep breath. "The Revolutionary Guards caught up to us. We had the men loaded and moved toward the ship. We were home safe. At least we thought we were. Instead we were pinned down by three Revolutionary Guards. Then unexpectedly your father came through the desert carrying the man we were supposed to capture. They didn't see him. He threw the guy on the ground and killed all three immediately. Your dad lifted the man up and rushed toward the boat. The other guards were getting closer and shot at him. If I remember right, a couple of shots hit him. He threw the man onto the boat and climbed in." McNulty smiled. "All he said was, 'I'm tired. Let's go home.' He slept all the way back. Anyway, he got our man and saved many lives. The terrorist was a member of a group in Iran who still has it out for America."

The server brought out their meal and peered at Myles. Willow rolled her eyes. She turned toward Myles and kissed him, then stopped and peered at the young lady. "This is my husband."

The lady blushed and quickly handed out the food. After she left, Brielle and Olivia laughed. "Good ole Willow," Olivia said.

"What do you mean?" she said batting her eyes at Myles. "I just wanted to kiss my husband."

Chapter 6

After lunch and goodbyes, the gang drove toward the three-mile span of the Chesapeake Bay Bridge. It connected Anne Arundel and Queen Annes counties. Olivia and Brielle scanned the boats on the bay as they drove over the bridge. Once off the bay bridge, they continued the trek south on Highway 50. Willow glanced at the Google map on her cell phone. "It's another couple of hours to Crisfield and then a boat."

"This is an amazing experience, Dad," Brielle said. "Thank you for taking us with you."

"I hope to do a lot more of this in the future."

"I hope you include me," Olivia said.

"Why wouldn't I?" Myles asked.

Olivia sat back and peered out the window. Brielle looked over at her. "What is it?"

"I'm not his daughter."

Willow turned to her. "Don't think like that. You're my little sister. Myles knows how important you are to me. You'll always be in our lives."

"You mean it?"

"Of course, I do," Willow said.

They all turned toward Myles as he pulled the car over to the side of the road.

"Is everything okay, sweetheart?" Willow asked.

"Yes, I just thought we could look at the anglers out in their boats in January. You'd never see this in South Dakota. You may see ice anglers bundled up along the river but not fishermen in shorts and t-shirts."

The four sat along the water's edge watching the anglers gather different fish in their nets.

Brielle glanced at Olivia. “Have you ever been fishing?”

“Nope. Never even thought about it.”

“Me neither.”

“Come on, Willow.” Brielle jumped up, and she and Willow walked down the trail a bit.

Myles sat down next to Olivia. “Is it okay if I put my arm around you?”

“Of course, it is. You’re Willow’s husband. You would never do anything to hurt me.”

“I won’t ever. Listen to me. You’ll always be part of my life. You’re the one who brought me to your sister. I’ve told Willow this. You’re the love of my life’s sister. I’ll always be there for you. Don’t ever worry about being part of our lives. You always will be. You were the one who helped me understand where Willow’s coming from. I’d never be able to navigate through her life without you. Thank you for that.”

“You mean that?”

“Yes, I do. I don’t lie.”

“You just don’t tell everything.”

“Yeah, about that.”

Olivia flipped a rock into the water. “I understand. You don’t want us to feel differently about you because of what you’ve done. You need to realize none of us here will ever feel any different about you. I have a hunch you’ll have to do something like what you’ve done in the past again. It’s okay. Willow will always love you.”

Myles scrubbed a hand over his face. “I’m not worried about Willow. I’m worried about you.”

“What do you mean?”

“I don’t ever want you to feel like you can’t talk to either one of us. We’ll always be there to help you. Now, about Trevor. How do you feel about seeing him again?”

Olivia scanned the bay. “I really don’t know. I’m so used to not showing emotions.”

“But you did, Olivia, when you were holding Joshua.”

“What? I was holding that…”

“Yes, you were.”

Olivia ran her fingers through her long, blonde hair. “I didn’t know. I just tried to help him. As for Trevor, I have feelings for him. But I also don't want to get myself into a situation where I'll regret it. Willow and I have been through so much of that in our lives. She much more than myself. Now I have both of you. And Brielle."

Myles took a deep breath. "Don't ever forget that. It's okay to have feelings about Trevor. I believe he's a good guy. He's just in a bad predicament like you were. Remember that. And it's okay not to have any feelings toward him. We're going here because I need to gather some information about what is happening."

They both turned at Brielle's voice. "Let's go, you two. What's the problem here?"

Myles jumped to his feet and pulled Olivia up. "I was just telling Olivia it was her turn to drive. I'm crashing in the back seat."

Brielle put her hands on her side. "What is this? Why Olivia? I'm your daughter."

"She's older," Myles said throwing her the keys. "Just don't kill us."

"I promise."

~

Olivia started south on Highway 50 once more. Myles leaned his head on Willow's shoulder and fell asleep quickly. Willow moved him so he could rest his head on her legs. She fell asleep against the window.

Brielle turned back to the two. "They're both crashed."

A couple of hours later, Willow rubbed Myles' hair. "Wake up, sweetheart. We're almost there."

He sat up. "I needed that."

"You slept peacefully, dear," Willow said. "We stopped and switched drivers, and you didn't stir. I also found us a place to stay on the island. Smith Island Inn. Rooms for all of us."

They took an hour-long boat ride to Smith Island, which was approximately twelve miles from Crisfield. The boat finally docked.

"Look at this." Olivia said. "Karts and bikes. No cars."

Smith Inn was down the street. They walked toward the Inn. Willow paid for their rooms. Each of the girls had a room to themselves.

"You're just in time for supper," the innkeeper said. "Go

ahead and put your bags upstairs and come back down, and we'll serve you some crabcakes and our world-famous Smith Island Cake."

"Can't wait," Willow said.

The family joined the innkeeper's family at a long table. Large platters of food passed around from person to person and they dug in.

"Wow, this is the first time I've ever had crabcakes, and they're very good," Olivia said.

Brielle nodded her head in agreement. She was chewing on her crabcakes.

The owner said. "Maryland is known for its crabcakes and our world-famous Smith Island cakes. The crabcakes you are tasting right now are crabs that we catch here in this area of the Chesapeake Bay." He took a bite of his own crabcake. "Our Smith Island Cake is a featured prize for our local fundraising cake walk. We play musical chairs. For each round the cake is cut in half and shown to the players who pay to participate in the game. It turns out to be a fun time for everyone."

"It sounds like fun," Willow said. "Is it a summer tradition?"

"Yes. It is."

The owner surveyed those around the table. "What brings you to Smith Island?"

Myles answered between bites. "Several things. It's sort of a history lesson for the girls. I'm a social studies teacher at a school in South Dakota. We've studied climate change and sea level rise. I understand Smith Island is going through that right now."

The owner peered up from his meal. "You're correct. The island has been shrinking in recent decades because of rising sea levels. It is estimated in the last one hundred fifty years, the island has lost more than thirty-three hundred acres of wetlands. By the end of the century, the island is projected to be completely eroded, should the sea level rise by another foot. We have been working on building jetties and improving island drainage to stop it. It seems like a long way to go from South Dakota for a history lesson."

"Yes, it is," Myles said. "We're here for another reason. We're looking for John and Sandy Hopkins. More importantly, his sister Holly and her grandson, Trevor Reynolds."

"We know no one on this island by that name," the owner said quickly.

Myles smiled. “I can understand your apprehension. This is a peaceful island where people want to live their lives in peace. You need to understand, sir. Two bombs detonated in South Dakota killing thirteen people. Reynolds here had nothing to do with it. I just need some answers to help solve the case.”

“Again, Mr. Cason. These people do not exist here.”

Myles sighed. “Okay. Let me make it clear. If they don’t talk to me, then they’ll have to talk to the federal government. And you're smart enough to realize that won’t end up well. The family will have their lives shattered, the people on your island will be upended, and your lives will change. My family does not want that to happen.” He went back to eating his supper. “I agree. This is wonderful food.”

~

Willow perched herself on the edge of a windowsill in their room. “I’ve been studying this man who has been looking up here for the past five minutes. I’m guessing it’s Mr. Hopkins.”

She took a deep breath and turned to Myles who was sitting on the side of the bed taking his socks off. “This place is beautiful and dangerous. Kind of like you.”

His eyes snapped up at her. “What do you mean?”

“Myles you’re so handsome, but there’s something about you that is so dangerous.”

“Are you sorry you married me?”

She hurried over to him and sat on the side of the bed taking his hand. “No, I’m not, sweetheart. The moment my eyes touched yours, my heart was yours. That will never change.” Willow sighed. “For the second time in my life, I’m scared. The first time was when I couldn’t find you after the bombing. The second time was today when the lieutenant commander told us the story about you in the Strait of Hormuz.”

“It’s okay.”

She blinked back tears. “I don’t know if it is. I’ve seen every part of your body over the past few months, and I wonder which of those scars came from prison, which came from an operation in the Strait of Hormuz, or any other operation.”

Myles pulled her into her arms. “You’ve given up so much for me. I’m sorry I’ve changed who you are.”

Willow stood up and pushed him down on the bed. She crawled on top of him and kissed him hard. "Listen to me, sweetheart, I'm exactly who I want to be. Sure, I've changed from who I was, but this is who I want to be. I'm your wife. I will be the mother of our children. I'm a county attorney or at least acting country prosecuting attorney. Most important, I'm married to the man I want to be with. The man who protects me, loves me for who I am, and has my heart. That's all I've ever wanted in my life."

"Are you sure?"

"Positive."

Willow rolled over and snuggled into his chest. He put her arms around him. She peered up at him. "I've needed you to hold me many times recently. Tonight is another one of those nights. I know some things about you but not everything. Someday I may. What I do know is that you're a wonderful social studies teacher and boys' basketball coach. I really didn't get into basketball until I started watching you coach those kids. More importantly, I've seen how those kids respond to you. Most of them have had a tough time with parental authority. You've broken through and helped them."

She reached over and kissed him on the forehead. "I sat on the windowsill thinking about what my life would become. I've always wanted to have children but not until I found the right guy. You're the right guy. When we first met each other, I was excited about all the possibilities. But now that I soon may have our children, Myles, I think more about their safety. You say I've given up a lot for you. I haven't. I've done everything I have because I love you. I want to continue this journey with you but not at the expense of people like Holly and Trevor Reynolds. Give them some peace. I know what it's like to live in a family hell like they are. At least think about it?"

She snuggled back into his arms. "I've also been thinking about not being pregnant. And it scared me. I'm disappointed. I didn't want to let you down ever. And I did."

"How could you say something like that?"

She sat up and gazed into his eyes. "I want to have a child because it would allow you to experience something you never did with Brielle. You never had to see her grow up, hold her when she was small, or any of that stuff a mother or father gets to do with a child. What if I never have a child? Will you still love me?"

Myles pulled her close again. "I'm happy with my life. You're in it. Truly that's all that matters to me." He kissed her lips gently. "Child or no child, you'll always be the only woman in my life. I promise."

Willow smiled. "I feel better when you promise. You never break your promises." She nestled close to his chest and fell asleep.

Chapter 7

Myles woke up early the next morning when the sun came through the windows. He glanced over at Willow who was sleeping peacefully. She was so beautiful. But she didn't realize that his life had changed also when she walked onto that volleyball court.

Willow opened her eyes and smiled into his. "Still the same sexy eyes I've been drawn to forever."

Myles laughed. "No, just for three or so months. Are you going to stay in bed all day, or are you going to get up so we can go on one of those fun cruises?"

She jumped up. "Are you sure?"

"Positive. Let's go on a cruise and travel to D.C. I'm not involved in solving this case, but we'll talk to the president and Senator Dawson."

Willow started to kiss him when she stopped.

"What?" he asked.

"Are you for real? You're the first man who ever cared what I had to say. And you didn't even ask for my body last night."

He smiled at her. "That doesn't mean I don't think about making love with you every night. Last night we just needed to sort some things out. Willow, you're my heart also. And I love you."

She kissed him passionately. "Let's go enjoy a boat ride."

He grabbed her before she jumped off the bed. "You fell asleep and didn't hear what I said last night."

She looked up expectantly.

"I guarantee nothing will push you away from me."

Her eyes glowed. "Thank you. I love you and guarantee you'll always be my man. Even if we never have a child."

The two dressed and headed downstairs to the kitchen. Brielle and Olivia were already there. "Mom, Dad, you should taste these pancakes. They're wonderful," Brielle said.

Olivia nodded, her mouth stuffed with food.

Myles waved at the innkeeper's wife. "Where's your husband?"

"He's outside taking care of a couple of things."

Myles thanked her and walked outside.

"Good morning, Myles."

"Good morning. Thought a lot about what you said last night. We've decided to take you up on the offer of one of your exciting cruises. Funny thing. We couldn't find anything out about the Hancocks or Reynolds. They must be enjoying their lives."

He peered up at Myles. "Thank you."

"What are you doing here?"

"Preparing for another group of tourists coming in this afternoon."

Myles smiled. "We've already worn out our welcome."

"Oh no. I thought you were leaving today."

"We are. I have to go back to my classes in South Dakota on Monday."

"You had better go eat. The cruise starts at ten-thirty."

It was after one p.m. when the Casons made their way back to Crisfield on a boat. Brielle and Olivia were letting the wind blow through their hair. Myles had his arms around Willow. She peered up at him. "This was wonderful. Thank you for all of this."

"You're welcome."

"I want to travel around the world with you."

"I know. For now, it will include those two goofballs over there with their hair blowing in the wind."

Willow eyed them and laughed. "Yeah, they're still young and they have their whole lives ahead of them."

"Whoa, young lady. *We're* young and we have our whole lives ahead of us."

"Yeah, you're right. I'm going to enjoy every moment of it."

The two went back to enjoying the Chesapeake Bay and its beauty. When they arrived at Crisfield, they climbed into the car and headed toward Washington, D.C.

~

The next morning Myles visited the president while the women toured the Smithsonian Institute. He waited outside the Oval Office. The door opened and Myles was ushered in.

"Myles Cason, nice to finally meet you," the president said shaking his hand.

"Mister President, same here."

"Have a seat. Would you like anything to drink?"

"A glass of water would be fine."

He brought him a glass of water and sat across from him. "What brings you to the capital?"

"Wanted to talk to you in person. Mr. Nelson had mentioned you wanted me to take over a task force."

"Yes, I do. He must have told you about becoming a liaison for me and working with other countries and fighting crime."

"Didn't say anything about fighting crime, but that's what's happening right now in South Dakota."

"How is that going?"

"I'm not involved in solving the case but have my theories."

"I'm sorry to hear that you're not involved in the case. You would be a tremendous help. What are your theories?"

"Sir, I'm almost positive families from Rosewood and River Valley are involved with it. Hopefully F.B.I. Agent Throckmorton will be able to figure out what's happening."

"Good. Because I'm ready to send you out of the country. Things have changed since Jack Nelson contacted you. Funds have been obligated specifically for the task force you will coordinate in our country and around the world. You'll decide who's on the team. I'm designing a committee you will work with to decide what projects are deemed necessary. It involves nothing covert. Think working with other countries in dire need."

Myles glanced at the president. "I understand Sweden was the first target."

"Yes, but I'm thinking more of Libya. The United States would like to build better relationships with the country."

"Wow, Libya. That's a surprise. Aren't they still a little angry at the U.S.?"

The president smiled. "That's why I want you to go there. You're rather good at repairing fractured relationships."

"Thank you for the compliment, sir."

"Think about it. Besides, it's much warmer than South Dakota."

"That's true."

Myles took a deep breath.

"What is it, Mr. Cason?"

"Sir, Senator Dawson may have something to do with what is happening in South Dakota."

"What? Are you for sure?"

"A bag was left at a cafe near the Target Center in downtown Minneapolis. I can't specifically say it was the senator's wife who left the bag, but I'm certain she's the one. Or did it for someone. A guy named Michael Comforti is collaborating with him on some land deals for casinos in northern Minnesota.

"Wow. Why doesn't any of this surprise me? Politics at its finest. You let me deal with Senator Dawson."

"And it goes all the way to your office, sir."

"My office?"

"Yes. There is at least one or maybe more people in your administration involved with all of this."

"What could they hope to gain out of it?"

"There has been some talk Senator Dawson has his sights set on the presidency."

The president stared at Myles. "That won't happen. I'll make sure of that." He took a deep breath. "Before you leave for South Dakota, I'd like you, your wife, and the girls to join the first lady and me for a social gathering this evening with the presidents from Morocco and Libya."

Myles laughed. "How were you able to bring those two countries together?"

"Easy." He smiled. "They need our money. I want to introduce you to the current Libyan president and his wife. You may actually know her."

"What?"

The president smiled. "She was one of the women models you guarded in Paris one year."

"Got ya. We'll plan on joining you with a couple of young seventeen-year-old girls."

"Good. I can't wait to see that beautiful wife of yours and the two young ladies. A security detail will come and pick your family up. Where are you staying?"

"The Radisson."

"Say five p.m. It is a dress-up affair."

Once out of the president's office, Myles called Willow on his cell phone.

"Hey, sweetheart. How'd it go with the president?"

"Piece of cake."

"Great. You'll have to tell me about it."

"Right now, we need to shop for some fancy clothes. We've been invited to a social gathering with presidents from Morocco and Libya tonight."

Willow laughed. "How is that even possible? I didn't think those two countries could coexist in the same room together."

"Exactly what I said. It boils down to money. It also sounds like the two countries have had some positive relations in the recent past and are moving toward that once more."

"Everything is about money. We'll meet you at a restaurant along the Mall area in fifteen minutes."

"See you then."

Myles walked out of the White House and down toward the Mall. He stopped when he saw Michael Comforti talking to an older man. Ducking behind a group of tourists, he quickly shot a cell phone photo. "Got you, Mister Inside Man." He strolled toward the restaurant and found the women waiting for him.

"Dad, how was your meeting with the president? Is he cool?" Brielle asked.

Olivia jumped in. "I hear we've been invited to a social gathering with the president. What should we wear? I've never been to anything like that."

Myles reached over and kissed Willow on the forehead. "Slow down, young ladies. Yes, we're going to a social gathering. You'll have to dress up special. Probably even must wear makeup, lip gloss, all that stuff."

"Wow, Dad," Brielle said. "Are you going to be okay with that?"

Myles winked at Willow and smiled. "Yeah, I'll be fine."

"Good," Olivia said. "We had better eat and go shopping."

The ladies ordered salads.

"What is this?"

"Come on, Myles. We're going to a social. Have to look our best," Olivia said.

"Got ya."

After lunch, the women headed to shops in Georgetown to buy some clothes for the evening. Myles wandered around the Mall looking at the sites of D.C. A couple of hours later, Willow texted him saying they were back at the hotel.

It was quarter to five when Willow came out of the bathroom in her dress—a lavish off-the-shoulder gown with strapless heels.

His mouth stood agape. "Wow, you are magnificent!"

She blushed. "You think so?"

"Yes. I do. What, no makeup?"

"No, sweetheart. That's not me anymore. This is me." She blushed once more. "Here, let me fix that tie of yours. You look awful handsome yourself. Wait until you see your daughter."

On cue Brielle and Olivia both walked out of the bathroom.

"Wow, I don't know what to say."

Brielle smiled. "Am I beautiful, Dad?"

"Oh my gosh, yes."

"And me?" Olivia said batting her eyes.

"Yes, you are too."

"Good. We did it, girls. We shocked your father, Brielle."

Brielle smiled. "That wasn't really hard. He is so old-fashioned."

Everyone laughed.

"Should we go?" Myles asked.

"You bet," Willow said sticking her arm through his.

A knock sounded on the door. Myles answered it.

"Mr. Cason. The president sent us to pick you and your family up."

"Security picking us up? How do you rate, Myles?" Olivia asked.

"Special, I guess." His eyebrows waggled.

The limousine took them to the White House where they marveled at all of the men and women dressed in elegant attire.

Brielle grabbed her father's hand. "This is what's it like to reach the top?"

"Yes, it is."

"Have you been to something like this?" Olivia asked.

"Several times."

Brielle grinned. "Wow, my dad is a social butterfly."

"Not really." He laughed. "Had to do it."

Willow interrupted. "Well, dear, I have you here, so I'm going to take advantage of it."

"What do you mean?"

She kissed him on the cheek. "Dancing later and more after that. You are so damn handsome."

The president and his wife came over to Myles. "Your wife is spectacular," said the first lady.

"Thank you, ma'am," Willow blushed.

The president turned to Myles. "I'd like you to meet my secretary of state and two senior members of the cabinet."

Myles shook their hands. "My wife, Willow, my daughter, Brielle, and Willow's sister, Olivia."

"Nice to meet you all," the secretary of state said. "The president has said you're the man who's going to coordinate the newly-formed task force Congress recently approved."

"The president has asked me about it, but I haven't talked to my family about it yet."

The secretary of state cast a glance at Willow. "I'm sorry, ma'am. I didn't know."

She smiled sweetly. "Sir, my husband will do the right thing."

One of the senior members kept staring at Willow.

"Do I know you, sir?" she finally asked.

"I'm sorry, ma'am. You just look familiar."

Before Willow could say anything more, Myles took her hand. "Sorry, sir. I promised her and the girls a gourmet buffet."

"By all means, Mr. Cason. Take care of your family."

Myles pulled Willow away with him. The girls followed. She peered up at him concerned. "What was that about?"

"Not yet. Girls, go ahead and grab something to eat. We're right behind you."

Once they were at the buffet line, Myles pulled out his cell phone and showed Willow the photo. She was stunned. "That's Comforti talking to that man. I've never met him before, Myles. But it looks like your hunch is correct. What are you going to do?"

"I'm not sure. I'll call Nicolas Parker and have him tail him and find out more. Nicolas has worked with me in the past tracking down information. And many times following people. I'll contact him before we leave. Let's grab supper."

"Myles, for a man who doesn't want anything to do with this case, you've dived in the middle of all of it."

"I just can't help myself."

They went through the buffet line right behind Senator Dawson and his wife.

"Myles, what are you doing here?" Cynthia asked.

Myles glanced at her. "The President invited Willow and me."

"Willow Cason, nice to meet you."

"Ma'am."

Senator Dawson's head tilted. "Myles Cason. I have heard your name before. Aren't you a basketball coach or something like that in South Dakota?"

"I try. I hear you're interested in economic development in Minnesota."

The senator put on his politician's face. "Always want to make Minnesota better. Dear, we have a couple of people I'd like you to meet."

Cynthia smiled at Myles. "Great to see you again."

After they left, Myles frowned. "You'd think she would have known you."

"I told you, dear. I've never met her. Even if I did, I wouldn't like her."

Myles shook his head. "Let's eat." He dished some potatoes onto his plate. "Funny thing—Cynthia not saying anything about our meeting. It must mean she doesn't want her husband to know."

They both turned at Olivia's voice. "Let's go find a table. We're hungry."

A hand touched Myles' shoulder. "Mr. Cason, you are invited to dine with the president and his wife, along with the presidents of Morocco and Libya and their families."

"Please join us, Mr. and Mrs. Cason," the president's wife said.

"Thank you, ma'am," Willow answered. Myles pulled out her chair for her.

The president took over. "Mr. Cason, Mrs. Cason, Please meet the presidents of Libya and Morocco. They are guests in our country and will be here through the weekend."

Everyone greeted each other. The Moroccan president stared at Myles. "I have seen you before," he said in his best English.

"Sorry, sir, I can't recall meeting with you."

The president frowned. "Maybe I'm mistaken." He turned toward Willow. "Have you been married long?"

"Just a month."

The Moroccan president turned toward his wife and said something in their language. They both laughed. Myles smiled and took Willow's hand.

"I'm sorry, ma'am," the Moroccan president said. "We didn't mean to be rude."

The president stepped in. "The leaders of the two countries are here to iron out some details for a loan between the three countries."

The Libyan president spoke up. "The president and his wife have been wonderful hosts. We look forward to doing business with your country."

"Our country wants to help other countries to succeed."

The Libyan president nodded with a smile. His wife peered at Myles. Then she turned toward Willow. "It's good you have a strong man by your side."

Willow smiled. "He's the perfect man for me. I love him with all my heart."

"That is good this woman loves her husband," the Libyan president said.

The group talked for the next hour before the music started. The president and his wife went out onto the floor. The Libyan president bowed at Willow. "Would you like to dance?"

Willow didn't hesitate. "I would be delighted." He stood up and reached out his hand and she took it. Myles did the same with the president's wife. "May I?"

She smiled. "I would love to."

They joined the president and others out on the floor.

"You dance well, Mrs. Cason," the Libyan president said.

"I enjoy dancing especially with my husband."

"Have you known him long?"

"Yes, for many months."

"My wife and I were meant for each other when we were younger. Was that the same for you two?"

"Yes, it was, sir. We were meant for each other."

"I'm glad that you two will work with our country. I can tell you and your husband will be a good asset."

"Thank you, sir. I'm not sure if that is what my husband will do."

"No? I thought it was already set."

"No, Mister President. Myles hasn't decided. He's considering how it will impact our family."

"I hope you do join us. You'll be a nice addition."

Willow held back her disdain of his comment. The two continued dancing through several songs. They both turned when Myles tapped on the president's shoulder. "May I?"

"By all means, Mr. Cason. You have a lovely wife."

"Thank you, sir."

Myles took her into his arms and started dancing with her. "Did you enjoy yourself?"

Willow smiled up at him. "He has to be the first guy I've danced with that didn't pat my ass or try to kiss me."

"You mean like this?" Myles said kissing her gently on the lips.

"Like that. You know you could always do more of that. And I sure wouldn't be opposed to your hand touching my backside."

"Later, sweetheart."

"I'll hold you to that." Willow snuggled against her husband's shoulder as they danced. She popped her head up. "You knew what the Moroccan president said, didn't you?"

"Yes."

"What did he say?"

"Do you really want to know?"

"I wouldn't have asked."

Myles sighed. "He said you would be perfect for a wife and would be fertile to provide him many sons."

"What an asshole. And his wife put up with him saying that?"

"No choice, sweetheart. Some countries are okay with that. Both Morocco and Libya allow more than one wife."

"How disgusting. Thank God, I live in America. No way would I share you with another woman."

Willow leaned her head on Myles' shoulder. The two were silent for a moment. Myles broke the silence. "I'm sorry I didn't get a chance to tell you about my conversation with the president before tonight."

"How would you have been able to?"

"Still."

"No worries. We've talked about it before. I'm pretty excited about this task force."

"You are?"

"Yes, honey. Imagine the cultures we'll be able to visit. The people we'll get to see. It will be an educational experience for the kids."

The girls were busy laughing and talking to the children of the two countries. Myles spoke up, "They're enjoying themselves. Are you?"

"Sweetheart, any time I'm with you I'm enjoying myself. So, stop worrying. It is late, and I sure would like to kiss you many more times before we go to sleep tonight."

Myles took her hand and the two walked off the floor. "Are you ready, girls?"

Brielle yawned. "Yes, we're kind of tired ourselves."

Myles smiled as the two girls walked ahead of them.

"What are you grinning about?" Willow said.

"You forgot one thing tonight. The girls are in the same room we are."

Willow stopped and laughed. "Yeah, I did. Never again will I make that mistake."

Chapter 8

It was late Sunday afternoon when the Cason family arrived back in River Valley. Myles had contacted the sheriff when he arrived. "How did the town meeting go?"

The sheriff smiled. "For a man who wants to remain low-key on all of this, you're sure interested about everything."

Myles grimaced. "Yeah. Willow said the same thing."

The sheriff spoke up. "Everyone seems to be putting their lives back together. Did you find the Reynolds?"

"About the Reynolds. Why didn't you say that you had sent them that way?"

There was a hesitation on the other end. "Yeah, I should have. I wanted so bad for her to get away from all of this. She had nothing to do with it."

"That's kind of how I felt. We were on the island but didn't look for them."

"Thank you, Myles. Hopefully, the two will find some peace in their life."

Myles took a deep breath. "Do you have time to meet after supper?"

"Sure. How about at the office here in River Valley? Say eight?"

"Sounds good."

Willow came over and asked Myles what he would like for supper.

"How about we go pick up a pizza?"

She smiled. "Funny, that's what the girls wanted to do. It's unanimous."

The four drove downtown to the pizza place along the river. Though the place was full, they were able to find seats quickly.

Brody hurried over. “Olivia, Brielle, how have you been doing? Great to see you again. How was your trip to D.C.?”

“Wonderful,” Brielle said. “We’ll tell you tomorrow.”

“Great. You know you all can join us if you want. Devin and his family are with us also.”

“We wouldn’t want to interfere,” Myles said.

“Coach, you’re never interfering. Please join us. The pizza’s already there.”

Willow touched Myles’ arm. He glanced at her. “Why not?” Other members of both the boys’ and girls’ basketball team and their families were there also.

“What’s the occasion?” Willow asked Mrs. Davis.

“School starts again tomorrow, and practice starts. The kids thought we needed something like this.”

Jacie Tuthill walked over. “Thank you for inviting me.” She smiled. “It was nice of you.”

James Bush peered up at her. “Ma’am, I know it’s been hard on you, and we wanted to show our support.”

Willow took Myles’ hand and smiled at him. She whispered to him. “That’s your influence.”

They all turned around when Elroy came running in. “I’m sorry I’m late. My father just got off work.”

“I’m sorry,” his father said.

“It’s okay, Sampson. We’re just starting,” Mr. Davis said.

“Myles, this is my father. He works for the city street department. He just finished scraping the snow after last night’s snowstorm.”

“Nice to meet you, Mr. Hubbard.”

“Thank you, sir. Elroy has been excited to be playing basketball. He just enjoys it.”

Sampson glanced over at Jacie. “Mrs. Tuthill, I’m sorry about your loss.”

“Thank you, Sampson,” she said. “It’s been a long time since I’ve seen you.”

He smiled. “Work has kept me busy. How’s your husband?”

“Gone. And that’s all I care.”

Nothing else was said. They all dug into the pizza and enjoyed the conversation. It was close to seven forty-five when Myles whispered in Willow’s ear. “Sweetheart, I have to go meet with the sheriff. I'll see you at home."

"You need a lift?"

"I'm good. I enjoy walking."

She smiled at him. "You don't have to do that any longer. Plus, it's January."

"I'll be okay," he said kissing her on the forehead.

"See you later."

Myles started to walk out the door. He turned at Jacie's voice. "Myles."

"What is it, Jacie?"

She took a deep breath. "I think my husband's dead."

"What do you mean?"

"I heard from him every hour the first couple of days after I kicked him out. Then it stopped. His last message said he needed help because they had found him."

"Do you know who found him?"

"No. I don't."

"Did you tell Throckmorton?"

Jacie grimaced. "I don't trust him."

"Okay. Stop by and talk to Jack and give him your statement."

"I'll do that. Thanks for everything you've done."

"I haven't done much."

"Yes, you have. You've helped keep this town together after what happened. And everyone appreciates it."

Myles hurried down to the sheriff's office. The sheriff was sitting in his office when he walked in. "Howdy, Myles. How was the pizza?"

He smiled at the sheriff. "Is there nothing you don't know about that's happening in this town?"

"Yeah, who set off the bombs?"

"What about Tuthill? His wife believes he's dead."

The sheriff jumped up off his chair. "What?"

"Yes. She just told me."

"I just saw him yesterday. He was talking to a couple of men."

Can you describe them?"

"Thirties, one tall and the other one short. The shorter one had a scar on his face. Both looked mean."

Myles took a deep breath. "That means Tuthill is dead. They're the group's hit men."

"Hit men?"

"Yes, the two tried to kidnap Brielle back in Rosewood last year. I just happened to be there, and she escaped. Since I had no authority, I couldn't arrest them. But I can almost guarantee Tuthill's dead. Probably dumped at the bottom of the Missouri."

"Damn it. There are only a couple of spots where they could dump the bodies unless they used a boat, and the boats aren't going anywhere because of the snow and ice. It'll be difficult to find a body now. I'll have a crew look at those two spots tomorrow."

"I wish I was wrong. Don't think I am."

The sheriff sighed. "What else have you found out?"

"The president now knows there's someone in his cabinet involved. And I happened to take a photo of a man talking to Comforti. He's a senior member of the president's cabinet."

"Can we prove anything?"

"Nope, can't prove a thing at this point. However, I have a man looking into it. Should have something soon. This man is thorough. Any word on Zachary Hunter?"

"He hasn't shown up. Nowhere to be found."

Myles took a deep breath. "It's a good possibility he set the bombs. We have to find him and find him fast. Anything more from the disk?"

"Nothing of any use as of yet."

"We have to find Hunter. We also have to find out if there are any other targets."

"I'll work on it first thing in the morning."

Myles climbed out of his chair. "What's the hurry?"

"Classes and practice tomorrow. Besides, Throckmorton is managing the case. I'm just here."

"If you say so. But that's right. Back to school for the kids. I'll keep you updated on what we find."

"Sounds good."

It had started snowing when Myles walked outside. It was a half mile to their house. He picked up his cell phone.

Willow's soft voice was on the other end. "Hey sweetheart, we're home now."

"I'm starting my walk to the house."

"Do you want me to pick you up?"

"No, I need the walk to clear my head."

"You okay?"

"Yes, I'm fine, honey. Lot of things to think about. Find Hunter first off and see if there are any targets on that disk."

"I'll look while you're making your way home. Please be safe."

"I will. I've spent more time walking in my life than anything else."

There was silence on the other end. "You don't have to do that anymore. Just be safe. I love you."

"Love you, also." Myles took his time. He arrived at the house close to ten. Willow sat on the couch in her favorite position with her legs up against her chest reading a book when he walked in. "I was about ready to send out the National Guard, or in your case, would it be the U.S. Navy or U.S. Marine Corps?"

Myles smiled at her. "Thanks for being concerned about me. Where are the girls?"

"Upstairs talking about their trip, boys, school—you name it. We're so fortunate our two girls get along so well."

"Yes, we are. What are you doing just sitting here in your favorite position?" he said.

"Reading and also thinking about us." Myles sat down next to her. She took his hand. "I want you to run this task force. You can do it. And we'll be together with our family."

"Is that what you've been sitting here thinking about?"

She smiled. "Yeah, that and plenty of other things. But we'll talk about those later. Right now, I think I may have some leads on the next targets. Or possibilities."

"Okay. Shoot."

"There is no rhyme or reason why the first two bombs were set. Except you were there. There is only enough dynamite for one more bombing. And if my theory is correct, it'll be something you're involved with."

"Why would anybody want to kill me?"

"I've thought about that. One possibility is your affiliation with what took place seventeen years ago. I found out the boy's name was Austin, and he was Cynthia Gold's brother. Everyone still believes you killed him with that car. Including his sister, Cynthia. Another possibility is Cadence and Ronald. You have destroyed their lives. Isaac Reynolds. His warped mind believes you stole me from him. And they're all part of the same group. Then there is a person who's been listed many times. No name. I 'll call him Mister X."

"Do you really think these are the reasons?"

"I don't know what to think. Part of me believes it's much larger than that, and it has something to do with your background. Something you've done in your past. But it isn't even connected to you. It's just something you've run across in your past experiences. And my gut reaction is it relates to my Mister X, whoever this person is."

"I'm sorry I've put you in danger."

She put her arms around him. "No, you haven't put me in any danger. We're in this together. We'll figure it out together. I'll keep digging."

Myles pulled her close and kissed her.

"Nice." She smiled.

He unbuttoned her top two buttons and massaged her breasts.

"Much nicer."

Myles kissed her once more. She wrapped her arms around him and responded. Then stopped. "Please upstairs. I don't want the girls to see us making out on the couch."

He lifted her up. She wrapped her arms around his neck and her legs around his back. He grabbed her back end. "Did anyone ever tell you that you have a nice ass?"

"A few times. But your opinion is the only one that matters."

Myles carried her upstairs and sat her gently on the bed. He dropped down to his underwear. She scooted back against the headboard. Myles crawled on the bed, unbuttoned a couple more buttons, and kissed her breasts and her body.

Willow rolled him over and climbed on top of him. She started kissing his scars. Then stopped. "Hold it a minute. I have something for you." She climbed off the bed with her shirt unbuttoned, went into the bathroom, and came back a few moments later.

"Please, roll over."

He did as she asked. Willow started rubbing the cream with two fingers onto the scars on his back. "I've always wondered where each of these scars came from," she said as she gently rubbed them in. "Was this one in prison? Was this one in

Afghanistan? Where?"

Myles rolled over after she was finished. "Lots of places. Please don't get bogged down on my scars."

"I can't help it. It's part of your body that I love. It hurts me to know that someone did this to you. But the doctor said this cream will help with the scars."

She set the container down on the floor. Myles gently slipped the shirt off her shoulders. Then he gently took off her panties. She did the same with his underwear and climbed on top of him. "You need to know I'm deeply in love with you. I've been since the first day I saw those gorgeous blue eyes. And I will deeply love you until those same eyes close for the last time and after."

The next morning Myles eyes popped open. He looked at the clock. It was five-thirty. Myles turned his attention toward Willow. She was snoring lightly lying in his arms. The blanket lay over them after last night's lovemaking. Willow opened her eyes and glanced at him.

"Good morning, dream."

"Good morning," he said kissing her gently on the forehead. "I need to take a shower."

"I'll make you some breakfast," she said sitting up on the bed.

"You don't have to."

"I want to."

Myles walked toward the shower but turned around at Willow's voice. "Did anyone tell you you have a nice ass?"

"Yes, but you're the only one who matters."

~

She wrapped her arms around her naked body. Willow had never been happier in her life. Even if she never had Myles' child, she wouldn't worry about it anymore. It was all about enjoying life with Myles.

Willow jumped off the bed, put on Myles's shirt, and pulled on her robe. She had breakfast going when Myles came downstairs. "Scrambled eggs with bacon in them."

"Smells good."

Willow placed his plate down with orange juice. She climbed into a chair next to him and curled her arms around her knees.

"Okay, what's on your mind?"

"Nothing really. I'm happy. Life is good."

"Yeah, about that. I don't know if I should take the president's job."

"And why's that?" Willow asked.

"You're so happy. I don't want to ruin that."

She grabbed his fork and stuffed some of the scrambled eggs into her mouth. "Please realize the reason I'm happy is because you're in my life. It doesn't have anything to do with this house. Or your car. Or even your job. It all has to do with you. Nothing more."

"Are you sure?"

"We don't lie to each other." She grabbed another bite of scrambled eggs and switched subjects. "It's going to be a busy day for me. A lot of court appearances, mostly misdemeanor stuff. Tomorrow is the criminal stuff."

"Good luck. We travel to Bluffton tomorrow for our first game after the holiday break."

"Yeah, I'm not sure I'll make it. Unless the judge decides to cancel it, or the attorneys ask for a continuance. Always possible. If not there, I'll be thinking about you."

Myles glanced over at the clock. "Basketball practice starts once more."

She reached over and kissed him on the lips. "I love you, sweetheart. Not any car, house, or job. Just you. Whatever you decide, I'm right behind you."

"Good to know. You're the best thing that happened to me, also. Love you."

Chapter 9

Myles stepped into the gym. Elroy sat on the bleachers. Myles could tell he was contemplating something in his mind. He took a seat next to him.

"Good morning, Coach."

"Elroy."

"Today is going to be strange. No Trevor. No Joshua. No Lydia. Why would people do something like that?"

"It's hard to comprehend why people do what they do. We must continue on. It's tough to hear this, but life goes on. And we must move forward. If we don't, the criminals win."

Elroy peered up at Myles. "Never thought of it that way. I hope you find who did this."

"They'll find them eventually. Now dress out. Practice starts in ten minutes."

Myles ran the boys through several drills. Some the same, others different because of the loss of two of their main players. He moved Elroy into Trevor's shooting guard position and inserted a couple of reserves into the varsity rotation. Then he stopped practice early. "Well, guys. Good workout. Let's talk some."

The boys sat on the bleachers. Myles scanned their eyes and could see the confusion in them. He took a deep breath. "This past week was horrible for everyone. Especially the families of those who lost loved ones. I don't know if I have the right words to help you through this, but I'll try." He sighed. "Before I came here, I spent several years in prison, as many of you know. Sad situations all the way around for those involved. One common theme for many in prison was resilience. Maybe that's what you were meant to have."

"What do you mean, Coach?" Devin asked.

"This group of young men could take it upon themselves to provide the school, the community, with the hope that things can get better. With your performance in the classroom, in the community, and especially on the basketball court, you can set the tone of how your friends and others move forward with this crisis. You're only young high school students, but you've been through adversity on the basketball court and have risen to the challenge. My gut tells me you can do it off the court also. The community and your friends count on someone to help them through this tragedy. Let's be the ones who help them. Now grab a shower and go to class."

Myles noticed throughout the day that the boys took what he said to heart. They talked to their friends, kept a positive outlook, and helped others when they needed it in his social science classes.

Mrs. Thompson hurried to walk with him to the lunchroom. "What's up with those boys?"

"What do you mean?"

"Michael Papport actually helped one of the girls in science with an experiment. He's never done that. And Devin Bush. He can't stand science. For the first time since I can remember, he asked questions about photosynthesis of all things."

"Maybe they're just eager to learn."

Mrs. Thompson smiled. "No, Myles. Elroy told Miss Roberts that you asked the team to step it up in the classroom and help their friends. They're doing it."

"Good for them. I always try to tell them there's more to life than just basketball."

"I'll pass it on to the members of the girls basketball team."

Myles glanced at her. "Brielle and Olivia are already doing that."

"What?"

"Devin is dating Brielle. At least I think that's what it is. I'm not sure anymore."

"Mrs. Thompson laughed. "Yeah, I hear you."

"Anyway, Devin told her what I said at this morning's practice. He asked her to help. And she will."

Mrs. Thompson sighed. "Everyone knows you've gone through tough times in your life. Believe me, you've helped turn this school around. The kids, even those who don't play sports, are excited about what's happening. They've seen Devin and Brody excel on the basketball court and realize that they can be someone too. Thank you." Mrs. Thompson rushed toward her classroom.

Olivia grabbed his hand. "We're not as bad as we believe we are."

He rubbed her hair. "We'll have to always remember that."

She peered up at him. "Mind sitting with me at lunch?"

"Love to."

When they entered the cafeteria, they stopped, their eyes wide.

"Wow, Myles. The lunchroom has never been this full." She pointed at Brielle who had saved a seat for her and Myles.

They joined her, then Myles asked, "What's for lunch?"

Brielle laughed. "Same ole stuff."

"Then what's this?"

"The boys on your basketball team have taken it upon themselves to do as you asked."

"And what's that?"

"Brody told me how you told them how resilient prisoners were in the state penitentiary. They said you made it through horrible situations. This community would also."

Myles laughed. "That isn't exactly what I said. I told them the prisoners were resilient not me."

Olivia interrupted. "You know high school kids. We take everything and twist it."

They all looked up as Willow strolled into the lunchroom. She had grabbed a salad and came and sat with them. "Mind if I join you?" she asked sliding down next to Myles. Willow scanned the lunchroom. "Am I dreaming or is this the most kids who have ever been in this lunchroom?"

"You'd be right, big sister," Olivia said. "Blame your husband."

Willow turned to Myles.

"I told them maybe the boys basketball team could take some ownership in what happens in their community after last week's tragedy."

Before Willow could say anything, a young girl came over to them. "May I sit down by you?"

"Please join us," Myles said.

"Thank you. I'm Clovis Papport. I'm a senior here. My little brother, Michael, said that it was okay for us to eat in the lunchroom with others now."

Myles turned to Clovis. "I don't understand."

"Sir, River Valley has many types of cliques. Jocks. Druggies. Brainiacs. And losers like myself and my brother."

"Whoa. Who said you were a loser?"

Clovis laughed. "Come on, Mr. Cason. Look at the women around this table. They're all beauties. Every boy wants to be with them. Me, I'm lucky if my brother wants to hang around me. Anyway, I just wanted to tell you thank you for thinking of everyone in the school, not just the popular kids."

She stood and started to walk away but stopped and peered back at Myles. "Mr. Cason, you've done wonders for my brother. He's always wanted to play basketball, but the cool kids wouldn't allow it. Devin and Brody joined the team and told him it didn't matter who the boy was. Their coach cared about each one of them for who they were. My brother will play his heart out for you, Coach. Just like everyone else on that team will. That's what you're seeing here today. You're giving kids who haven't had a chance hope."

All four sitting at the table grew silent when she left. Willow peered over at Myles and smiled. "I've told you you're good for these kids and this community. And this salad is extra good."

Everyone laughed.

"What?"

Olivia smirked. "You come up with some of the corniest, off-topic things all the time."

Willow laughed. "Non sequiturs. That's what my husband says all the time. It's one of the things he loves about me." She continued eating her salad. "I had a break and thought I'd come over here and join you all for lunch. But I actually do like their salads."

"How's courtroom drama?" Brielle asked.

"Nothing too much this morning. A woman sued her husband because he signed a prenup when they first got married that he wouldn't have sexual intercourse with another woman. If it happened, he would lose all of his wife's estate."

"What?" Myles asked. "They can do that?"

"Yep. Anything's possible. She's rich. And the rich do bizarre things."

"How'd it turn out?" Olivia asked.

"Weird situation. He argued he didn't have sexual intercourse with another woman. It was a man, so the judge dropped the suit."

Myles frowned at Willow. "You're making this up."

"As sure as I'm sitting here, it happened. The attorney for the man pointed out that the contract specifically said sexual intercourse with a woman. It didn't say not being able to have sex with a man. Those are some of the things I deal with every day in the courtroom." She took another bite of her salad. "This afternoon will be better."

Myles studied Willow. "Okay, explain to me how the woman would have known her husband fooled around on her if he didn't tell her."

"Come on, Dad, Olivia and I know when you and Willow make out with each other. And we're only seventeen."

His brows furrowed. "What?"

"Dad, Willow has this glow. Just like she did this morning."

Willow coughed on her salad. "Time to return to work. I'll walk you to class, Myles."

The two girls laughed as Willow grabbed Myles' hand and pulled him away.

~

That afternoon Willow completed her court work in her office. A call came in from one of her department staff. "Willow, the judge would like to see you in his office."

"All right, on my way up. Did he say what it was about?"

"Nope, just said to stop by when you had a moment."

Willow walked out of her basement office and up the stairs to the third floor. She was stopped on the first floor by Rhonda Papport, who worked in the treasurer's office. "Willow, good to see you."

"Rhonda. How have you been?"

"Doing good. I wanted to thank you for helping Clovis and Michael out at school. They both have said that you and Myles have done everything you can to help them through this recent tragedy. Michael's especially pumped about playing basketball. Coach told him he'll see some action in Bluffton tomorrow. We plan to catch the fan bus to the game. Usually, we don't go out of town because we can't afford the cost."

"I'm glad that you're taking an interest in Michael. So many parents don't do that with their children. Is Clovis still considering USD and law school in the future?"

"She is actually."

"If she's interested. I do need help in the office. Some simple things. It would give her a chance to see if she's interested in law after all."

"I'll tell her. Thanks."

Willow started to climb the steps to the third floor.

"Willow, I forgot to mention this. I saw a couple of guys carrying something near the River Valley bridge the other night. I just caught a short glimpse and am not sure what it was. Just thought you may want to know."

"Thanks."

Willow climbed the next set of stairs and stopped. She pulled out her cell phone and dialed Myles' cell phone. Brielle picked it up. "Hey, Mom, Dad is kind of busy right now."

"It isn't Miss Roberts again?"

Brielle laughed. "No, writing something on the chalkboard. You really need to help him with his printing. We students have a tough time reading it sometimes."

"Okay, Brielle. I'll tell him. Can he talk or is he in the middle of class?"

"He can talk. The bell just rang."

Brielle handed the phone to her father. "Some light brown-haired, gorgeous woman wants to talk to you."

Myles picked it up. "Hey, sweetheart. What's up?"

"So, I'm a gorgeous, light brown-haired woman?"

"Yeah, that's what our daughter thinks. And she would be right."

"I just talked to Rhonda Papport a few moments ago. She mentioned that she saw two guys carrying something near the River Valley bridge. I thought I'd pass it along to you."

"Thanks. I'll let the sheriff know. Are you done with your exciting court cases?"

"Yes, heading up to the judge's chambers. He called me up for some reason. I'll talk to you tonight. Love you."

"Love you, also."

Willow continued her trek to the third floor. She stopped and said hi to the court clerks. "Is the judge in?"

"Yes, he's expecting you."

Judge Quinten Townsend was from East River. He had taken over the court after Willow had gone over the former judge's head to help Trevor Reynolds. The boy needed protection from his family. Other improprieties had arisen with Judge Garner so the state had suspended him until the issues could be investigated. Now Willow headed into his office and knocked on the door. Judge Townsend peered up. "Come in, Mrs. Cason."

Willow entered, surveying the dark wood bookshelves full of casebooks.

"Have a seat."

"Thank you, sir."

"No sir, Mrs. Cason. You can call me Quinten when we're out of court."

"And you can call me Willow."

"Now that's settled, I have some issues I wanted to talk to you about. I'm happy with the way you have handled the court docket over the last couple weeks after the former country prosecuting attorney Reginald McKenzie was suspended for the incident with Mr. Reynolds. It makes it much easier for all of those involved. Especially for those who have been wronged or are seeking justice."

"Thank you, Quinten."

"I've talked to colleagues of mine on the Supreme Court in South Dakota. I wanted to gauge your interest in filling the seat as district court judge. You're well known in this area of the state, you're very thorough in your briefs and opinions, and you're fair in every part of your job. Your department staff has admired you since you set foot in the courthouse."

"I don't know what to say, sir."

He smiled at her. "I'm sure it's a shock right now. Realize you're nothing like your family. You care about people, and you want justice to be served. You would serve the remainder of the term which would be close to three years. Then after that, you would have to be reelected."

"Can I think about it?"

"Of course, you can. I'll give you a month or two to let me

know your decision. Right now, continue to do your job as the county prosecuting attorney. Another thing."

"Yes, sir?"

"Court has been cancelled for tomorrow."

"What? Why?"

The man smiled at her. "It seems there's a big boys basketball game tomorrow night in Bluffton. And unbelievably, many of the attorneys have filed for a continuance because their clients want to see the game. I guess it's pretty big."

"Wow! Basketball even supersedes court hearings."

"What your husband is doing has attracted national attention. More importantly, he and those boys are providing some life in a community that tragedy struck recently. You two are special in this community. In this region. Thank you."

Willow stepped out of the judge's office stunned. She slouched against the wall not sure what to think.

"Willow, are you okay?" one of the clerks asked.

"What? Oh yes."

"Are you sure?"

"The damnedest thing just happened."

"Were you asked to be the judge in district court?"

"Yes. How did you know?"

"The judge has questioned us extensively for the past two weeks. Everyone is in agreement you'd be great for the job."

"Would I?"

"Of course, you would. You care about people. You want to serve justice but also care about those who are hurting, whether they be a victim or the perpetrator. You've rubbed off on your husband, or he's rubbed off on you. Either way. Thank you for what you've done to help us get through the tragedy."

Willow peered at her. "Everyone keeps saying that. What is it that we're doing any different than what anyone else is doing?"

The clerk smiled at her. "You two are at the forefront of every activity here in the community. Who was it that put together a banquet after the boys won their first game? In an opposing gym, of all places. Who was it that brought a meal for the boys in Pineview? Who was it that kissed the hell out of her husband not once, but twice to help raise money for the community? You and the two young girls in your family spent last week in the gym helping those in need after the bombing. Your family cares about this community. Many of us do. But you two work harder than most to make sure our kids have a better opportunity." She took a deep breath. "Rhonda Papport has been telling everyone how her son is going to play in his first varsity basketball game tonight. The kid is so excited. The whole courthouse is taking a fan bus down tomorrow tonight to cheer the boy on along with the others."

Willow laughed. "So that's why there are no court cases tomorrow?"

"Justice will be served. It can wait. We realize what your husband has gone through and the hits he's taken from his past. He's a good person and is the best thing that has come into this community in a long, long time. We all just hope it continues."

The clerk hurried away back to her desk. Willow was just too shocked to move. Finally, she made it down to her office. A judge? She had always dreamed about being a judge someday. Now it was here.

She stopped. What about Myles? How would he react? What was she thinking? He would be happy for her because he loved her. And that was all Willow ever wanted. Someone to love her.

Chapter 10

After classes were over, Myles called Sheriff Watkins. "Have some information for you."

"Go ahead."

"I may know where Tuthill was dumped."

"Yeah. Where?"

"River Valley bridge."

"I'll meet you over there in ten. Throckmorton is joining us."

"Will do." Myles headed out the classroom door. Brielle was walking ahead of him in the corridor. "Brielle."

She stopped and turned toward Myles. "Hi, Dad."

"Hey, sweetheart. Can you tell Walter or James to go ahead and start practice without me if I don't make it back in time?"

"Sure. What's up?"

"Some stuff to deal with the sheriff."

"Okay."

Myles was out the door and headed over to River Valley bridge. It was only a few blocks from the school, so he hoofed it. He had given his car keys to Brielle earlier so she and Olivia could ride home after practice. He arrived as a group of scuba divers went into the water.

He saw the sheriff and stood near him. Throckmorton was directing the divers.

The sheriff was watching with his hands in his pockets. "How did you find out?"

"Willow called me about it. Seems one of the ladies at the courthouse saw two men carrying something the other night."

"We'll see. By the way, we have a hit on Zachary Hunter."

"Yeah?"

"Bluffton."

Myles' head snapped toward him. "Are you serious?"

"Yes."

"Damn. The basketball game tomorrow night."

"You have to be kidding?"

"Willow has this theory that I'm the one they're after."

"If so, why would he kill hundreds of kids and their families?"

"Who knows? Can you contact law enforcement in the area and check out the gym and school?"

"I'm on it."

"I'll try to contact Vicki Hunter and see if there is anything she can tell us."

Jack slowly turned his head toward Myles. "That won't happen."

"Why?"

"She and her family have disappeared."

"What?"

"Yes, right before Zachary left prison, my contact in the Sioux Falls area said she asked for protection from her husband, and they took her away from there."

"I don't understand. This is becoming weirder and weirder."

Throckmorton came running over. "Sheriff, they're not only bringing up one body but two."

The trio waited along the shoreline. Sure enough, two bodies came up. One was Tuthill. The other…

"Damn. That's Vicki Hunter," Myles said. "How did she get here? Where are her kids?"

The sheriff stared at Myles. "And the plot thickens. We'll handle this. Go to practice."

~

Myles made it into practice just as the boys started shooting their free throws. More spectators filled the bleachers. One group of at least twenty or so sat up in one corner of the bleachers. He walked over toward Brielle and Olivia who were watching the boys warm up.

"Hey, Dad. What do you think?"

"Think about what?"

"The cheering section."

"Who are they?"

Olivia jumped in. "They're cheering for Michael Papport."

"He has his own cheering section?"

"It looks like it."

"Well, I'll be…" He stopped before finishing the sentence. Myles hurried over to the team who had been shooting free throws.

James Bush walked over toward him. "Few sprinters today. They're hitting their free throws."

Myles glanced at the boys. "Elroy, please come over here."

The sophomore ran over to him. "Yes, Coach?"

"I'm going to put Michael in your spot during practice tonight for tomorrow's game against Bluffton. There will also be times I'll use both of you together to give Brody a break. I want you to handle point-guard duties tonight."

"What? Me?"

Myles smiled at him. "You were the only one who could keep up with me on our first run. I'm sure this will be simple for you. Keep your eyes on Brody throughout the first part of practice."

"Yes, Coach."

Myles started practice with Michael at the shooting guard. Every time he touched the basketball, his cheering section erupted with cheers. After about ten minutes, Myles stopped practice. He substituted Elroy for Brody.

He pulled Michael Papport aside. "Michael, you can shoot the basketball."

The teen grimaced. "I'm afraid I won't even hit the rim. They'll laugh at me."

"If you don't, keep trying. Besides, it doesn't matter what you do. Those kids up there will be right behind you every step of the way."

Brody stood next to Myles and watched the practice. Elroy passed the ball to Michael who dribbled and put up a shot. The ball bounced off the rim. Everyone turned when the kids roared and applauded. The next time Michael hit his shot.

Myles placed his hand on Brody's shoulder. "Watch what Elroy does when he passes the ball. See how quick he moves the ball to spots."

"He makes it look so simple. Why isn't he the point guard?"

"Because you are, Brody. I wanted you to take a step back and see how easy playing point guard can be. Elroy doesn't realize it, but the kid is as gifted as can be. He just wants to fit in."

The two watched for fifteen minutes. Brody peered over at Myles. "I can see what you mean. The kid is good."

"Yeah."

"He should be our point guard. We can be so much better. I'd be willing to switch positions with him."

Myles smiled at him. "Brody, your folks would be so proud of you. You're growing into a fine young man. If I switch you it will mean you'll score more points."

This time Brody smiled. "And it would mean maybe some colleges would scout me."

"Bingo." Myles hollered for Devin to come to the sideline. "Go in and take his place."

Devin hurried to the sidelines. "What's up, Coach?"

"Oh nothing. Giving you a break. Wanted to see how this matchup would work. Trying to find different combinations."

"Coach, Elroy has his passes exactly where I need them for a quick shot."

"Good. I plan on moving him to point guard and Brody is going to move to shooting guard."

The boys went through the drills for another half hour before Myles called it quits. He sat them down on the bleachers. "Good practice, team. Tomorrow night will be another tough one. Bluffton's crowd is loud and obnoxious. Be prepared." He took a deep breath. "I'm going to move Elroy to point guard and Brody to shooting guard. At times Michael will join the pair. We're going to an even smaller, quicker lineup. Grant Black, I'm keeping you in at the low post. I'm counting on you to clog up that middle. Micah, you'll do the same when Grant needs a breather."

"Okay, Coach," he said.

"I want to reiterate that tomorrow night will be possibly the toughest game you'll ever play. Only Rosewood will be tougher."

"Even tougher than Pineview?" Devin asked.

Myles nodded.

"Why's that, Coach?" Elroy asked.

Myles took a deep breath. "Neither school can stand me."

~

The sheriff bopped into the gym as practice was wrapping up. "Do you have a minute?"

"Sure."

"Both were strangled."

"What? That means Zachary Hunter is nearby."

Myles turned quickly toward the bleachers. The girls were sitting there. He picked up his cell phone and dialed Willow. No answer.

"What is it, Myles?"

"Willow. He's after Willow!"

The sheriff called one of his deputies immediately. "Get over to the Cason house. See if Willow is there."

Myles hurried over to the girls. "Stay in the gym with the others until we return."

"Is everything okay?" Brielle asked.

"Not now, Brielle. You two stay with Devin, Brody, and the others. All of you, please stay here in the gym until I come get you." Myles and the sheriff hurried out the door. "To the courthouse."

"On the way."

They two arrived at the courthouse several minutes later. Willow's car was there. The two hurried toward the front door.

"Damn, it's after five. Everything's locked," the sheriff said, then fumbled in his pocket for his key.

~

Willow was working on some of her court papers when she heard a creak as if something was opened. What was that? Everyone was gone. She climbed out of her chair and walked over to the door. "Anyone here?" A glance at her phone showed that Myles had called, and but she'd missed it because she'd silenced the phone. Her breath caught. Zachary Hunter stood at the door banging on it. Willow raced to the door and locked it. The man continued to beat on it.

"Willow Cason. It's your time."

She tried to dial the office phone for help. Damn it. The phone line was dead. Glass shattered from the door's window. Zachary! The man's hand tried to unlock the door. Willow grabbed a letter opener and slammed into his hand.

He howled. "You bitch. This is going to be even more fun than I thought. Just like my wife."

"What about your wife?" Willow asked.

"Yes, Raped. By me. She didn't want to put out one night. It just happened another guy came into the house. I didn't know my wife was such a slut. Broke his neck."

"Myles trusted you."

"No. He just wanted information. I provided him what he wanted to hear. Almost all."

Willow tried to keep herself calm. "Why are you trying to kill him?"

"People are paying big money to end his life. He escaped two attempts. This one he'll never escape. It won't matter to you because you'll be dead before him. But not until after I've ripped those clothes off you and have my way with you." He laughed. "Isaac Reynolds always said you were good in bed. But of course, while he was screwing you, he spent many times in Mitchell sleeping with other women. Seems like he had a new one every day. Most recently the English teacher in River Valley—wasn't worth his time. Then of course there was your mother. Samantha, isn't it?" Hunter shrugged. "A little too old for my taste. But now that Cadence woman—she was a nice piece. Had her a couple of times. She enjoyed me more than she ever enjoyed Ronald Halter. Now I'll make my dream come true with you."

Just like that Hunter busted the door in. Willow pointed the letter opener at him. "You'll never touch me. The only one who will ever touch me is Myles."

He glared at her. "What is it with Myles? Don't know what you see in him. He should be dead. The one mistake I made was putting the dynamite too far away from the actual ceremony. Won't make that mistake again or the next one. A town called Bluffton. No way he'll escape because the man will be sitting on the bomb. Kaboom. He'll be shredded to pieces."

"Okay, if I'm going to die tonight, at least give me the satisfaction of telling me why, and don't say money. That really gets old."

"Wow, you're a sharp woman. That's why you two make a good pair. He's sharp also. You see, Mrs. Cason, the organization I work for has high aspirations. As high as putting their man in the Oval Office someday."

"You? Not likely."

"I didn't say me. Senator Dawson."

"Why do we have to die for him to become president. Myles

has nothing to do with any of this."

"It's not necessarily you, Mrs. Cason. I just wanted you. So once that happens, I can't let you live. Now Myles is the key. He has so many things locked up in that mind of his."

"For instance?" She moved back.

"He knows a lot of the evil doings of Dawson and others that include your father and Brielle's father."

"You're mistaken there, Hunter. Brielle is Myles' daughter."

"What about Jasmine?"

"Jasmine? What does she have to do with it?"

"You didn't know? She's Myles' sister. Not Joanna. In fact, Myles' is Jasmine's only sibling. Casey and Joanna are the products of affairs their father had over the years. Just like your father and mother. Who knows whose daughter you are? Or for that matter, whose father is Olivia's?"

"You leave my little sister out of this."

Hunter lunged toward her. She bolted to her left. "I told you Myles is the only one. Now get out of here."

Hunter snickered. "Do you really want to know why I have to kill Myles?"

"I don't care. Just get out of here."

"It's because Senator Dawson, your father, and others are all involved in international activities. Didn't you just meet the President of Morocco recently? He is looking for help from the U.S."

Willow was caught off guard, and Hunter jumped on her. She tried to stab him with the letter opener, but he was too quick. He started to tear her dress off her, but a strong arm wrapped around Hunter's neck.

"You son of a bitch. Get your hands off my wife." Myles lifted the man up and slammed him on Willow's desk. The sheriff quickly put the cuffs on him. Shaking, Willow jumped into Myles' arms. "It's okay, sweetheart. I'm here," Myles said caressing her hair. "He won't harm anyone again."

She continued staring in terror at the man. Finally, Myles softly moved her face toward him. "I'm here. No one will ever touch you."

She finally broke down and buried her face into his shoulder.

There was a smirk on Hunter's face. "Myles, you know it's

not over. They'll be coming after you. You know too much to live."

The sheriff took over. "Okay, Zachary Hunter, you are under arrest for the attempted rape of Willow Cason and also for the attempted murder of Myles Cason." He read Hunter his rights, who whipped around toward the sheriff. "You have nothing on me dealing with murder."

He smiled. "You should have thought about that before you attacked Willow here in the courthouse. She has set up surveillance cameras in this office. You'll be going down big time. And attempted murder charge will keep you in Sioux Falls for a long, long time. Of course, you killing your wife would take care of that."

Hunter glared at him. "Like I told Myles, you have no idea who you're messing with."

The sheriff smiled. "You have no clue who Myles Cason is, do you? You're toast. You'll either rot in prison or in a black-op site somewhere around the world. Either way, good riddance."

They peered up as two deputies arrived. "Take him away. And make sure he's never let out of these chains."

"Understood, Sheriff."

Once he was gone, the sheriff turned toward Myles and Willow. "Do you want us to get her some help? Someone to talk to?"

Myles took a deep breath. "Can you keep the girls tonight?"

"Yeah, the wife will love to have those two with them. I'll take care of it."

"I'll take Willow home. See if I can help her through this."

"If you need me at all for anything, call."

~

Myles helped Willow to her car. "Where are your keys, honey?"

"In my handbag, I think."

Myles reached into her purse and helped Willow into the car. "Buckle up."

Willow tried, but her fingers were shaking so bad she couldn't attach the seat belt. Myles reached over and buckled it for her. She stared forward all the way to the house.

He sat her down on the couch. "Can I bring you something to

eat?"

"I'm not hungry."

"You need to eat something."

She glared at Myles. "I'm...not...hungry. What don't you understand about those three words, Myles?" After she said it, she broke down sobbing. Myles sat down by her, and she crawled into his lap. "I'm so sorry I snapped at you. I'm so sorry."

"It's okay. How about I just hold you?"

"Will you? Will you never let go?"

"I'm always there for you."

She peered up at him. "You always have been. I don't know why. I deserved everything I would have received tonight. It's my karma after all the men I've used and abused."

"Whoa, sweetheart. Don't think like that. No one deserves what that man was going to do to you."

"Why not? I've always been a whore. Just like my mother. Do you know Isaac Reynolds slept with my mother? My mother, Myles." Willow started to tear off her dress.

"Whoa. Stop. What are you doing?"

"I need you to touch me, check my body, to make sure I'm okay. He didn't touch me, did he? I told him no one would ever touch me but you." She peered up at him. "Did he…did he rape me?"

"No sweetheart, we arrived in time. No harm came to you."

"How do you know? You weren't there. I couldn't even call you for help. Did he rape me?"

"He didn't touch you. I promise."

She stared into his eyes. "You're always promising me things. I never promise you anything. You deserve better than just a whore for a wife."

"You're not a whore."

"I'm not? Do you know how many men I've slept with? Seven...count them. And each one of them I felt nothing. I'm a whore." Myles continued to stroke her hair to try to soothe her. She glanced up once more. "Zachary tried to rape me. He killed his wife and he also raped her and killed a man who didn't rape her."

"We'll straighten it out. Why don't you try to get some sleep?"

"I can't. After tonight you'll never want to touch me again.

It's ironic—for the longest time I didn't want the seven men I slept with to touch me. Now the only man I want to touch me will never touch me again because I'm damaged goods. No one wants to sleep with a rape victim. That's all I'll ever be to you again. I don't ever want that, Myles. I'm not just a quick jump in the bed with you. You're the one I love."

"You'll always be the one I love. Nothing happened to you tonight. I've always said you're the strongest woman I've ever met."

"Am I?" she asked. The glow slowly crept back into her eyes.

"Yes, you are."

"Please hold me." She buried herself into his shoulder. "You promise. You won't ever think I'm a whore. A slut. Someone you sleep with because you feel sorry for me."

"Never. You're the only one I've ever loved. I promise."

She tried to smile again. "You've never broken your promise." Willow stood up and started to take her clothes off. Myles jumped up. "What are you doing?"

"I'm taking my clothes off. That's what you want to do. That's all I've ever wanted to do with the seven men I've slept with."

Myles lifted her dress back on. She crumbled into his arms; tears flooded her eyes. "Please just hold me. Never let me go."

Myles held her in his arms. She snuggled in tightly. A few moments later, she was snoring lightly. The emotions had been too much for her. He kissed her on the forehead. "You'll be okay."

The phone rang. He answered it. "Is Mom okay?" Brielle asked. "We need to be there to help her."

"It's better you spend the night there. She needs some space. She'll be okay."

"She had better, Dad. You said you'd protect us."

"Okay, Brielle. Get some sleep. Tomorrow will be a new day."

"I'm sorry, Dad. I'm scared. I can't lose my mother. I love her and I love you."

"Is Olivia okay?"

"Mrs. Watkins and I have been trying to calm her down. She finally fell asleep."

"Okay, do the same, sweetheart."

"I promise. Good night."

Myles stared at Willow. Her glow was coming back to her face. Willow was a strong woman. She would be okay. They would be okay. With that thought he fell asleep. His eyes popped open. "How long have you been staring at me?"

"Not long enough," Willow said with a smile. "I broke your heart last night, didn't I?"

"What do you mean you broke my heart?"

"All the things I said."

"You remember what you said?"

"Much of it. I didn't mean any of what I said. Myles, it would only be a matter of time before something like this would come back to haunt me."

"What do you mean?"

She didn't move from his lap. "I've been playing with fire my whole life. The men I slept with. None of them were good for me. None of them. Until you came along. You're the only good thing I've had in my life. Last night I thought was the end of us. All my past life finally caught up with me. You didn't want me anymore because I'm a whore. At first, I slept with men because I was told to do it. Then it just became natural. I didn't know any different. If Zachary Hunter would have raped me last night, it wouldn't have been anything different than what happened to me before you came along." She sighed. "Why didn't you want to make love with me last night?"

"You were hurting, sweetheart. No way was I going to take advantage of you after such a traumatic experience."

She peered at the wall. "That's what makes you so essential to my life. Any other man I slept with would have jumped at the opportunity, and I wouldn't have cared. It would have broken my heart last night if you would have taken advantage of me."

Myles pulled Willow close to her. "You can move forward. What happened with those seven men is over. What happened last night. That's your past. You and I are the future."

"It is, isn't it? Thanks for being here for me and being understanding."

Myles frowned. "I hope you're as understanding with me."

"What do you mean?"

"Hunter said some things that are going to come back to haunt me. I've done some things that I can't get away from. That's part of the reason I've tried to keep things away from you. I didn't want to have you hurt in anyway."

Willow had to smile. "Well, it didn't work very well not telling me, did it?" She reached up with her hand and touched his face. "I was emotional last night, but you need to realize you're the only man I would have let hold me and would talk about those things with. When you're history comes out, I'll be there for you. I can handle any baggage you have because I love you that much. But I was just afraid you couldn't do the same with me—afraid you would never want me again because of the sexual misdeeds in my past."

Myles frowned. "Okay, Willow Sage Cason. You're not a whore. You're not a slut. We're fine. I love you dearly. Move forward."

She smiled. "Are you sure?"

"Yes, I am. Every time I look into those eyes, I see the only woman I could ever be with. I could raise a family with. I could spend the rest of my life with."

"Funny, I see that in your eyes also." She reached over and kissed him with pent-up passion. They both turned as the door burst open.

"Are you okay, big sister?" Olivia asked.

Brielle laughed. "I would say the two are just fine."

Willow buried her head in Myles' chest. "And I told you I didn't want the girls to catch us making out on the couch."

Chapter 11

Tuesday morning, Zachary Hunter was arraigned in District Court. He was charged with two counts of murder, attempted rape, and two acts of terrorism. If convicted, he would either face life in a federal penitentiary or death by lethal injection. Rare in South Dakota. Willow was taken off the case because of her involvement, but she was in the courtroom when Hunter walked in. Hunter was to be transferred to maximum security in Sioux Falls. The man glared at her. After he was arraigned, he stormed past Willow with the deputy.

"Can I have a word with him?" she asked.

The deputy nodded.

"I have only one thing to say to you. My husband will bury you and everyone associated with you, you son of a bitch." Willow turned and strode out the door.

Her staff jumped out of their chairs when she came in the office. "Are you okay?"

Willow smiled. "I'm doing better. Last night was rough, but Myles was there. Like he's always promised."

"I'm glad."

Everyone turned around when the judge came walking through the door. "Ladies. Willow. Can we talk?"

"Yes sir. I'll be right up."

"No, Willow. We can talk in your office."

He followed Willow to her office. Once they were both in, he shut the door and turned to her. "Most likely the man will be executed for what has happened. I just wanted to make sure you were okay."

Willow looked surprised. "Last night was rough, but Myles helped an emotional, hysterical woman through."

"I'm not surprised. I've cared about you for a long time."

"What? What do you mean?"

He frowned. "Yeah, perfectly inappropriate words after what happened last night. What I meant to say is the court system has had its eyes on you for several years. A person who would be good for the state. And you do it honestly and the right way." The judge stared at her. "May I sit down?"

"Please do so."

"Willow, you're fortunate to have Myles in your life."

"You know Myles?"

He smiled. "I've known him since he was a little boy. His father and I were best friends."

"He can't stand his father, Your Honor."

"No, not his stepfather. The Gulf War hero. I know it was hard for you last night. Realize it was just as hard for Myles. The man has been through a lot of shit. Stuff he'll never be able to tell you because he works for the U.S. Government. And that's what's happening here. They're coming after him because of his past. You know some of his past issues, and you must make a choice, Willow. Either stay with him and help him fight or walk away."

"There's no question, I'll never walk away from Myles. I would have done that in the past with any other man I was with. But not this guy. I'm deeply in love with him. I'll be right beside him."

~

The team bus was scheduled to leave River Valley at one for Bluffton. The kids were ready to go, but the bus was on hold waiting for their coach. The fan buses would leave an hour later. There were five of them.

Myles and Sheriff Watkins sat across the desk from Throckmorton. "Hunter gave a surprisingly good description of where the bombs have been placed. The bomb squad found them, so you're good to go."

"Bombs?"

"Yeah, three of them."

Myles laughed. "He wanted to make sure I didn't escape from this one."

Throckmorton frowned. "Yeah. But we both know it's far from over. We just solved one piece of the puzzle. You had better get going. There's a cheering section of your own down there."

"Yeah. Who?"

The sheriff smiled. "You'll just have to wait and see."

Myles headed toward the team bus, arriving fifteen minutes late.

"Ready to roll," he said climbing on the bus.

"About time, Coach," Devin said with a smile.

"We thought you had forgotten about us," Brody said.

"Never."

The bus started the three-hour drive toward Bluffton. It arrived at the Bluffton High School just outside of Sioux City close to five-thirty. The fan buses had arrived earlier, and the fans were in the gym. Willow and the girls had provided another sub meal for the team. This time other mothers of the players were involved.

After their meal, the team headed into the gym. Myles took a deep breath. Elroy walked by him and tapped him on the back. "We got your back, Coach," he said.

Micah, who followed behind him, added, "I'm sure the coach feels good now. We all have your back, Coach."

The gym was almost filled for the game. Myles glanced around the facility. Signs were everywhere. "Devin, you can't hit squat." "River Valley who?" Myles stopped and stared at one sign in the corner. "Myles Cason is a murderer."

~

Willow put her arms around the two. Brielle peered at her with moist eyes. They watched as the sign was taken down. "Why would they say that about my dad?"

"Sweetheart, some people will never forget or forgive."

Olivia sniffed. "That's sad, Willow. The guy didn't do anything, and he still has to suffer."

"I know."

The three walked toward the River Valley section to a chorus of boos. "Hey, Cason's daughter, we know who your father is. Do you?"

Brielle halted and glared at the student section. Willow grabbed her hand and pulled her with her. "Oh yeah, you need a mother like that?"

This time Olivia stopped. "Knock it off. My sister doesn't deserve to be treated like that."

"Wow. Which Konnor girl would you settle for? I'd prefer the older one."

They all turned to a man's voice. "Back off, boys."

"Oh, which one are you dating?"

The man turned toward security and waved at them. They came over. He whispered something to them. The security guard waved for the two to come down.

"Who, us?"

"Yes, you two."

"We didn't mean nothing by it," the two said coming down.

"Son, you should check out who you're talking to before you do something stupid and not mean it. These three are under my protection."

"What? We didn't know. We're so sorry, Mrs. Cason."

The man glanced at her. "What do you think?"

"Let them go. Waste of time dealing with them."

"My sentiments also."

The two boys scrambled back up into their seats. "Thank you, sir," Willow said. "We were okay."

"Yeah, but Myles wouldn't have been happy with me if I didn't do something about it."

"You know my dad?" Brielle asked.

"Yes, ma'am. You must be Brielle. Nice to meet you, young lady. Myles and I have been together for sixteen years now."

"Sixteen years?" Willow asked.

"Yes, ma'am. We've been best friends."

"What are you doing here?" Olivia asked.

"A couple of reasons. I have info for Myles and am tasked with watching you three."

"Wow!" Willow said. "You just show up out of nowhere and expect us to believe that. Let's go, girls."

~

Several moments later there was a deafening booing when the River Valley Eagles came out onto the court. It continued for several minutes.

"Wow, this is loud," Olivia said almost hollering.

The boos turned to the roar of cheers a few moments later. It was as loud as they had heard in any gym they had been in.

Willow turned to the girls. "They hate Myles here."

"Why's that?"

"This is where he literally ended Bluffton's best season ever and eliminated them from the playoffs."

"That was seventeen years ago," Olivia said.

"Little sis, you know as well as I do small towns don't ever forget."

The teams continued warming up. Willow glanced over at the man who'd walked in after them. He was talking to Myles. Myles was laughing at whatever the man was saying.

Brielle jumped down off the bleachers and hurried over to her father. "Dad, this is crazy."

"Yeah, Brielle. It'll get louder and stay that way throughout the game." He turned to Nicolas. "Sweetheart, this is Nicolas Parker. He and I have been good friends for a long time."

"We've already met," Brielle said. "He helped us out of a pickle."

Myles frowned. "Are you okay?"

"Nothing we couldn't handle." Nicolas smiled.

Nicolas and Myles hugged each other. "It's great to see you. We'll talk soon."

"Yeah, I have a lot to tell you. I'll be in River Valley in a couple of days."

~

Brielle spun toward Nicolas Parker. "Would you like to join us?"

"Are you sure the spunky Konnors will be okay?"

"Yes, as long as you don't call them Konnors. Especially Willow."

"Noted. Let's go."

The two walked over to the others. "Mom, this is Nicolas Parker. Dad's best friend."

Willow frowned. "I'm so sorry about the way we acted."

He smiled at her. "Don't be. Myles has told me you're pretty protective of the two girls."

They all turned at the starting lineups. The Eagles were booed when they were announced. It grew even louder when Myles was announced as coach.

"Wow, there's some hatred for the guy," Nicolas said.

"Yeah, he kind of broke this community's hearts when he was

a senior," Willow said.

River Valley controlled the tip. Elroy found Micah streaking through the lane, and he slammed the ball through the net for the first points of the game. The two teams battled back and forth throughout the first half. River Valley held a three-point lead at halftime.

~

Willow headed over to the concession stand to grab something for her and the girls.

"Well, lookee here, if it isn't Willow Konnor."

Willow turned and glanced at a man she had not seen in several years. "Daniel Rexalt. It's been a long time. And the name is Cason. Willow Cason."

"Willow Cason? You mean you married a murderer. Your mom and pop are probably totally disappointed that you married the man."

"I don't care what my folks think about my life. I'm happy with who I am and what I've become."

"I'm glad to hear that. You'd be happy to know I'm shacking up with Constance Brewster."

"Vincent's sister?"

"Yes, I'm sorry about what happened to him."

"Yeah, it was tragic. I should go. It was nice talking to you."

Willow hurried back to her seat. She could never stand the guy.

~

The second half was more like the first half. The teams battled evenly and were tied, 80-80 with thirteen seconds left in the game. Myles called a timeout. "Well, guys, you battled through it and are one shot away from winning the game. Michael Papport, you're in for Elroy. Brody, you move to the point. Devin, you'll be double-teamed. Michael, you'll be open. Hit the shot."

Everyone clapped hands and walked out to the court. Myles turned to look at the crowd right above them. They stood and yelled when they saw Michael in the game again. Michael looked up and over at Myles who waved him over.

"You can make the shot. I've seen you do it every night in practice. Everyone of your teammates have seen it, and your cheering section will be carrying you through the halls tomorrow."

"Are you sure, Coach?"

"Look at that crowd out there. They've been hostile all night long. They've yelled at Devin, Brody, Micah, and even yourself. Wouldn't you love to be the one to shut them up tonight?"

"Yeah. I would."

"Good, then do it. Tonight's your night. We need you."

Myles was right. They double-teamed Devin, who scored forty-three points for the evening. Brody found Michael cutting across the lane. At first, he dropped the basketball, then quickly picked it up and got off the shot as the buzzer went off. Swish. The Eagles remained unbeaten.

The crowd went silent, but the group in the corner supporting Michael went crazy. Devin and the rest of the team ran over to Michael and lifted him up. Brielle and Olivia rushed over to the team.

Willow glanced at Nicolas. "Don't you dare do anything to harm my husband!" She bolted out of the bleachers and hurried toward Myles, then wrapped her arms around him and whispered in his ear. "Michael did it. You have to be so proud of him."

Myles pointed to the crowd. "More importantly, those kids up there are proud of him."

She reached up and kissed him. "And I'm so proud of you. This had to be tough for you."

"You know, it wasn't. It was high school basketball. Then the real world came tumbling around." Myles eyes stared ahead. Willow followed his eyes. Jasmine, his sister. He walked over toward her.

"Myles, is that really you?"

"Jasmine!" He lifted her up and held her tight.

"I thought you were dead. Everyone said you were. Then I saw your daughter, Brielle."

"She's here. And you remember Willow?"

Jasmine smiled at Willow. "How could I forget. She helped me through everything in the Halter household."

The two hugged. Jasmine turned at Brielle's voice. "Jasmine, I'd hope you'd come and watch my father's game."

Myles' eyebrows lifted. "You called her?"

"Yes, Dad, I did. I thought you'd want to see your sister. Your real sister."

"How did you know?"

Willow whispered in his ear, "The book."

Myles turned back to Jasmine. "How's school going?"

"Right now, not too good."

Myles was alert. "What happened?"

"Money kind of ran out."

"What are you doing now?"

Jasmine glanced around the gym. "Looking for a job. No luck."

Olivia come running over. "Myles, we don't have a girls basketball coach anymore."

"What are you talking about?"

"Mrs. Thompson and her family are moving away. She resigned."

Jasmine touched Myles' arm. "Sorry, big brother. I still have another year and a half before I earn my teaching degree. Have to find someone else."

"Their problem. It's great to see you."

"And you also. I've missed you so much."

"We can help with your education. You realize that."

"You would?"

"Of course, we would. Just let me know what you need."

She kissed his cheek. "Now I need to talk to Willow."

~

Jasmine and Willow sat down in an empty bleacher. "How did you connect with my brother? You didn't even know him in high school."

"No, I didn't. I met him in October, and everything clicked."

"You and Olivia are not like the rest of your family."

Willow sighed. "That life is over. I'm happy with your brother. More than happy. I love the guy and always will. We've all had it hard. None harder than your brother."

Jasmine studied her eyes. "Is he serious about helping me with my education?"

"Your brother would do anything for you and Brielle."

"And you're okay with that?"

"Why wouldn't I be? Your brother is my dream."

Jasmine smiled. "Thank you for being there for me. And especially for Brielle. I couldn't help her because of Cadence.

Willow, she's evil. My brother did the right thing in not hooking up with her."

Willow eyed the others. "Yeah, our lives haven't been the greatest. I still fight my demons."

"Willow, don't. You're with my brother. He needs you."

"And I need him."

"Willow, you know you could coach those girls. And do a better job."

"Yeah, I could. But Myles and I have big plans in our future."

Chapter 12

Myles went through his Wednesday morning classes, then headed toward the lunchroom. Olivia and Clovis Papport invited him to join them for lunch. Brielle had a couple of makeup tests to do.

Grant walked up. "Mind if I join you?"

"Sure," Myles said. He introduced Grant to Clovis.

She smiled at Grant. "Coach, we know each other."

"Right. Sorry."

Willow popped in and sat down next to Myles. She kissed him on the cheek. "Hey, handsome. How's school?"

"Wonderful. Now ask *me*?" Olivia asked.

"How's school, little sister?"

"Wonderful. I aced my Civil War test. And Myles didn't even help me."

"Why would I?"

Olivia frowned. "Everyone believes since I live with you and Willow, I get preferential treatment."

Clovis interrupted, "Mr. Cason doesn't give preferential treatment to anyone. I've heard from classmates that he's the toughest but fairest teacher in school."

"There you go," Olivia said. "You need to tell everyone else that."

Myles smirked. "Do you want me to announce it over the loudspeaker?"

"Yes. Do it."

Everyone laughed.

"You're quiet, sweetheart," Myles said to Willow.

"Sorry, busy morning. Lot of things on my mind."

"Can we help?" Myles asked.

"That's sweet. Just court stuff. I wanted to stop by and say hi to my favorite guy and favorite girls. Missed one but will catch her at home tonight." She grabbed a bite of her salad. "I did hear something interesting."

"What's that?"

"We're in for a major blizzard starting tonight and running through Friday."

"So now you're a weather forecaster?"

"One of us has to keep up on things. Someone I know didn't remember to call me this morning about a particular item."

"Crap. You wanted me to grab something. I don't remember what."

Willow laughed. "I got it, sweetheart. Go back into your own little world." She glanced over at Olivia. "Did you remember what you were supposed to do?"

"Oh shoot, no. My bad. I'll take care of it at home."

"Thanks."

Willow took her husband's hand. "Come on, dear, I'll walk you to class."

Grant glanced up at the Casons. "Coach, your wife walks you to class more than any of the other girlfriends in school."

Myles blushed. Willow smiled. "I enjoy walking him anywhere. Besides, I get to hold his hand."

Once they were out of earshot, Myles said, "Okay, Willow, what's on your mind?"

"Lots. Need to talk to you. Tonight though. I can tell you that Zachary Hunter will be tried in federal court, so that's good news. There's only a question—will he receive the death penalty?"

"He won't."

"What?"

"Not in the federal system. He would have had a better chance in South Dakota. One good thing with the federal system. He won't be released for a long time."

"Good."

"How are you handling all of it? I haven't noticed any flashbacks."

"Getting it out of my system that night helped immensely. Thank you. I could have never done it without you. I would have held it in. In fact, I thought I handled myself well in Bluffton. I ran into a man who I'd partied with in college. We did some stupid things. Drinking, drugs, etc. He brought some things up, but it didn't faze me. For the first time, my past didn't haunt me."

"You'll make it through."

The two were at Myles' classroom. She closed the door after her. "I'm so sorry about what happened with your friend, Nicolas Parker."

"Don't be. He's fine."

"Does it bother you I told Jasmine you'd help with her college tuition?"

"No. Why?"

Willow squeezed his hand. "I didn't want to step out of bounds."

"Okay, what's wrong with you?"

She trembled. "Sweetheart, I thought I had my life together with you. Now I feel everything's out of control. I wanted to have your child so bad. Now I'm not pregnant."

"Hey." He took her hands. "Someday it could happen."

She peered up at him. "You don't want to have a baby, do you?"

"That's not it at all. If you have a child, I'll be ecstatic. I'm just saying slow down, take a breath, and let's see what happens. You're the most important person in my life. Don't you ever forget that."

~

After practice, the school board president stopped Myles as he walked out of the gym.

"Join me for a cup of coffee in the common area."

Myles nodded and they headed to a round table in the high school lunchroom.

"Wonderful game last night. It was exciting to see that young Papport hit the game-winning shot. He's on Cloud nine today."

"He's worked hard to play. The whole team has."

"I've noticed we've had some scouts on campus. In fact, Principal Alexandria Newcombe said a recruiter stopped by yesterday to access one of the kids' records."

"Oh?"

"Yeah, your daughter's."

"Wow. It must have been Spencer Graham."

"No, it wasn't actually. A lady from University of Connecticut."

"Big time."

"Yep. Myles, you've done a wonderful job here."

"Thank you. Any luck on the superintendent search?"

"Hoping to fill the vacancy in the next couple of weeks. Two candidates left to interview. I hope you and Willow would be able to sit in on the last two interviews?"

"We'd be glad to."

"Both are on Saturday. At one and then at two here in the boardroom."

"I'm sure we can handle it."

"I hoped it would work out for you."

Swanson paused. "Any luck on what's happening with the bombing?"

"We arrested the bomber."

"I heard that. He also tried to rape your wife. I'm so sorry about that. She's okay?"

"Willow's strong. She'll be okay."

"Great. See you later."

Myles headed out of the boardroom. He picked up his phone and called the sheriff. "I'm on my way to your office."

"I'm here, Myles. I'll see you in a few."

Myles arrived at the station around nine p.m. He walked in and dropped in the chair across from the sheriff. "Busy as my day, I see."

"Yep. What's new?"

"The two bodies were Vicki Hunter and Jordan Tuthill. It was easy enough to notify Hunter's other half. Jacie Tuthill didn't seem a bit surprised or show any remorse. She's glad it's over."

"Hell of a way to go. Lose your whole family in a month. I wonder what she'll do."

"She's going to work for me."

"What?"

"Yeah, she'll handle public relations, reports, etc. She's always wanted to do it. So why not let her. On another note, Judge Townsend has approved my request for a search warrant. Will do that tomorrow."

"You know as well as I do everything has been cleaned up."

"Probably at his home. But the warrant also includes his places of businesses and Jeremiah's rendezvous points including Mitchell, Geddes, and Rapid City."

"Damn, the guy gets around."

"He does. But the warrant also includes all his assets including those in Rosewood. And Myles, he has assets connected with Konnor, Halter, and Cason. Willow did a thorough job. And Hunter is starting to talk to the F.B.I. and to Throckmorton."

The sheriff sighed. "One of my deputies overheard Throckmorton asking him about a book."

"The same book we have. Do you think we should turn it over to Willow and let her turn it over to the judge?"

"It may be a good idea."

"I'll talk to her about it when I go home tonight. The one thing that has me puzzled is Senator Dawson, Comforti, and the senior advisor in Washington, D.C."

"One step at a time, dear friend. One step at a time."

"Yeah, it works that way."

"I'm heading home. Do you need a ride?"

"No, I'd rather walk."

Jack shook his head. "You're the most walking fool I've ever known. Tuthill's funeral is on Thursday evening."

"I'll make sure the basketball team is there."

"That would be a good thing. Jacie will need support. She's handling it pretty well considering."

Myles crossed his arms. "The loss of her children has devastated her, but her husband, I don't think so."

"Probably right there. Now the Hunter lady. We can't find any relatives of hers at all."

"How long do you wait before you do anything? I know she has children. Just don't know where."

"We'll give it another week."

~

Myles made his way the three quarters of a mile to his house. It was close to ten p.m. when he left the sheriff's office. His cell phone rang right after. "Do you have ESP?"

Willow laughed on the other end. "What do you mean?"

"I just left the sheriff's office, and you're calling."

"The warrants were one of the things I had to tell you about.

Sheriff Watkins probably told you."

"Yep. Excellent job, sweetheart."

"Thank you, my love. Do you want me to come pick you up? We could go parking. I wasn't in high school with you, so I didn't have the opportunity to go parking with you."

This time Myles laughed. "Why not? I'll be sitting on the benches in front of the school."

"Pick you up in ten."

Myles sat on one of the benches and scanned the sky. He had drifted off into neutral zone when headlights from a car pulled up. The lights shut off and Willow hurried over to him.

"What's this? Are you staring off into the stars?"

"It's so peaceful."

She sat next to him and snuggled into him. "Someday you're going to have to explain to me why you are such a goofball walking everywhere and now just staring into the stars."

He pulled Willow close to him. "I probably owe you explanations about a lot of stuff."

"Only if you want to talk about it." She reached over and kissed him on the forehead.

"I always walk because I didn't have a car in the last several years. It was just easier not to have one because a car is a way to track me."

"You've never really told me what you do."

"I haven't? After what happened with Hunter I don't know if I ever want to."

"Please, don't keep anything from me. I'm in all the way with you. I'll protect you anyway I can."

He sighed. "That night in the gym before we were married, I tried to tell you who I was."

"I remember."

Myles stared into the sky. "At eighteen I was pulled out of a prison cell and swept away into a secret operation task force to a small island in the Pacific Ocean. They figured out I was on my way to prison and was the president's cousin, so why not? I've been around the world. Received the scars on my back in Afghanistan, Morocco, and China."

"China?"

"Yep, China. Almost made it out but was caught. Found out

later Ronald Halter told the Chinese government who I was. I won't feel good about myself until the man is put away." Myles took a deep breath. "Everything points to Ronald Halter and the others. Once he's done, we can move forward. I'll finally have a future. Unless I bring him down, I won't have a future with the one person I love in this world."

Willow gazed into his eyes. "Let's get one thing straight here. You have a future with me. There is nothing you could ever do that could drive me away from you. Let the guy go. He's not worth it. You're married to a woman who deeply loves you and is going to have your children one day. You are the head coach of a damn good basketball team and have found a home here."

"What about the task force?"

Willow hesitated. "If it'll make you happy, sweetheart."

Myles peered into Willow's eyes. "What aren't you telling me?"

"What do you mean?"

"Your expression changes on your face when you have something you want to say, but you let it pass. Kind of like Samantha on *Bewitched* when she wiggles her nose."

Willow laughed. "You really are a goofball. I've never seen *Bewitched*, and my nose doesn't wiggle."

"I never said it did. It's just an expression." He tried to imitate it.

She giggled. "You mean like this?"

"There you go again."

"You're right."

"What is it?"

"It's not important."

"Now you listen to me, dear of mine. If you have something to say that's important. Just say it."

"Judge Townsend called me into his office the other day and told me he loved the work I was doing. Then he told me he recommended me to become the interim judge for this district court. Can you believe it?"

His eyes opened wide. "You're great at what you do. I'm so proud of you. Take it."

"What about your dream?"

"I would never stand in your way. You've worked hard to

achieve the position you have."

"I'm thrilled. You're the one I love. I don't want to lose you. First, I can't have your child. Now I'm in line for a judgeship."

Myles brought her close. "Remember when we had this discussion about whether or not I could be with you because of my past? What did you tell me?"

"We need to move past our past because we're better people."

"Correct. You're a wonderful woman. It's everything about you. It's not because you can have or not have a child. Or because you're a judge or not a judge. Or anything else you believe you can do or can't do. My heart belongs to you."

Her eyes opened wide. "And I have your heart?"

"You sure do." He took her hand and placed it against his heart. "Feel that. That's all yours. And it will always be yours no matter what happens in our lives. I can't put it any simpler than that."

She wiped away a tear. "Okay."

"You still up to parking?"

Her lips twitched. "You mean you want to still go parking after the bombshell I dropped on you?"

"Of course, I do."

"I know a cool spot we can park down near the river."

"How would you know a cool spot?"

Willow grinned. "I heard about it from our two daughters when I told them we're going parking."

"And I'm a goofball."

"What is that supposed to mean?"

"You gather your information from two teenagers who've probably never been parking."

Chapter 13

The blizzard that was expected to hit the area arrived on Thursday. Snow started after lunch and picked up steam after five. The funeral for Jordan Tuthill, which was switched to earlier Thursday because of the impending blizzard, was sparsely attended.

Myles and Willow attended with the girls along with members of the boys and girls basketball teams and their parents. The sheriff and his family along with members of the school board attended to show support for Jacie. The snow had caused difficulty for those outside of the community. After the funeral people gathered for a small meal put on by members of the church.

Jacie walked over to Myles during the wake. “Thank you for bringing the basketball team to show their support for Jordan. He’s done many horrible things. One good thing he did do was bring you to River Valley. I hope you never leave this place. You’ve done so much for those kids, for this community. Thank you.”

“We did it to support your family. It’s been a tough couple of weeks for you, but the kids have seen the character and strength you’ve shown. It’s helped them also.”

“Thank you. That was nice of you to say.”

Willow walked over. “Hi, Jacie. Our sympathy for your loss.”

“Thank you, Willow.” She hurried away to talk to others.

“Notice who Olivia is hanging out with?”

“Brody. Nice guy. And tall.”

Myles rolled his eyes. “So, what does tall have to do with anything?”

Willow giggled. “I don’t even know why that came out.”

“What do you think of that pairing?”

Myles stifled a yawn. “I gave up trying to understand high

school dating. Clovis likes Grant. Or I should say, Grant likes Clovis. Brielle still likes Devin. Or she likes Elroy now. Who knows? And really, why are we talking about this at this venue?"

"Yeah, you're right. But it is a wonderful place to pick up guys, or in your case, girls. Many people who don't even know the deceased stop by for food and to hit on women."

Myles was dumbfounded.

She laughed. "I wish you could see your expression right now. I was just being a goofball."

Myles started to walk away. "You haven't seen anything until you've made out on a tarmac."

"What?"

"This time your face is priceless. And sweetheart, I have made out on a tarmac."

She stood there with her mouth open while Myles ambled over to talk to some of the boys' parents.

~

"Willow, what's wrong?"

She turned to Mr. Swanson, who'd just joined her. "Nothing. Myles just said something ridiculous. Left me flabbergasted."

He laughed. "Myles and you two make a wonderful couple. I'm happy for the two of you."

"Thank you. I love the man dearly. But at times he drives me bonkers."

"I can imagine. I understand you're in line for a judgeship."

"I'm excited."

"How does Myles feel?"

"He's happy for me. It caught him off guard. Myles needs his space to process. He wants me to take it, but he also has a dream of his own."

"It's not being a basketball coach or teacher?"

Willow frowned. "He's afraid I won't want him anymore because he's a teacher and I'm this sophisticated judge. What will people think? Anyway, that's his thinking."

"I can relate to that. My wife had a wonderful opportunity to become a senior advisor for an accounting firm in Rapid City. She passed on it because I wanted to be a superintendent of a school near where Myles played basketball. Worst decision I ever made. I should have thought of her and let her take the job. I'm not saying she's not happy with her life, but occasionally I see that faraway look in her eye that lets me know she should have taken the job. This is a wonderful opportunity for you. I'd hate to see what happened to my wife happen to you."

"I'm sorry it didn't go the way you wanted it to."

"You're the one who has to make the decision. Don't let Myles make it for you. If he loves you, he'll understand how important it is to you."

The school-board president darted away to talk to someone else.

Brielle put her arms around Willow. "My father will be just fine with whatever you decide, Mom."

"I don't know. I may break his heart if I take this job."

"There are only two things that will break his heart. One, you find another guy."

"And the second?"

"Something happens to you."

"He'll never have to worry about me finding another guy. But I can't control what happens to me."

"What happened to you at your office the other night nearly killed him. If the sheriff hadn't been there, Myles would have snapped his neck. He almost did it to a guy who tried to molest me in Rosewood last year."

"I'm sorry that happened to you. How did you know it was your dad?"

"I didn't at the time. Then it dawned on me it was him because of his voice and how scared the man was of him. People are afraid of my father. I can't figure out why. He's not an evil man by any means."

Willow held the girl. "It's always great talking to you two girls. You both provide me some perspective."

"How was the parking spot we told you about?"

"Let's just say wonderful."

~

It was around ten o'clock when the family made it back to their home along the river. The school principals had called off the school for the next day. Meaning Friday's girls game would be rescheduled for Saturday as part of a boy-girl basketball doubleheader.

Olivia sat in the living room with Myles. Brielle had homework to do, and Willow was catching up on some court papers. “What do you think of my sister becoming a judge?”

Myles twirled a pencil. “Wonderful. I’m so proud of her.”

“Do you want her to take the job?”

“I do.”

Olivia glared at him. “Then why don’t you tell her that? She really believes you don’t want her to take it.”

“I never said that.”

“She takes it that way.”

Myles eyes rolled. “How did you come to that decision?”

“I’m her sister. I know how she thinks. And Brielle and I know how you think.”

“Double whammy.”

“You’re probably worried about what people think—she being a judge and you just a teacher, but Willow doesn’t think that.”

Myles stared at her confused. “What are you talking about?”

“This is small-town America. A social studies teacher married to a judge. Wow! How degrading for Willow. That’s so far from the truth with you two. And it would be unbelievable if you ever thought like that. What month are we in? January. She’s been in love with you for four months and in her thirty-three years of life, she’s never been in love with anyone but you. She is so proud of you.”

“Don’t you have homework to do or something?”

“No, tomorrow’s a snow day. We’re going to play Monopoly.”

Olivia jumped up off the couch. “Think about it. Nothing you can ever do will break my sister’s heart. Unless you decide to sleep with the English teacher. That would be a game-breaker.”

“If you don’t have homework, go read or something.”

Olivia giggled. She hurried over to him and hugged him tightly. “Don’t ever forget you’re the best thing that has happened to Willow. She loves you. Not a job. She even likes this old house. It’s pathetic she feels that way. You’ve actually corrupted her.”

“Go away.”

Olivia giggled once more, kissed Myles on the cheek, and ran up the stairs.

~

Myles checked the house and locked it up. He stared out the back window along the river and shook his head. Olivia was a crazy but wonderful young girl.

Willow put her arms around her husband. "Which one are you shaking your head at this time? Brielle or Olivia?"

"Your sister."

"What did Olivia do now?"

"I've corrupted you because you moved into this dumpy house for me."

"In a heartbeat," she said wrapping her arms around him.

"Would you ever think I'd cheat on you?"

"Where did that come from?"

Myles hesitated. "She said the only thing that would be a game-breaker is if I slept with the English teacher."

Willow laughed. "So, let's see, the English teacher on the tarmac. Must be like a Clue game or something like that."

"Wow, and you think I'm a goofball."

"Hey, handsome. There is nothing that would break us apart. It would kill me if you screwed around on me, but I won't worry about it because it'll never happen. I'll tell you many times you'll never have anyone as good as me. That's the only thing in our lives I can guarantee." She hesitated. "Where did all of this come from?"

"Your opportunity to be a judge. I'm so excited for you. If you'd ask me what you should do, I'd say take it."

"What about you, sweetheart? Would you still feel that you're beneath me?"

"Wow, so that's what this is all about? You won't take a wonderful opportunity because you're afraid I'll be unhappy and pout like a big baby. Willow Sage Cason, there is nothing in this world that would make me happier than for you to achieve all the dreams you've ever had. So there, I said it. I'm going to bed. Good night." He turned around, kissed her, and headed up the stairs.

Willow wrapped her arms around her body, glowing inside. She had hoped he would want her to take it.

~

The next morning Myles was up early cooking breakfast for everyone. He decided to go all out with pancakes, eggs, sausage, and hashbrowns. Brielle was the first one down.

"What's this all about, Dad?"

"Wanted to do something to congratulate our new judge."

Brielle smiled. "You know she loves you, Dad, and just wants you to be happy."

He held his daughter. "I'm happy because I get to spend time with you and Olivia. And, Brielle, I love Willow with all my heart. I want her to be happy. She's good at what she does. Willow can do this and do an excellent job."

"I'm proud of you, Dad. You're the first person in my world who's ever put the ones they love first. Willow has done the same thing for you. Now that's she's a judge, there will be plenty of social events you'll be going to across the state and the country. Can you handle it?"

"Ugh." He turned around and flipped the pancakes over. "Why don't you go wake your mother up."

~

Willow was sleeping peacefully when Brielle sat on the side of the bed and gently shook her. "Hey, sleepyhead. Breakfast is almost ready."

"What?"

They both turned around when the door opened, and Myles walked in. "What's this?" Willow asked.

"I wanted to be the first one to congratulate, Your Honor, with breakfast in bed. All your favorites. Juice instead of lemonade."

"Classy, Dad," Brielle whispered.

Willow sat up in bed. "How sweet." She glanced down at the meal and then peered up at Myles. "Are you sure you're okay with all of this?"

"You're going to do an excellent job, and I'm happy for you. Enjoy your meal." He climbed off the bed and kissed her on the lips.

Myles started to walk out the door but stopped at her voice. "This means the world to me."

"I tried to cook the eggs the way you like them."

"No, goofball, supporting me for this judge's position."

~

Willow enjoyed every mouthful of her breakfast in bed. Myles had made her feel so good with this gesture. With everything they'd endured in their first month of marriage, at times she wondered if their fairy-tale romance would outlast their troubles. In her line of work, Willow had seen so many marriages fall apart after even shorter periods of time. The Tuthills had been married for more than twenty-five years and their marriage ended so tragically. It would never happen to her and Myles' marriage. They had each waited for the right person to come into their lives.

As she was nibbling on her eggs, she thought about being appointed a judge. This is what she had worked for, but it was before Myles had come into her life. There was part of her who craved the excitement that Myles' job with the task force would bring. Would it be wise to take the girls from place to place? But the girls would only be in their household for another year and then off to college.

She and Myles had found this home in River Valley where they were both respected. They were nothing like their families. Myles had made this house something special. Olivia was finally somewhere she could feel comfortable.

Willow finished her breakfast, crawled out of the bed, and climbed into the shower. The warm water felt good running over her body. Once she finished her shower, she slipped into a dress. Since she and Myles had married, Willow had never even thought about makeup. Like many things, that part of her past was over. This was her new life. A life where she'd found happiness with the man she loved. She climbed down the stairs and strolled into the kitchen. It was close to eight. Willow turned toward Myles. "Sweetheart, I'm heading to work."

"Do you need me to drive you?"

"That's sweet. I'll be okay. I promise to call you when I arrive at work."

"Sounds good. I'm going to learn how to play Monopoly the right way today. No cheating."

She smiled at his grin. "What?"

"I'm happy. I have everything I want."

She kissed him. "I love you so much."

"I love you also. I'll take you to lunch. What time?"

Her eyes perked up. "That's sweet. Say twelve-thirty."

Myles turned back to Brielle and Olivia. "Okay, girls, are you ready to get stomped on?"

Chapter 14

Willow pulled into her doctor's parking lot at the River Valley Clinic, which sat on the edge of town, for her annual checkup. She hadn't told Myles about the appointment. As she waited for the doctor, Willow wondered if she should have. She still had work to do to overcome her past.

"Mrs. Cason?"

Willow's head shot up. "Sorry, I was daydreaming."

The young nurse smiled. "It happens. Let's take your vitals."

Willow stood on the scale and glanced at her weight. One hundred forty-three pounds. The nurse smiled. "Healthy as can be for a woman almost five-ten."

"Thank you."

"We drew blood earlier this week. Doctor Browning will be able to determine more information from the blood work." The nurse led her to a room. "Strip down to your underwear and put this on." She handed Willow the paper robe.

"Thank you."

"The doctor will be in a few moments."

Willow glanced at the different hospital instruments and a couple of photos on the walls. Really inviting room. She snapped out of her reverie at the knock on the door.

A tall man ambled in. He stopped to stare at Willow. "Sorry, Mrs. Cason. Dr. Ledyard Browning," he said shaking her hand. "Please have a seat. I'm going to do a thorough exam today."

Once he finished, he smiled. "Everything looks good. You're in great health."

She frowned. "But—"

"But your ovaries aren't ovulating like they should."

"Meaning I can't get pregnant."

"You have a premature ovarian failure or low ovarian reserves. That doesn't mean you can't get pregnant with your own eggs. However, there are some people who are unable to conceive using their own eggs and will need IVF treatment with an egg donor. If you're planning to have children, it would be best to deal with that now, because the older you get, the harder it will be."

"Thank you, Doctor."

After he left the room, she slowly put her clothes on. Willow slipped out of the clinic ready to burst into tears. She climbed into her car and drove toward the courthouse. Once she reached the parking lot, she took a deep breath. Willow had a job to do. Myles would always be there for her.

The snow came down harder, and the winds were strong. There were a few people out but not many. The courthouse was still open. In South Dakota, everyone dealt with the winter blizzards the best they could. Most everyone who worked at the courthouse lived in River Valley or close by.

She edged through the side door and slid into the office. Her two-department staff were there already.

"Good morning, Willow."

"Ladies. You decided to brave the winter snow and cold."

"Yep. Need the money."

Willow knew that had been the case for many people who lived in the River Valley area. They barely made enough to scrape by. Both the ladies who worked in her office were single mothers. She headed into her office and turned on her computer to check any important emails. The phone rang. She picked it up. "Sheriff, good morning."

"Good morning, Willow. Great news."

"Tell me about it."

"We found a small piece of paper from our warrant issued for Reynolds' Black Hill residence that mentions locations. Or I should say coordinates to the three locations where the bombs detonated. And Willow, Myles' name was on the piece of paper. He was the target."

"What?" Willow shrieked.

"Yes. It's evidence that will put Reynolds away for good."

"How do we know it's Reynolds for sure?"

"Maybe it would be best if I stop by the office in the next ten minutes."

"I'll be here."

The sheriff was prompt as usual. Willow heard him greet the ladies up front who ushered him back to her office.

"Have a seat, Sheriff."

He dropped down into a seat on the other side of her desk. She pushed her chair back and circled her desk to sit by him.

She looked confused. "What?"

"After I talked to you, more information popped through my email. I printed that out also."

Willow was excited. "Let's have it."

Sheriff Watkins handed Willow a folded piece of paper.

"Where did you get this?"

Jack smiled. "Nicolas Parker."

"He's Myles' friend."

"Correct. He has been following Michael Comforti and the X-guy—that's what I call him. Comforti happened to meet with an executive from Libya the weekend his president was in town. Thus, the photo of the two. More importantly, Comforti is recorded as saying Halter would make sure the goods reached him at the deadline."

"What goods?"

"I'm not sure. Comforti drove to a warehouse in Upper Marlboro, Maryland." He laid down another photo. "Isaac Reynolds."

Willow ran her fingers through her hair. "It sure looks like him. It does tell us he's mixed up with Comforti. With what we're not sure."

Jack jumped in. "Nicolas plans on checking out the warehouse today or tomorrow."

Willow's eyes darted up at the sheriff. "Wait, he was just in Bluffton on Tuesday night."

"He was. Parker flew out later that night to D.C. after he heard Reynolds was on his way there."

"How did he find that out?"

"Myles."

"Whoa. Now I'm confused even more. How would Myles know?"

"Despite the F.B.I. handling the case, Myles and I continue to have conversations about the case. Throckmorton's still in charge. He asked that I follow up on Reynolds who happened to be at the basketball game on Tuesday night. He met with one of your good friends at one time, a Daniel Rexalt."

"What?"

"Nicolas Parker was in town to deliver information to Myles. Never was able to, and lo and behold, he saw you talking to Rexalt. He's been on our list of possibilities for a couple of years."

"You mean you've been working with Myles for a couple of years?"

"Actually, ten years to be exact."

"Okay, back to Rexalt."

"Nicolas Parker and Rexalt have known each other over the years. The two went to high school together in the Bluffton area. Rexalt had information for Nicolas. That's another reason he was there. Rexalt told Parker about talking to Reynolds earlier in the evening and the meeting with Comforti the next day. He didn't know what it was about. Parker trusts Rexalt, so he talked to Myles and was back on the red eye to D.C." The sheriff glanced at Willow. "Do you have some coffee? Black."

Willow paged the receptionist. "Please bring in a cup of black coffee for the sheriff?"

A minute later the sheriff held a cup of coffee. "Now back to this piece of paper I just handed you. Notice the dates and times and Myles' name. And more importantly the Reynolds logo. Unmistakable."

"This is evidence he was involved in the bombings," Willow said. "But there has to be more."

"Right, who authorized it?"

"Halter of course."

The sheriff sipped on his coffee. "I don't think so."

"What do you mean?"

"There's someone else involved. The mastermind is a person we don't know about. It's not the senior advisor. It's someone else."

"Who?'

"Someone who knows Myles or even someone close to him that he wouldn't suspect."

"Why would you think that?"

"Look at the scribbled-out piece on the note."

She held the note up to the light. "*He has the book*. Jack, no one knows I have the book except you and Myles."

"Someone found out. And as tight-lipped as Myles is, it's someone close to him."

"Sheriff…" She stopped.

"What?"

"It can't be."

"What are you saying?"

"Walter Crocket. He and Myles are like this," she said crossing her fingers.

"What do you know about him?"

"He's been close to Myles and has always watched over Brielle for him."

"Do you think he may have found out Brielle had the book?"

"Brielle would have never said anything to anyone. She would never do anything to put her father in danger. That's not Brielle."

"Maybe it's someone else."

"Sheriff, Nicolas Parker and Walter Crocket are the only two he's even close to. Other than you, the girls, and I."

"What about Trevor Reynolds?"

"What about him?" Willow asked.

"He stayed with you for a bit. Maybe he found out."

"I don't think so. Myles did clean out some bugs in the house in Rosewood. Someone could have known about the book through the bugs. Walter Crocket has been in our house to spend time with the girls. But one of us has always been with them."

"You may have to consider that Walter Crocket is our man. He knows everything about Myles. Everything."

Willow peered up at the sheriff. "How can I ever tell him that the only man who's ever been beside him is the one trying to kill him?"

"That's tough."

Willow blew out a breath. "Let's put this information together and seek permission from the judge to issue warrants to arrest Isaac Reynolds and Michael Comforti?"

The sheriff smiled. "Good thing we law enforcement personnel stick together. I have a great friend in Washington, D.C.

who will arrest the man. The question is—how tough will it be to get extradition papers?"

Willow stared at the sheriff. "You let me worry about that."

"Okay."

Willow smiled. "I'm sorry. Comforti is a scumbag, and he's tried to harm my Myles. There isn't anything I won't do to bring him to justice."

"I can tell, young lady." The sheriff stood up. "Can I be candid with you?"

"Please do."

"You've changed a lot. You care about something in your life. And it's not just about the law."

She smiled at him. "Yeah, Myles has that effect on me. Can I ask you a question?"

"Of course."

"Myles wants me to take over the judge position here. I'm not sure if he's sincere about it, or if he wants me to follow my dream."

"Myles loves you deeply. And the Myles I know is sincere about following your dream even if it means he'll have to give up this task-force opportunity."

"You knew about it?"

The sheriff laughed. "Hell, he had even suggested I join him. I'm fifty years old. Why would I want to jet around the world when I can just take it easy in River Valley?"

"Because he trusts you. And he doesn't trust many people. If Walter Crocket is the mastermind out to destroy him, the only person who would shatter his heart more is if I betrayed him. Or you."

"You're not that girl anymore. You'll never look at another guy."

"No, I won't."

"You get some warrants. I'll work on arresting the son of a bitch."

After the sheriff left her office, Willow walked up the stairs to the judge's chambers and knocked on the door.

"Good morning, Willow. Come on in."

"Judge. Couple of warrants for you to sign."

"What do we have here?"

He read the warrants. “I’ll be damned. Michael Comforti.”

“You know him, sir?”

“Oh yes. His father engaged in multiple weapons deals with African countries many years ago. Finally convicted him and he’s still spending time in jail. Like father like son.” He signed the two warrants and handed them back to Willow. She hesitated for a moment.

“What is it?”

“Sir, how well do you know Walter Crocket?”

“Walter Crocket. He’s been close to Myles for many years. Other than you, Walter could be the only person Myles trusts. Why do you ask?”

“Just asked. No reason.” She started to walk out.

“Willow, please stop.”

She turned to him.

“What is it? You don’t ask a question without a reason.”

“Sir, I’m not sure. They’re after Myles. I believe Walter Crocket may be the mastermind.”

The judge studied her face. “You’re a good judge of character and have a good gut instinct. What does your gut tell you?”

“It’ll devastate Myles, but my gut instinct is he’s the one.”

“Then go with your gut instinct. Myles will understand.”

“Will he or will I lose the only man I’ll ever love?”

Chapter 15

Willow walked back down to her office. She ambled through the door to smiling faces. "What?"

"Oh, nothing."

Willow strolled back to her office. Sitting on the chair in front of her desk was Myles.

"Sweetheart, is it lunchtime already?"

"Twelve-thirty to be exact. And a salad that the girls put together especially for you."

"That's sweet," she said reaching down and kissing him on the cheek. "I'm hungry." She pulled a chair next to him to eat her lunch. "This is nice."

"I thought maybe I'd join you for lunch at your office since you're always coming to join me at school."

She offered a half-edged smile.

"What is it? You don't like the salad? And the lunches I provided your employees?"

She peered up at him. "You brought them lunch? How nice of you. No, it's been a busy morning."

"Arrest any criminals?"

Her smile was brighter. "Served warrants on Isaac Reynolds and Michael Comforti."

"Great news."

"Maybe. You're the target."

Myles took a bite of his salad. "No surprise."

"It doesn't bother you?"

"Nope. Used to it."

"It downright scares me that my husband is targeted for death."

He smiled up at her. "One of my unique qualities."

She had to laugh. "Why are you eating a salad?"

"You're going to be a judge. The girls and I made a pact we would never disappoint you."

Willow dropped her fork in her salad, and her eyes brimmed.

"What?"

She peered into his eyes. "Please, don't. I don't want any of you to change who you are because of me."

"What is all this about?"

She stared into his eyes and then took a deep breath. "I'm not sure I want to be a judge." Willow waited for a response. Myles didn't say anything, so she continued. "I love you and don't want you to ever think differently of me. You're accepting this because you believe it's my dream. It *was* my dream. But now you're more than that dream. You're my everything."

He set down his fork. "Let's go for a walk." Once they were in the waiting room, Myles took her hand. The two department staff members smiled at the two.

"I'll be back in a bit," Willow said.

"Take your time."

The two walked up the stairs and out the front door. It had stopped snowing a bit, but it was cold. "Where are you taking me?"

"Shh," he said. The two walked over to a little gazebo that was outside of the courthouse. Myles brushed off the bench, sat down, and pulled her onto his lap.

"What's this all about?"

He held her close. "You've told me everything about you. Me hardly anything about myself."

"That's okay."

"Maybe. Maybe not. Every morning I open my eyes and there you lie. The most beautiful woman I've ever been associated with. And believe me I've seen beautiful women."

"You have?" she said shocked.

"Yes. In Paris."

"You were in Paris?"

"Yes. There was a young model who was being stalked by an up-and-coming Libyan executive. The same man you met in D.C. My job was to guard her. The U.S. government asked me to do that. Actually, the Libyan government asked me to." He held

Willow close to keep her warm. "Those models are beautiful, but they don't hold candle to how gorgeous you are."

"Thank you. What happened?"

"The two ended up marrying each other. You saw that woman at the White House. I danced with her." He could tell she was confused. "I'm trying to tell you a bit about myself. You've done everything you could to tell me about yourself. You've changed who you are because you wanted to be with me. I can do the same thing. I *want* to do the same thing."

Myles made her look at him. "Your seventeen-year-old sister told me I needed to tell you how I feel about this opportunity. This is it. I'm so proud of you. I want this for you because it's your dream to become a judge. I'll always be in your life. You've worked so hard to become this person. Now you have the chance. Don't throw it away because of one man."

"You're not just one man. You're my heart and soul."

"I will always be that."

She reached over and kissed him lightly on the cheek. "Are you sure?"

"Yes, I'm sure. I can happily be a social studies teacher and basketball coach." He smiled.

"What?"

"I've thought about this a lot. How many times do you see women driving her man around because he lost his license?"

"I deal with it a lot."

"I can be that man. You can drive me everywhere. I'll be fine."

She slapped him gently on the shoulder. "You goofball. I already do that. Because for some reason, like in the middle of a blizzard, you walk everywhere." Willow wrapped her arms around him. "I'm happy with my life because you're in it." She kissed him again on the lips a bit more passionately. "I'll always be in your life."

"Then it's all settled. You go catch criminals, and I'll try to keep criminals off the streets."

"I'll think about it. No one would have ever talked this through like you have."

He winked at her. "I wonder what it's like to sleep with a judge."

"You can try it right now."

"Wow! Bold, aren't you?"

"Nope I just wanted you to realize that I'm much better than any model."

"No question about that."

Myles started to crawl off the bench. Willow pulled him back down. "Sweetheart, I stopped by the clinic before coming to work today."

"Are you okay?"

Her bottom lip trembled. Myles pulled her close to him. She wrapped her arms around him.

"What is it?"

"I may not ever be able to have a baby."

"Okay, slow down. Calm down. Explain it to me."

She took a deep breath. "The doctor told me I have premature ovarian failure or low ovarian reserves."

"And he said you couldn't have a baby?"

"He said some people are unable to conceive using their own eggs and would need an IVF treatment with an egg donor. I don't want to do that. I want to have our baby naturally."

"After the bomb went off in The Depot, Brielle and I sat in the hospital waiting for you and Olivia. She was pretty upset because of the tragedy. It was a setback. I almost lost you. But we survived. This is just another setback in our lives. We don't know what will happen. You're a strong woman. If anyone can have a child, you will. If you don't, it's not because of anything other than it wasn't in the plan."

Willow frowned at him. "How can you be so nonchalant about all of this? You do it all the time."

He shrugged. "I'm sorry. If it was a choice between you and a child, you'd be my choice every time. That may seem harsh, but I'm nothing without you in my life. Olivia told me one time she was going down a dangerous road until I came into her life. That's how I feel about you."

"It's going to be tough, but I can appreciate your explanation and how you feel. I will keep making love with you any chance I have. You won't ever stop making love with me because of this, will you?"

He smiled. "I promise. Besides, you've always said you're the best I'll ever have."

Willow smiled weakly. "I did. But right now, I don't feel like that. I feel like a deformed woman."

"You're not, sweetheart. You're still the most beautiful woman in the world both inside and outside. This will never change how I feel about you…ever."

The two walked back into the courthouse. She kissed him goodbye. "Thanks."

Myles left and Willow headed back to her office. The two ladies smiled at her.

"What?"

"There has been a glow on your face since that man came into your life."

"Yeah, there has. I love him deeply."

"Everyone in this community can tell."

~

Myles strolled back home. He walked past the high school. There were several cars parked in the parking lot. He entered the gym. Members of the boys' and girls' basketball team were on the court shooting baskets and socializing.

He smiled as he watched what was happening. Even in the middle of a blizzard, the kids were working on their basketball skills. And with friends that weren't out for basketball. Willow was right. They were making a difference.

After watching for a few moments, he headed downtown. Not much was open because of the blizzard. He noticed a figure staring at the site where The Depot had been. "Everything okay?"

A man turned around. "Myles Cason? This damn bomb was supposed to have killed you. You're still walking around."

"Curtis Cain. What are you doing here?"

"Just wondering where my life turned. I never wanted to be a killer. I had no choice."

"Everyone has a choice, Curtis."

Myles eyed the man who along with a man named Paul had contracted to take care of people who were detrimental to Ronald Halter's operation. The problem was no one could prove their dirty deeds.

"No, they don't. My wife and children are still held hostage by those madmen. Nothing I can do about it."

"You can help us end their reign."

Curtis stared at Myles. "Can I? What can I do? One word, and my wife is toast. I'll lose them all."

"Why are you standing here in the middle of a blizzard?"

"Partly hoping I freeze to death. Maybe wishing I was here dead like thirteen others. That way my family would be free."

"I need a cup of coffee. So do you. If we both stand out here, we'll freeze to death. And neither of us want that for our families' sakes."

The two walked toward the bar and grill which was the only restaurant open. Myles found a booth in the back out of everyone's way. "Just a couple of cups of coffee."

The two sat down. Curtis stared at Myles. "Why did you let me live after what I tried to do to your daughter?"

"I really don't know other than I don't kill people in cold blood."

Curtis laughed. "That's the difference between the two of us. You kill but do it honestly."

"Not necessarily true. There have been times I've had to kill someone because it's required. I understand what you're going through."

"Your family isn't held hostage."

"Zachary Hunter tried to rape my wife in her office. If the sheriff wasn't there, I would have snapped his neck and not felt a bit of remorse."

"How was what I did any different?"

Myles shrugged. "I really can't answer that now, but I didn't know my daughter."

The two sipped their coffee.

"Curtis, I'm tired and want out as well. I have no clue how to."

"Amen."

"You know who's behind all of this. If I rescued your family out and brought them here, would you help me? Help both of us get out of the mess."

Curtis laughed. "Dream on. No way you'll get close to my family."

"If I can, would you help me?"

"If that happened, I'd become the biggest rat you've ever

known."

"Tell me everything you can about where your family is and who has them."

"They're in Cheyenne, Wyoming."

"That close?"

"You didn't know we're from Wyoming, did you? Ran into Halter and Konnor at a ski lodge in Yellowstone."

"Did you know Willow?"

"Oh yes. She's a beauty. Nothing like her folks. Wanted no part of anything that was happening. Especially after she met you."

Myles eyes popped up. "What do you mean?"

"Willow's hounded that group since October after she saw you at that volleyball match. She's had law enforcement knocking on doors ever since. They're all scared because they can't keep up with her. There's someone else in the picture. Always keeps himself in the background. This person knows everything about you. I mean everything. From your trip to Paris to your capturing the terrorist in Iran to your daughter, Brielle, and her friends playing basketball in an old barn."

Myles stared at him. "No one knows anything about me. They can't. All my records are sealed."

"This person does."

Myles blew out some air. "You go about your business and do what they've asked you to do. Once you see your family in my house, then we'll work together to destroy them."

Curtis glanced at him. "They want us to kill you."

"How's that going to happen?"

Curtis sipped his coffee and took a deep breath. "Through your daughter."

"How much time do I have?"

"Three days."

Myles jumped off his chair. "You don't touch Brielle. Is that understood?"

"I don't want to hurt her, but Paul has different thoughts. The man is hung up on her and her looks."

Myles glared at the man. "Brielle is off-limits."

"I'll do what I can. Do you really think you can get my family out of there?"

"If I don't, I'll have to kill the two of you."

As soon as Curtis left, Myles was on his cell phone. “Address for you. Bring the family here.”

Chapter 16

When Myles reached his home, Brielle and Olivia were cooking spaghetti and meatballs with garlic toast. "What's this?'

"Our treat for Willow," Olivia said.

Brielle added. "You really need to be a lot nicer to the woman. She's given her heart to you and changed lots of thing about herself."

"Okay, you two. Enough. Just today I told her I wanted her to take the job as a judge."

Brielle and Olivia glanced at each other, then ran over toward Myles hugging him. They all turned as the door opened.

"What's all this?" Willow came in.

Brielle spoke up. "Dad told us some wonderful news."

"What's that?"

"He talked to you about the judge job and told you take it."

"Yeah, about that," she said moping.

"What?" Olivia asked with a concerned look.

"I have until Monday to take the job as district judge." Her eyes brightened.

The girls ran over to her and hugged her. "Good for you, big sister," Olivia said.

After the girls were done jumping around, Willow asked what was happening.

"We're cooking spaghetti especially for you," Olivia said. "It's cold out, blizzardy, and I know how much you love spaghetti."

She turned around at Brielle's voice. "If you don't come over here, we may have to think of something else."

"Oh shoot," Olivia said running over to her.

Willow inched over to Myles. "I love you. Thank you for

supporting me. The judge came down this afternoon and told me the job was mine if I accept it. They'll start looking for a county prosecuting attorney as soon as I give them my answer."

"What about your friend in Minnehaha County?"

"Wow. Never thought of Gabrielle. She'd be perfect. I'll call her after we enjoy our spaghetti and meatballs."

Myles held her. "So, what's your first case?"

"Believe it or not, if I take the job, my first case will actually be a rape."

"Wow."

"Yeah, sad situation. Good news. Isaac Reynolds and Michael Comforti are now in custody. Isaac is sitting in the county jail. Comforti is fighting extradition. He'll be back in South Dakota."

"Good job, sweetheart."

"Thank you. You and the sheriff have been a tremendous help."

"Yeah, we need to talk later tonight."

"I have something to talk to you about also. And this will be tough for you to hear."

"How about we eat now and talk later?"

~

Right after supper Willow called Gabrielle.

"Hi, Willow. I thought about calling you this week. You must have read my mind. How are things going in the river city?"

"Wonderful. I have some great news for you."

"What's that? You found me a hot guy?"

"No. Haven't even been looking at hot guys," Willow said, thinking of her one and only.

"Yeah, I figured that much out at the Minneapolis conference. What is it?"

"I'm being appointed judge for this district court on Monday. That is, if I accept it."

"That is great. I'm so proud of you."

"It gets even better. It's up to me to pick my successor. I'd hoped you would consider being the next county prosecutor. It would be for the remainder of the three-year term and then a possible election."

"Are you serious? You would consider me?"

"Yes, I would. Not only because you're my best friend, but

because you're good at your job. And you'll be a big contributor to this district. Please think about it?"

"When would I have to start?"

"Monday is when I start my job as the judge."

"I'll be there over the weekend."

"What? Are you sure? How can you leave without a two weeks' notice?"

"I made sure in my contract with this office if I found something of higher value, I'm released automatically. I'll be there on Sunday."

"Great. I'm so happy."

"No, Willow. Thank you for the opportunity. A county prosecutor and a judge in our mid-thirties. That's amazing."

Willow clicked her cell phone. Finally, her life was coming together. But still in the back of her mind, all she could think of was her husband. He was giving up so much for her.

~

Later that evening, Myles and Willow sat snuggling on the couch. The girls were upstairs doing their homework. Willow reached for a drink of lemonade. She had to laugh.

"What?"

"I imagined doing this all my life. Lying here with my husband, but with a martini or wine in my hand, not lemonade." She sat up. "Why don't you like alcohol or wine?"

"Never liked the taste. I saw what it did to people, so I stayed away. It was critical for me to keep my wits."

"Makes sense," she said crawling back into his arms. "Gabrielle accepted the job as county attorney. She's on her way here next weekend."

"Don't they have an election of sorts or something like that?"

"No. On Monday, Judge Townsend will swear me in as judge, and I'll turn around and do the same to her. That simple." She took a sip of her lemonade. "So, what exciting news do you have to tell me?"

"Ran into the man who tried to rape Brielle today."

Once more, Willow bolted up. "Are you okay?"

"Yes, I am. He was just standing looking at The Depot pondering why Curtis Cain wasn't there. They have his family. I sent Nicolas there to rescue them and bring them here. In exchange, he'll tell us all he knows about everything. Halter recruited him."

"That's good news."

"Yes, it is. There was something disturbing he said. He said there's another person involved, someone close to me, who knows everything about me. You're the only one—" He stopped. "Walter."

Willow took a deep breath.

"What's wrong?"

"The sheriff said the same thing. There is someone involved that no one knows. We both believe it's Walter. I talked to the judge about it, and he told me to follow my gut instinct. I'm sorry, honey, my gut instinct tells me Walter is the mastermind behind everything."

She waited for a response. Both turned at the knock at the door. Willow opened the door, and three young children were standing there shivering.

"We're searching for Myles Cason," the oldest girl said.

"Please, come in out of the cold," Willow said.

Myles hurried over to help them.

The older girl eyed Myles. "Are you Myles Cason?"

Myles nodded.

"My mother said you would protect us."

Myles and Willow glanced at each other.

"Let's get you three warmed up. Sweetheart, can you grab some blankets?" Willow asked.

He raced upstairs to grab some blankets. Brielle came out of her bedroom. "Are you okay, Dad?"

"Need blankets."

"Here, I'll grab one out of my room."

"Please bring it downstairs."

Both girls hurried downstairs and helped Willow with the three kids. Olivia said, "I'll heat up some hot chocolate. That will help."

"Thanks, Olivia," Willow responded.

After the children had eaten some food, they settled down. The two youngest fell asleep. The oldest girl stared up at them all. "Mom said Myles Cason would protect us if anything happened to her. We couldn't find Mom anywhere. Then we found out she was killed. We started our way here."

"From Sioux Falls?" Willow asked.

"Yes, ma'am. People would pick us up."

"You walked all this way?" Brielle asked.

"Yes, ma'am. I'm only thirteen. I can't drive."

Myles took control. "Okay, little miss. What's your name?"

"I'm Natasha. Tabitha is my ten-year-old sister, and Ricardo is my six-year-old brother. I don't know where my father is. Mom said he was no good and to stay away from him. She said you would protect us. Will you protect us?"

"We will," Willow said. "Nothing will happen to you here."

Myles turned to Olivia and Brielle. "Can you two set up the extra room? We'll put the kids there for tonight."

"We can do that," Brielle said.

Myles lifted Tabitha up and carried her up the stairs. Natasha watched closely. Willow touched her. "Natasha, Myles won't let anything happen to your little sister."

"Mom said he was a good man. She talked to him several times. He also gave her money to help us."

"He did that?"

"Oh yes, ma'am. He's a good man."

Willow held her. "He is."

Myles came back and grabbed the younger boy. "The girls made a bed of sorts for him on the floor, Natasha. He'll be near the two of you."

"Thank you, sir."

"Why don't you get some sleep?"

"I am tired."

Willow helped the young girl up the stairs. Brielle and Olivia waited for her. "We fixed the bed up so you and your sister can sleep together," Brielle said. "We're right down the hall there. My mother and father are on the other side of the hall. You'll be safe here."

"Thank you, ma'am."

Brielle smiled. "I'm Brielle. This is Olivia."

"You're both very pretty."

"Thank you," Olivia said. "Remember if you need anything, don't hesitate to find us."

"I will."

Natasha started to close the door, stopped, and glanced at the girls. "Right down there?" she pointed.

"Yes, right there," Brielle said.

Willow held the two older daughters in her arms. Brielle peered up at Willow. "Who would do something like this to their children?"

"Girls, families do the damnedest things. Brielle, Olivia, we're lucky Myles is in our life. Tomorrow we'll figure out what to do."

Olivia glanced at her big sister. "You know what to do."

"What?" Willow said.

"Protect them."

"We will. Good night, girls."

"Good night," they said hugging her.

Willow hurried down the stairs to Myles who was locking up the house. She went around to the back to check the sliding door. It was locked also. "What is happening here?"

"I don't know. We'll investigate it tomorrow. Right now, the best thing we can do is hope they get a good night's sleep."

"How about you? Are you okay after what I said earlier?"

Myles wrapped her in a hug. "The one true thing in my life is you."

Willow was stunned.

"I'm more concerned about you," he said.

"What do you mean?"

"Having a child is so important to you."

She framed his face with her hands. "I've thought about it this afternoon, and I feel the same as you. If there was a choice between a child and you, I'd choose you one hundred percent. I'll be okay. If we have a child, that'll be wonderful. If not, I'll be happy. I'm happier than I've ever been because you're in my life. I just thought a child would be fulfilling for both of us. But we have Brielle. We have Olivia. That's enough right now. Thank you for being there for me. Don't you dare leave me."

"I promise."

~

Tabitha woke up and crawled out of her bed, then opened the door and walked down the hallway. She opened another door, ran into the bedroom, and shook Brielle.

Brielle's eyes snapped open. "It's okay, Tabitha."

"How do you know my name?"

"Your sister told me it."

"I'm thirsty. And I don't know where I am."

"How about we go down the stairs and get a drink of water?"

"Would you go with me?"

"You bet."

Brielle climbed out of the bed and headed down the stairs all the while holding the girl's hand. "It's okay now."

"I don't know. Your family is in danger because of us."

"Don't you worry about that. My dad will protect us."

"My mom said he's a hero."

"I don't know about that. He's my dad. And he loves me. He loves everyone in this house."

"But he doesn't know us. How do you know he'll protect us?"

"I know my father." Brielle grabbed the girl a drink of water. She slowly let it fall through her throat. "This is good. We didn't have much to eat because we didn't have much money. Natasha helped us."

"You're brave traveling across the state like this."

"Natasha said we needed to come here because your dad was here. My mother trusted him."

"How about you get some sleep? You'll feel better tomorrow."

Brielle started up the stairs. Tabitha ran over to her and grabbed her hand again. Brielle smiled down at her. "Okay, I'll hold your hand."

They made it up to the room where Brielle tucked her in. Natasha had not even moved. Later Brielle crawled into her own bed. Just then she heard little footsteps and opened her eyes to see Tabitha.

"I'm scared. Can I sleep with you?"

Brielle smiled. "Come on and join me."

Tabitha crawled in. Brielle put her arms around the little girl. She waited until she could hear her silent breaths before she fell asleep.

~

"Tabitha? Where are you?"

Myles and Willow bolted out of their bedroom at the voice.

"What is it, honey?" Willow asked.

Natasha was in tears. “I can’t find my sister.”

“It’s okay. We’ll find her.”

Olivia came out of her room. “What’s wrong?”

“We’re looking for Tabitha.”

Olivia wiped her eyes. “She’s in with Brielle. I heard them going downstairs last night.”

Myles peeked in Brielle’s room. Brielle had her arms around Tabitha, and the two were sleeping peacefully.

“She’s okay. Let her sleep, Natasha,” Willow said.

“Let’s go make some breakfast,” Myles said. “I’m cooking pancakes.”

Little Ricardo’s eyes grew large. “He cooks?”

Willow nodded. “He does.”

“My father never did. He just yelled at Mother.”

Willow hugged the little boy. “Let’s see what my hubby has planned.”

Ten minutes later, they piled down the stairs. Myles already had pancakes going on the stove. He put in some bacon along with hashbrowns. The two younger kids gathered around the table waiting for the pancakes. Myles set a couple plates out for Natasha and Ricardo. They dug in.

Olivia stepped in. “Okay, you two. Slow down. They’ll be plenty for everyone.”

“I’m sorry. We haven’t eaten for a while,” Natasha said.

“How long?” Willow asked.

“Almost two days,” Natasha said quietly.

Willow smiled. “I’ll make sure Myles makes plenty of pancakes.”

She went over and kissed Myles on the cheek. “I’ll grab a shower. Have to be at the courthouse before seven-thirty.”

“I’ll take the kids to school with me.”

Olivia glanced at Natasha. “Feel like joining me in my classes?”

“Can I do that?”

“Of course. It’ll be fun.”

Brielle and Tabitha came downstairs. Tabitha ran over to her older sister. “I’m sorry. I was scared.”

“It’s okay. We’re going to school today. Olivia said I could go with her.”

Tabitha frowned. “We haven’t been to school in a long time.”

“Maybe now we can.”

Tabitha spun around and ran to Brielle. “Can I go to school with you?”

“Sure can. Right now, let’s eat breakfast. My dad cooks fantastic pancakes.”

Everyone glanced up as Willow hurried down the stairs. She almost fell trying to get her second heel on.

“Slow down, Judge,” Myles said.

She smiled at him. “I’m running late.” Willow stuck a pancake in her mouth, kissed Myles, and told the girls to have a wonderful day at school. She came running back in the door once more. Myles held out the keys.

“Missing these?”

“Thanks. Love you, sweetheart.”

“Love you.”

Once she was gone, Ricardo’s eyebrows rose. “Is she always like this?”

Olivia smiled. “This is one of her better days. Let’s take quick showers and get ready for school.”

Natasha pulled on Myles’ shirt. “We don’t have any school clothes.”

Brielle spoke up. “We’ll buy you some clothes this weekend. You’ll be fine.”

Ricardo joined Myles in his first period history class. Several of the students walked in wondering what was up. Myles opened the class. “This is six-year-old Ricardo, and he decided to help me with my classes today. Ricardo, these are the students in my first period geography class. Let’s see what they’ve learned.”

Myles walked around the classroom. Ricardo followed him and tried to imitate what Myles was doing. Then Myles sat on the side of the desk and talked about South Dakota geography. Ricardo tried to climb on the other side of the desk. Micah lifted him up and put him on the desk.

“Thank you,” the small boy said.

Micah smiled. “Seems like Coach should take lessons from you on how to sit properly on a desk.”

It drew a laugh from the class. By the third period, Ricardo was able to fit in with the students. The bell rang, and several started walking out.

"What now?"

"Lunchtime."

"Pancakes?"

"Not sure, but we'll find out what they're having."

Ricardo grabbed Myles' hand as they walked down to the lunchroom. As they started to walk in, Myles saw Brielle and Tabitha were already at a table. Olivia and Natasha joined them. Several of the kids stared at their table.

Three boys walked over with smirks on their faces at Natasha, Tabitha, and Ricardo.

"What's the problem?" Randolph Two Flaggs asked walking past them. "

"It's hard enough to deal with Randall," a freckled-faced boy replied.

Randall stood his ground. Brielle jumped up and talked to the two boys. "Back off."

One of the boys raised a hand to slap Brielle. Randall blocked the attempt and threw the kid on the floor, then jumped on top of him. He was getting ready to punch him when Myles grabbed his fist. "Whoa. Slow down."

Randall narrowed his eyes at Myles. "No one touches Brielle Cason. I was protecting her, Mr. Cason."

"Understand. Let him up."

The boy did as Myles asked. The other two boys helped up the boy. "Are you okay?" Randall asked Brielle. She nodded.

The principal hurried over to the ruckus. "What happened?" she asked Myles.

"A little misunderstanding."

The principal surveyed the scene. "Okay. No more nonsense."

Myles spoke to the three boys. "Go eat your lunch."

He touched the older boy's shoulder. "There won't be a second chance."

The boy scowled at him and stormed out of the room with his two friends. Myles hurried toward Brielle. "Are you okay, sweetheart?"

"Yes, caught me by surprise."

Myles sat down with the group. "Ricardo and I are hungry men. He's been teaching up a storm."

Ricardo beamed. Myles smiled. "Let's eat, big guy."

They dug into their lunch. A few moments later, Willow dashed in. "Am I late?"

Natasha and Tabitha looked at the others. Brielle explained. "She loves to join her family for lunch"

"We're not her family," Natasha said.

"As of right now, you are," Olivia said.

Willow kissed Myles on the cheek. "I really love their salad," she said smiling at Natasha.

"Can I try it?" Tabitha asked.

"You bet."

Devin and Brody stopped by. "Coach, looks like we have some new folks in our midst?"

"We do."

Devin smiled at Brielle. Brody did the same thing at Olivia. The two boys left. Natasha and Tabitha smiled at each other.

"What?" Willow asked.

Natasha spoke up, "The two boys like the two girls."

Myles's face screwed up. "Now how would you know about that? You're what? Thirteen and ten?"

Tabitha answered for the others. "Sir, in Sioux Falls you know lots of things at ten years old."

"Ugh," Myles said.

The rest of the table laughed.

The lunchroom bell rang, and everyone scampered to classes. Willow took Myles' hand. Ricardo took Willow's other hand. She looked down at the little man. "How lucky can I be? Two handsome boys escorting me to class."

Once they arrived at the classroom, Willow kissed Myles goodbye. "Love you."

"Love you back."

Ricardo glanced up at the two. He looked sad. Willow bent down and kissed him on the cheek which brought a big smile. Willow hurried away.

"Wow," Elroy said. "No one gets kissed by Mrs. Cason other than Coach. You must be a special boy."

The afternoon classes went quickly. There was basketball practice after school for the boys and girls. Both teams would play on Saturday at home against Ashton. The girls' game was a makeup from the blizzard cancellation.

Myles and Ricardo headed toward the gym to watch the girls practice. Principal Newcombe called Myles into her office when he passed by. He and Ricardo walked in.

"Miss Stewart, can you watch over Ricardo?"

The business manager smiled at him. "Of course, I will."

The principal closed the door after him. "Myles, what happened in the lunchroom today?"

"A difference of opinion."

"That isn't what I understood. There was some racial tension amongst the kids."

"Yeah, a couple of them got out of hand. One boy tried to push Brielle. Randall stuck up for her and put him to the ground."

"Is Brielle okay?"

"She's fine. It just kind of surprised her."

Principal Newcombe took a deep breath. "I was afraid something like this would happen sooner or later."

"What do you mean?"

"I had mentioned to the former principal that we need to do something about race relations in the school district. He didn't think it was needed. Couple of questions for you, Myles. Who are the young kids?"

"Ma'am, their mother was the one recently found in the Missouri River. Their father is in jail waiting to be charged with the killing of thirteen people in that bombing here."

The principal's eyes popped up. "He was the one?"

"Yes, ma'am. He'll be shipped out of here soon to be tried in federal court in Sioux Falls. The kids don't have a family."

"What does that mean?"

"I don't know at this point. We hope to start them at the elementary school and middle school on Monday. They're good kids, Alexandria. Just bad parents, or I should say, father."

"I can understand that." She hesitated. "Would you and Willow be willing to establish a cultural exchange program in the school district? A race-relations class to help others adjust to the diverse cultures in the area. Native Americans have been shortchanged for so long. The eighteen-year-old boy is Randall Two Flaggs. He's asked me several times to start something like this because it's needed."

"I've been here only a couple of months. Wouldn't there be somebody better?"

Alexandria smiled. "We both know you've had experience in this sort of thing."

Myles let out a breath. "I'll talk to Willow."

"Thank you. I'll talk to the elementary principal and middle school and get the kids enrolled. How old are they?"

"Natasha is thirteen, an eighth grader, Tabitha is eleven, a sixth grader, and the little guy, Ricardo, is six. He's a first grader. They've had little educational experience in the past year or so because of their parents' problems."

"I see," she said. "You know, you and Willow are the ones to help them."

He rolled his eyes. "Our house is turning into that *Seventh Heaven* show."

Alexandria laughed. "More like *Different Strokes.* But you two can handle it."

Chapter 17

Myles and Ricardo made it down to the gym to watch the girls' practice. Devin and Elroy sat with Natasha and her sister. The two headed toward them.

"Coach," the two boys acknowledged from their seats.

Natasha and Tabitha jumped up and hurried over toward Myles and their brother. Myles glanced down at them. "Are you okay?"

"Yes," Natasha said. "The two boys watched over us."

Elroy laughed. "Coach, Brielle and Olivia made it clear if anything happened to them, we'd be in trouble."

Myles smiled. "Thanks, guys. What do you think?"

Natasha's eyes surveyed the court. "Your daughter and Olivia are good. The others not so good."

"They're still learning how to play."

Devin spoke up, "Where's Coach Thompson?"

"She's moving away."

Elroy interrupted. "No wonder Miss Roberts is coaching. Was she the only candidate? Because she knows nothing about basketball?"

Myles gave Elroy a look. "That's enough, Elroy."

"Sorry, Coach."

Myles smiled looking at Natasha. "Have you ever played basketball?"

"I wanted to, but Mom and Dad said no."

"Would you like to?"

Natasha's eyes widened. "Could I?"

"Next year, but you'll have to wait until after then, but I'm sure Miss Roberts will be glad to have you."

Natasha wiped a tear way from her eye.

"What's wrong?" Elroy asked.

"No one has ever said I could try something."

Tabitha put her arms around her big sister. "Remember, Mom said Mr. Cason would help us."

"Yes, you're right."

After the girls finished practice, Myles waited until either Brielle or Olivia joined them. Willow beat them both to the gym.

"Hi sweetheart, I thought I'd come and watch my favorite guy's team practice."

She reached over and kissed him and looked at the trio. "How was your day?"

They didn't say anything. Myles spoke for them. "Girls, Willow is kind of nosy, so my advice is—just answer her questions. Ricardo, you want to help me with the team?"

"Can I?"

"You bet. Let's go." He turned toward Natasha. "Is it okay?"

"Of course."

Tabitha shrugged, her eyes travelling to Willow's face. "We promised we would always ask Natasha for permission."

"Understood. Now let's watch this awesome team practice."

~

"Where's Walter?" Myles asked James.

"He said he had to take care of some business."

Myles quickly waved toward Willow. "I'll be right back."

She hurried down the bleachers. "Willow, please call the sheriff and have him send someone to this address. Protect the man no matter what."

"Okay."

Myles went back to coaching the boys. He moved Elroy back to the point guard. Ricardo stayed by the coach as he watched the boys. He looked down as Ricardo tugged on his sweats. "What is it?"

"Too slow."

Myles smiled. "Guys, come in a moment. Coach Ricardo has something to say."

Micah spoke up, "Tell us, Coach."

"Too slow."

"You heard the man," Micah said. "Speed it up."

The boys did as he asked. Both the first and second team were everywhere contesting all their shots, playing defense, and scrambling after loose balls.

Ricardo sat with James and Myles.

"What do you think, son?" James asked.

"Devin very good player, but Elroy better. And the guy on second team better than everybody."

Myles and James eyed each other. After another half hour, Myles called it quits. "Hit the showers."

Micah came over to him. "Coach, we're going to continue shooting around. Is that okay?"

Myles nodded.

"Do you want to join us, big guy?" Micah asked.

"Wait a minute?" Ricardo held up a finger.

Micah nodded. He and Myles watched as the little boy scampered up to the bleachers to talk to his sister. Micah shouted at the boy, "Big guy, tell them to join us."

The next thing, they were all down shooting baskets. Myles and Willow watched as the kids shot around. Several players, in particular Elroy and Micah, helped Tabitha and Ricardo with their stance. Half an hour later, Brielle and Olivia ran over to Myles and Willow.

"Ready, Coach?" they said grabbing him by the hands.

Myles rolled his eyes. "Okay. Okay,"

"Willow?"

Willow put her hands along her side. "Come on, sweetheart, I'm in a dress."

Brielle and Olivia both laughed.

"What?" Willow asked.

Olivia grinned. "Myles had us drop our heels and play in our dresses."

Willow smiled. "I can do that." She kicked off her heels and joined the rest.

Elroy took charge. "Boys against girls."

Brielle smiled. "You're on."

Elroy gave the girls the ball first. Myles covered his wife. Devin covered Brielle, Brody, Olivia, and Elroy, Natasha. Micah helped Ricardo and Tabitha.

Brielle hit a basket, and then the boys had the ball. Elroy passed the ball to Myles, who made a move and tried to go toward the basket. Willow grabbed his sweats, spun him around, and kissed him.

"Whoa," Micah said.

Willow smiled. "Defensive move."

Everyone laughed. Toward the end of the game, Elroy stole the ball and passed to Myles. Brielle and Olivia hurried over to Willow. "Mother, watch it."

Just like that Myles rose in the air, did a spin, and slammed the ball through the hoop backwards. Everyone jumped up and down. "Oh my gosh," Willow said covering her mouth.

"Isn't he good?" Olivia said.

Micah and Devin ran over to them. "I've never seen anything like it. Even during the dunk championship," Micah said.

Ricardo started running toward Myles but stopped and ran back to Natasha. "Go," Natasha said.

He grabbed Micah's hand. "Help me dunk it."

Micah handed the basketball to Myles. "He wants to dunk it, Coach."

Myles heaved the ball toward Micah who grabbed it, handed it to Ricardo, and lifted him up. "Slam it through."

Ricardo did just that. Everyone cheered him on. He ran back to his sisters.

Myles smiled at Micah. "Thanks."

"No problem, Coach. It's worth it see a young boy happy like that. You've done it for me and others."

"Micah, you're fourteen and only a ninth grader. You keep working hard, and someday you'll be better than Devin."

"You mean it?"

"Yep. You're six-six and will grow more. And you're a team player."

"Thanks, Coach. I saw what happened in the lunchroom. Coach, Randall is not a good kid. He just acts that way. His aunt and uncle are good people and are trying to help him. His little sister, Monique, is in my grade and just trying to fit in."

"What are you trying to say?" Miles was confused.

"Coach, you've helped a lot of people since you've been here. Randall's talked many times about starting programs at school about race. I'm part Native American also. Actually ten percent."

"Do you think it would be something that would work?"

"It could. And, Coach, one last thing. The reason Randall did what he did in the lunchroom was because of your daughter."

Myles had his hands in his pockets. "What do you mean?"

"Randall will protect her. He's not wanting to date her or anything like that. Many of the students have vowed to protect her and Olivia because of what you've done for us. Your family has given us a chance. Many of us will never forget that. You're more than a coach. When you first came, Olivia told us you cared about her. You talked to her about sex, drugs—everything high school kids deal with. We're trying our hardest not to let you down because you've always been there for us."

~

That night, Myles sat next to Willow on the couch.

"What a day," she said. "And to see my man do a reverse dunk. That topped my day. Damn, at thirty-five you're still good."

"We're not old. How was your afternoon?"

"I'm continuing to prepare for the big change that starts a week from Monday."

Myles looked confused. "I thought it was Monday."

"The judge agreed to push it back one week in order for Gabrielle to work out some details."

Willow kissed him gently. "The sheriff called me back. He reached that address before Walter did, then kept his eye on the place for a half hour. Walter never showed up, but two other men did. He arrested them for trespassing. I have to deal with them on Monday."

"I wonder where Walter is."

"The two men didn't know who Walter was. They said they were told to go to this place to pick up some gear."

"Where's Curtis?"

"In a safe house."

They turned at a knock on the door. Myles answered it. "Nicolas. Good to see you."

"Brought some friends with me." He turned to his friends. "Myles, Willow, this is Mrs. Curtis Cain and her family."

"Nice to meet you," Mrs. Cain said. "Is my husband safe?"

"He is, ma'am. You'll see him tomorrow."

"Can I at least talk to him to let him know we're safe?"

Myles glanced over at Willow. She nodded. He stepped out of

the way and called the sheriff.

"Ma'am, are you hungry, or would you like something to drink?"

"We're hungry," the oldest boy said.

"Nathan, watch your tone." His mother said with a glare.

He glared at his mother.

Willow smiled. "We have some leftovers from last night's spaghetti and meatballs."

"It'll have to do." Nathan looked at the food.

"Quit being such a jerk, Nathan," a younger girl said.

"Okay, you two," their mother said.

"Here, I'll help you." Willow led them into the kitchen.

The young girl glanced at her. "I can help."

"Thank you."

"I'm Sadie and this is my younger sister, Kyrie."

"Nice to meet you both."

"Kyrie's always been shy."

Sadie dished out a meal for each of them. Willow noticed the boy grabbed his own plate and went to the table without offering to help his sister. She touched Sadie's arm. "It's okay."

Her eyes became stormy. "No, it's not. My father is a killer. Here, Kyrie, let me help you."

Kyrie's plate slipped from her fingers and fell to the floor. She started whimpering. "It's okay, Kyrie," Sadie said.

The young girl buried her head in her hands.

"I'm sorry, Mrs. Cason. I'll clean it up."

"I can help."

Sadie stared at her. "You and your husband have done enough. I'll make sure we pull our share."

Willow didn't say anything for a moment. "How old are you, Sadie?"

"Fifteen. Kyrie is seven. Mrs. Cason, she's been scared for so long. I'm trying to help her."

"What about your mother? Your brother?"

Sadie didn't respond. "Where do you want us to sleep?"

"I'll show you after you're done eating."

Thirty minutes later there was a knock on the door. Myles opened it to see the Sheriff. "We've got it all set up," the sheriff turned to the woman and said, "Okay. Ma'am, you and your family can join your husband in the safe house."

"About time," Nathan said. He spun toward his two sisters. "Are you coming?"

Neither moved.

Willow wrapped her arms around the girls' shoulders. "Maybe they would like to stay here?"

The boy rolled his eyes. "Mom, you might as well let them. I can handle you and Dad together."

The sheriff peered at Mrs. Cain. "Ma'am, there is a bedroom for your son and one for your daughters."

She looked over at her daughters. "If they want to stay here, I'm okay with that. Let's go see my husband."

The sheriff shrugged. Once they left, Myles turned to Willow. "We'll have to figure out something for this evening."

Sadie spoke up, "We can sleep on the floor if we need to."

"No, honey," Willow said. "We'll work something out."

Brielle and Olivia came down. "I thought we heard something more than Mom's and Dad's voices," Brielle said.

Olivia jumped in. "We have sleeping arrangements made for all of us."

"You have?" Myles asked.

"Yep, the three Hunters are fast asleep. Brielle said she would sleep with Olivia. That leaves the other bedroom open for the two young girls. And Myles, you and Willow have to figure out a way to share the couch."

Myles took a deep breath. "It's settled then. Tomorrow we'll figure something out."

Chapter 18

Myles opened his eyes and saw Sadie clamoring around in the kitchen. "Do you need help?" She jumped at Myles' voice.

"Mr. Cason, I'm looking for some pans to cook breakfast."

"Here, let me help you."

The young girl nodded at him.

"What do you plan on cooking?"

She shrugged. "I don't know. Maybe eggs or French toast. Really anything so Kyrie and the rest of you will have some breakfast."

Myles grabbed some utensils. "You don't have to do this."

She wiped her nose. "Yes, I do. No one else takes care of my little sister. She's all I have. I'm all she has."

"What about your mother and brother?"

She didn't say anything. Myles let it go. "Okay, since we'll have a lot of hungry bodies coming down later, let's make a bunch of scrambled eggs and bacon. Sound like a deal?"

Sadie nodded.

"And Sadie?"

"Yes, sir."

"You have help now."

"No, I don't. You don't know my family."

The two scrambled up some eggs and added bacon into them.

Myles had a grin on her face. "Sadie, you're a pretty good cook. You're hired."

She finally cracked a smile. "For what?"

"To be the household cook. Or at least the sous-chef. This family continues to grow. It's always nice to know we can count on someone else to fill in if need be."

"Thanks, sir."

"Okay. I'm older than you are, but I'm not that old. Myles will do."

This time her smile was full. Sadie's head turned when the first group came down. Every time she heard footsteps, she spun toward the door.

~

When everyone else was down, Sadie looked around with frantic eyes. "Where's Kyrie?" She scrambled up the stairs and into the room they had slept in. "Kyrie? Kyrie."

Willow sat in the corner with the little girl. She glanced up at Sadie. "She's okay now."

Sadie slid down next to her sister. "I'm here now. Please, it's my responsibility to take care of her."

Willow climbed off the floor. "I'll be downstairs if you need me."

~

Sadie held her little sister. "Are you okay?"

The little girl just nodded.

"It's okay to talk to me."

Kyrie stared blankly into her sister's eyes without saying anything.

"I can't help you if you don't say anything to me."

Kyrie buried her head into her big sister's shoulder.

"Let's go get you something to eat. That will make you feel better."

~

"Everything okay?" Myles asked when they came down the stairs.

"She'll be fine."

"Breakfast time for you two. Kyrie, your sister scrambled most of the eggs. Heck of a cook." He glanced over at Willow. "I told her she was hired as the family cook."

Willow gently slapped him on the shoulder. "You know I'm a good cook too."

"Yep. You all are. But Sadie could be just a little bit better." The teen smiled.

Willow kissed her husband on the cheek. She knew exactly what he was doing.

Everyone turned at the knock on the door. Myles answered it.

Standing there was the sheriff. He didn't look too happy.

"Can we talk?"

Myles stepped outside.

~

"Everything okay?"

"Not really. The man will turn state's evidence. But he has certain conditions."

"Okay. That is something Throckmorton will have to deal with."

"I know. But before we bring him into this, we need to talk about the two girls in your house."

"What about them?"

"That's one of the conditions. The parents don't want them. The younger girl is disabled, or at least that's what they said. Her mother says she hasn't talked in several months."

"Wow. And they're going to dump their daughters?"

The sheriff sighed. "There's more. The little girl was molested."

The comment caught Myles off guard. "Who would have done something like that? Seven years old."

"They don't know. But my gut reaction is her brother. We can't prove it because the girl won't talk."

Myles peered out at the river. "Do they have a family? Relatives?"

"The girls have no family. Or at least none who will claim them. Cain is a hired killer. His son is going down that road also. And the wife. She's a basket full."

"What do you mean?"

"All she can think of is bedding with her husband. She doesn't care about any of the kids."

Myles let out a breath. "Damn, I promised him. I wished I wouldn't have."

Jack tapped his pistol handle and peered at Myles. "You're trying to end this so you can move on with your life. We all want to find out who did this."

"Correct. But damn it, look at how many children's lives are being destroyed. This whole house is full of young ones who have had raw deals."

"You could say that. But you and I both know that you and

Willow are two strong individuals who can help these kids move forward. As you've already done that with your daughter, Willow's sister, Devin, Brody, even Trevor. Hell no, it's not fair, but we have to do whatever it takes to solve this case and help as many people as we can."

"Are you telling me we're going to have to adopt the Hunters' children and now two other girls? We're not made of money. I'm a damn schoolteacher."

"You are. That woman in there will soon be a district judge, and she'll do whatever it takes to help those kids."

Myles took a deep breath. "Let's stop those assholes before they harm someone else."

"I agree."

Myles opened the door and asked Willow to join them. She hurried outside.

"Hi, Jack, good to see you once more." She smiled.

The sheriff smiled. "Always enjoy talking to you."

"What are the conditions Curtis wants for his testimony?"

"He wants to go into the witness protection program and of course, he wants all charges to be dropped."

Willow stared at the man. "Freedom from charges after he tried to rape Myles' daughter and tried to kill my husband? Is he nuts?"

The sheriff gazed at her. "If he gives us what we want, isn't it worth it? Don't think with your heart."

Willow turned to tamp down her anger. "What else?"

The sheriff took a deep breath. "He wants nothing to do with either of his daughters. The little girl was molested."

Willow's eyes ballooned. "What a son of a bitch! He's just going to let them go? Throw them out like they're trash?"

"That about sums it up."

Willow stormed toward the river.

"Let her have some time, Jack. She'll make the right decision."

"And what's that?"

"She'll take the girls, but she'll bury his son if he's the one who molested his sister."

~

After the sheriff left to talk to Throckmorton, Myles headed down to the river. Willow sat in the snow with her legs against her chest staring at the river. He dropped down next to her, swiping away her tears with the edge of his shirt.

She glanced up at him. "One night when I was fifteen years old, one of my father's cronies came into my room and started to undress me. I was so scared I didn't know what to do. He turned to sneeze, I jumped off the bed, and ran as fast as I could. It scared him enough that he left. From that night on, I locked the door in my room. Then when I was sixteen, a man named Cyrus Vincent forced himself on me. He hurt me, Myles. It was so painful when he went into me. Now I can't have a child. Your child."

She wiped away another tear and peered up at Myles. "Those events shaped who I became. I always felt dirty. It was okay for me to sleep with men, but I told you I never enjoyed it. And I didn't. Sometimes I'd cry when a guy was on top of me. And now I'm thirty-three, and I lay with you on the snow, and we made love all night. My whole life changed. I wasn't that same scared girl anymore."

Willow hesitated. "I also became an attorney to stop people from doing what that man tried to do to me. I can't do this. I can't just let the guy go who knew about his son molesting his own daughter. And the mother. Where was she? I can't do it. I won't do it. Kyrie or Sadie could end up just like me."

Myles drew her close to him. "Do you really feel that way?"

Willow peered up, her jaw tight. "I do, Myles. I do."

"I'll tell Jack that. When you become the judge in this district, you can grant us temporary custody for the Cains and the Hunters. You always wanted to move to the six-bedroom mansion along the river."

She peered up at him once more. "You wouldn't hate me?"

"No. Maybe instead of having children of our own, we're destined to help youth who don't have anyone. Just like you and I," he said kissing her on the forehead. He stood and pulled her up. "Please, give me a few minutes with Cain."

"Okay," she said under her breath.

"Let's go get some breakfast."

"I am kind of hungry. Remember we have the interviews with the two superintendent candidates and the big doubleheader tonight."

"Even Saturdays are busy."

She looped her arm with Myles'. "Thank you for listening."

"Always."

After breakfast, Myles drove to the safe house where the sheriff and Throckmorton waited for him. Myles noticed there were two guards stationed nearby.

"Must think he's pretty important."

The sheriff laughed. "Curtis is scared spitless. He'll only talk to you, Myles."

"Good to hear."

The sheriff stopped. "Why did you say that?"

"We'll see what happens when I tell him we're about ready to let him go because he hasn't provided us anything concrete."

"This should be interesting."

The three opened the door and walked inside.

"Myles, thanks for bringing my family. You did what you promised. I'll keep my promise."

Throckmorton took control. "Okay. Jack, will you take his wife and son to another room?"

"Why?" his wife asked, angry lines forming on her brow.

"Proper procedure, ma'am," the sheriff said.

Myles sat across from Curtis. Throckmorton sat next to him. Once his two family members were out of the room, Myles started the conversation. "I have a couple of questions for you before we start."

"Shoot."

"What happened to your youngest daughter?"

"I don't know what you're talking about."

"I think you do."

Throckmorton intervened. "And why are the two girls not included in your request for the witness protection program?"

"They chose not to be."

"Chose not to? That makes no sense."

Cain's eyes looked scared. "I can't answer for them."

"Could it be your son harmed one of the two?"

Cain got defensive. "I have no clue what you're talking about."

"I think you do." Myles said standing up glancing at Throckmorton. "Let them go, Lynus. If he's lying right now, you can't trust anything he has to say that will be of any use."

Throckmorton walked over. "You're free to go."

"Whoa. Myles, you know they'll kill me."

"Not my problem now. I did what I said I'd do. Hoped you would be honest. Your son molested his little sister, and you two knew about it. So now you're on your own." Myles opened the door.

"Myles, stop. You're right. Nathan fondled his sister a year or so ago. We put him in counseling so it's over."

"What about your daughter?"

He hesitated. "We didn't get her help."

Myles took a deep breath. "If Agent Throckmorton is agreeable, you and your wife will go into the witness protection program, your son will be charged with molestation of a minor, and you'll relinquish all rights to the two girls to Willow. That's the deal. Do you need time to think about it?"

"No, I agree to your terms."

Throckmorton turned to Jack who had just walked into the room. "Sheriff, send a deputy to secure a warrant for the boy's arrest?"

"Will do."

Throckmorton turned to Myles. "Thanks for your help. You can leave right now."

Curtis's eyes went wide. "I won't talk if Myles isn't in here."

Throckmorton eyed Myles and then turned back to Curtis. "Okay, Mr. Cain, start talking."

Curtis sighed. "Ronald Halter hired me and Paul to carry out hits on certain people who they deemed were detrimental to what the group was trying to accomplish."

"Who's this group?"

"Halter, Myles' stepfather, Cason, Jackson, Jeremiah and Isaac Reynolds, the Konnors, and Cadence Halter. The group also included Senator Dawson and his wife, Cynthia, Michael Comforti, and a member of the president's senior staff who works for the secretary of state, Marcus Sloan. I think that's his name."

"No one else?"

"Not that I know of. Hold it, there was one man who they called Mr. X. No one knew his real name. But he does know a lot about you. He provided Halter and Jackson details about Myles' life. Of course, you know Myles has been the prime target of these men."

"Did they ever say why?"

"They're all involved in illegal activities around the world. Myles disrupted many of their operations. The main ones they talked about were located in China, Libya, and Afghanistan."

Throckmorton frowned. "Your just naming names. What evidence do you actually have?"

"I kept track of all the money when it came in, who authorized it, and who sent us out. Every one of those people signed off on one or more of those receipts. I still have them on a Jump Drive." He handed Myles the drive. Myles handed it to Throckmorton.

Throckmorton continued. "Do you know anything about a book?"

"Oh yes. Cynthia Gold, I mean, Dawson, kept the book to cover her and her husband's ass."

"How was Senator Dawson involved?"

"Dawson wasn't directly involved. Comforti was his contact in D.C. He'd meet with Sloan and tell him the plans. Sloan's job was to make sure all avenues were secure for them to operate. He had tons of resources and information from the secretary of state's office."

"Was the secretary of state involved?"

"No. He knew nothing about it. Just Sloan."

Myles interrupted. "Can you tell me anything about this person who is supposed to know everything about me?"

"If you have the book, it provides clues as to who this person is."

Throckmorton jumped in quickly. "Do you know where the book is?"

"No, Dawson's wife kept it. She probably has it."

"What part did Zachary Hunter play in it?"

"The guy is best friends with Paul. The two served in Afghanistan together. Zachary is a demolition and arms expert. Paul confiscated weapons and demolition materials for us. They both have connections."

Throckmorton glared at him. "I'll need a list of those connections."

"There are several of them. And they're all over the world."

"We'll need them." Throckmorton glanced toward the sheriff. "Can you think of anything else?"

He shook his head.

Throckmorton turned toward Myles. "I'll collect the information. We'll dispatch it to the U.S. attorney's office. Your new identities will be here in the next couple of weeks if your information pans out. For now, they'll take you to your new homes."

Myles eyed Cain. "Oh, one more thing, Curtis. Where is Paul?"

"He's staying at a woman's house. A Miss Roberts. I think she's a teacher."

A weird look passed over Throckmorton's face. "We'll bring him in."

Myles headed toward the door and waved for the sheriff to follow him. "Have your men available just in case."

"Got ya. Right. You don't trust him."

"Don't let the son of a bitch escape. If he does try to escape, make sure Throckmorton goes nowhere."

"I'll take care of that. You have some interviews to sit in on and a game to coach."

Myles walked back toward Cain. "Curtis, you're going to be a free man. This is your chance. Make the best of it."

"Thanks, Myles. What about my son?"

"If it were up to me, he'd serve as much time as the system would allow. The only reason I didn't release you to your own fate is I promised to rescue your family. I don't break my promises. You're just fortunate my wife isn't the judge in the district where this occurred."

"Why?"

"Because he'd be spending most of his life in prison."

Chapter 19

Myles drove back to the house. On the way he stopped by the realtor's office to check on the six-bedroom house that interested Willow. They would be able to see it at three-thirty. It was eleven-thirty when he arrived at home.

No one was there. Willow had left a message saying there were out shopping, and there was lunch meat in the refrigerator for him if he wanted a sandwich. She'd meet him at the school at one.

He made himself a lunch and sat down and relaxed. Myles was finally bringing Halter to justice. All these years of chasing down the perp was ending. Willow was right. Cadence wasn't who she said she was.

His cell phone buzzed. It was Sheriff Watkins.

"Myles, the magistrate issued all the warrants, and the cops are in the process of arresting everyone mentioned around the state. Paul has been caught. You were right. Throckmorton tried to help him out. We arrested him also. His arrest opened a whole new can of worms. The only missing piece is Mr. X."

"Maybe that person's name will come out from their interrogation. Everyone will be trying to cop as much of a plea deal as they can."

"The one good thing we have going for us is Townsend will be the judge. He won't let them get away with anything."

"They'll call him in. Not Willow?"

"Yep. She'd have to recuse herself because it would be a conflict of interest."

"Yeah, right. Anyway, enjoy the rest of the day. Don't worry about this stuff. We've nabbed them. And because the judge signed the warrants for acts of terrorism, there will be no bail."

Myles ambled upstairs for a shower before the interviews. He had just climbed in and wet his hair when he thought he heard something. Not hearing anything more, he stepped out and dried himself. With a towel around his waist, he headed into the bedroom but stopped immediately. Lying on the clothes he had laid out was a note. He opened it.

"The games have just begun."

Myles had not locked the door so anyone could have come up the stairs. He sat on the side of his bed. Wow, he'd have to do a better job of protecting his family.

He arrived at the school several minutes before the first interview at one. Willow sat on a bench in front of the school. She hurried over and took his hand. "Everything good?"

"Yep. Tell you after."

The two headed into the school boardroom. The peered around. Along with school board members, there were a couple of teachers and community members.

The first interviewee was from a large school in Wyoming. Gerald Renault had been an administrator for eleven years. He said he wanted an opportunity to move closer to home. He was from the Geddes area, which was located southeast of River Valley.

"Have a question for you, sir?" Myles said. "What is your philosophy on race relations in schools?"

Renault thought about it. "I'm fifteen percent French and another thirteen percent Native American, so I understand how difficult race relations can be. I'm pro-communication. It's best to talk through issues. I'm also a proponent of setting up a task force to deal with the communication to foster good race relations. Good question, Mr. Cason."

Willow followed. "Your thoughts on where the curriculum is going in our school district?"

"I don't understand the question, ma'am."

"Mr. Renault, this school district continues to struggle with mandated test scores and scores in general. How would you improve test scores?"

"More training for teachers on the curriculum. Workshops quarterly and more strict teacher guidelines. I hope that answers your question."

"Thank you, sir."

Mr. Swanson glanced around the room. "Are there any more

questions?"

No one had any others. Mr. Renault stayed around and talked to the school board and others. He took Myles aside. "I understand you're the boys' basketball coach."

"Yes, sir."

"You're doing a wonderful job. Our athletics can go a long way with your help."

"Thank you, sir."

Willow linked arms with Myles.

"And you're the new judge?" Mr. Renault turned to face Willow.

"Not yet, sir. Another week."

"That's good to know."

Myles rolled his eyes after Renault left. She smiled. "Same feeling."

At two, the second interviewee entered the room. Garrett Horn came from a small school in North Dakota, even smaller then River Valley. He had five years of experience and was in his early forties with a wife and two sons.

Myles and Willow both asked the same questions they did earlier.

Horn was thoughtful about his answers. "Test scores are always difficult to address. Many students need extra help. To help them succeed, we must find ways to help them buy into the education process. For example, from what I've read after the tragic bombing, a group of students rallied with teachers to help failing students. It takes the community—teachers, and students working together to bring the scores up."

He took a deep breath before addressing the racial question. "To be truthful I don't have an answer for you when it comes to an issue that has plagued this country for hundreds of years. Since our first conquest of the Native Americans and then the tragedy in the Civil War, race relations are at an all-time low around the country. There is a significant Native American population in this area. My first reaction would be to set up multi-racial teams to generate ideas to help the situation. This would include adults as well as youth."

After the formal interview, Principal Newcombe hurried over to Mr. Horn. "Thank you for your insight, sir. Especially about the racial issue. Our social studies teacher, Myles Cason, and his wife, Willow, have agreed to spearhead the same task force you are considering."

"That's good to know. If I do become superintendent, I'll lean on his and your expertise to work toward a better understanding of this issue."

Myles strode over to Mr. Swanson. "Patrick, Willow and I have to run."

"Thanks for being part of the selection process. Your thoughts?"

"Horn by a landslide."

"They'll both be at the basketball game tonight. We hope to decide soon. Good luck."

Myles grabbed Willow's hand. "What's the hurry?"

"Surprise."

Myles and Willow walked quickly to his car and drove down the Main Street and then took the River Road. He pulled into a driveway of a house with four dormer windows on the second level and a three-car garage.

Jill Morgan was waiting for the two. Myles shook her hand.

"Glad you made it," Miss Morgan said. "Willow, good to see you again."

"Jill."

"Please let's take a walk through." She opened the door and Myles let Willow go through first. An open-living room plan led to a back sliding-glass door. She grabbed Myles' hand as they walked through the first floor.

"This is magnificent," she said, her voice barely above a whisper.

Jill explained the layout of the house. "There is a master bedroom on this floor. The remaining five bedrooms are on the second floor."

They walked into the master bedroom.

Willow's eyes were wide. "Wow, I've never seen a bedroom this large."

"Let's take a look upstairs," Jill said.

They viewed all five of the rooms. Three of them were large while the other two were just a bit smaller. They walked back downstairs and opened the sliding glass door to a large back patio.

The spacious backyard led down to the river where there was a boat dock.

"Myles, Willow, the house has been on the market for six months. They have dropped the price down to six hundred fifty thousand dollars. You possibly could get it for six and a quarter."

Willow glanced at her. "Are there any offers?"

"Not at this point. We did have a couple come in earlier this morning. It was little out of their price range."

Myles interrupted, "A lot to think about. We'll let you know tomorrow."

"That quick?"

Willow even popped her head up.

"Yes, we should be able to make a decision by then. I'm sorry, but we must run. The girls' basketball game will be starting in a half hour."

"I'm heading that way also."

Myles and Willow hopped in the car and headed toward the high school.

"Sweetheart, I love it. But that's too steep of a price for us. We can't afford that."

Myles shrugged. "If you like it, we can afford it."

"What do you mean?"

"I served thirteen years for the U.S. government. Because I had no one—no car, no cell phone, no house——I was able to bank lots of money."

"You never told me you had any money?"

"I don't really. It's my stock portfolio for you and our kids."

"What are you talking about?"

"Over the past sixteen years, I've built a stock portfolio. My broker has done a wonderful job. If something should happen to me, you and Brielle will receive the stocks equally."

"You didn't have to do that."

"Yes, I did. You're my wife and the one I love."

"How much is it?"

Myles frowned. "Close to two million dollars."

"What? My family never that much money in their accounts. Of course, they spend money as soon as they get it."

"I made a lot of good investments. Or I should say I had a good broker who made some good investments."

"You continue to amaze me."

He smiled. "I hope so. We have a lot to think about. I have other stuff to tell you about but will wait until after tonight's games."

"Okay. Thank you."

"For what?"

"This wasn't the house I envisioned, but it is one we could spend the rest of our lives in. That is, *if* we decide to stay here."

"Whoa. You're a judge now. That's what you wanted."

"We'll talk about that tonight also."

Myles peered at his wife. "Are you okay?"

"Sweetheart, let's talk about it tonight. Please focus on the basketball game. And enjoy the girls' game."

Chapter 20

The two hurried into the gym. The girls sat with Ricardo.

"Myles, Willow, I thought you were going to miss the game," he said.

"Not on your life," Myles said.

Willow slid next to Sadie and Kyrie. "I see you saved us a seat. Thank you."

"You're welcome, Mrs. Cason."

She wanted to add more but stopped. "Sadie, I'll tell you everything after the games. Is that okay?"

"Yes. I've never seen a basketball game before."

Myles sat on the other side of Kyrie. "You will tonight."

Natasha and Tabitha sat in front of them. Ricardo was sitting there but climbed up to sit on the other side of Myles. The tip-off started the game. River Valley trailed most of the first half, and at halftime Ashton led 37-32.

Tabitha looked up at Willow. "The coach has a lot of work to do with those girls."

She smiled. "I see that. Maybe you can help them."

"I'm too young, but Natasha can. She's old enough."

"We'll see. Maybe she doesn't want to play basketball."

Tabitha peered over at Natasha. "You want to play basketball, don't you?"

"No one's ever asked me to."

Willow smiled at her. "If you wish, Miss Roberts would be glad to have you on the team next year."

Natasha smiled and her eyes brightened.

At the start of the second half, Kyrie moved closer to Myles. He looked at her. "Are you having a tough time seeing the game?"

She nodded.

"Here, you want to sit on my lap?"

Kyrie quickly glanced over at her big sister. "It's okay, Kyrie. Myles won't hurt you."

When she finally climbed on his lap, Sadie peered up at Willow. "She still has a tough time with boys."

"I understand."

Halfway through the third quarter, Myles set Kyrie down and started to get up. She quickly grabbed his hand. "Kyrie, I have to prepare for the next game. Willow will be right here with you and your sister."

Kyrie glanced over at Sadie. "I don't think so, Kyrie." Willow asked what she wanted. "She wants to go down with him," Sadie said.

Myles glanced at Sadie. "She can't come into the locker room, but if she wants, Kyrie can come down and sit with Ricardo on the bench."

Sadie eyed her sister. "Is that what you want to do?"

She nodded.

"Deal," Myles said. "As soon as this game's over, Sadie can bring you down and you can sit on the bench next to me. It'll be great to have another scorekeeper."

"I'll show you how to do it," Ricardo said. The boy took Myles' hand, and they walked down the bleachers into the locker room.

~

Willow stared at Sadie. "Is Kyrie okay?"

"Yes. It's weird. She's never taken to anybody like she has Myles."

"When I first met him, he was such a calming influence on me. Your sister will be okay."

"What will happen to my father and mother and brother?"

"I wish I could talk to you about that, but I can't. At least not now. Let's just say things will be okay."

"What about us?"

"You may have to go into the court system."

Sadie's eyes teared up. "Please don't let that happen. Kyrie will not survive."

"We'll see what we can do."

They turned back to the game. Natasha commented, "They

seem to be out of sync. Isn't that what they call it?"

Willow winced at what Natasha was seeing on the basketball floor. "You're right. They're having a challenging time getting into their offense. And their defense isn't that good."

Tabitha said, "Brielle is doing well."

"She's like her father. A good athlete."

"I saw that the other night when he did that twist-around dunk or whatever it was called."

Willow smiled. "Yeah, he always was a good athlete. He holds many state hurdle records and was the MVP for his basketball team that won the state championship his senior year. Unless something happens, this team isn't going to win a state championship."

~

Ashton pulled away in the second half and won the game, 65-51. Fifteen minutes later the boys came racing out onto the court to the cheers of the crowd. Kyrie grabbed Sadie's shirt and pointed down.

"Okay, if you're ready."

The two started to walk down the bleachers. Kyrie stopped and quickly hid behind Sadie and pointed, her face frantic.

"That man. You know him?"

Kyrie nodded.

"We'll stay up here until he leaves."

The two walked back up to where they were sitting.

~

"What's wrong?" Willow asked.

"She knows that man."

"Who?"

Sadie pointed to Walter Crocket. Willow whipped around to Sadie. "How would Kyrie know Walter?"

Sadie shrugged. "She must have seen him when we were watched by the men."

Willow took a deep breath. "It'll be okay, Kyrie. You can stay up here with us."

The first half of the boys' game went like the girls' first half. Ashton controlled every aspect of the game and led by ten points at halftime. Myles made his way to the locker room.

"Myles!"

He turned to Willow's voice.

"What's wrong?" Willow ran down to meet him,

"Ashton's playing well." He shrugged

"Are you sure that's it? Your mind isn't in the game. It's elsewhere. The boys need your guidance. Shut it down and focus on the game."

~

Myles hurried into the locker room. He scanned the room and saw a despondent group of boys. "Guys, I let you down this first half."

Devin's head popped up. "No, Coach, you didn't. We all understand you have a lot on your mind deciding whether to stay here or move on to the president's offer of a job."

Myles stared at him, shocked.

Brody intervened. "Come on, Coach, we spend time together with Brielle and Olivia. We know what's going on. And it's okay."

"It's okay?"

"Yes," Elroy said. "You're human like we all are. It's okay to have an off day."

"Not when you need me."

Micah raised his hand. "I can say this for all of us. Coach, you've helped us in so many aspects of our lives. You've told us we can be whoever we want to be. So can you."

Devin spoke up. "If you're worried about letting your daughter down, don't. She and I do date, but both of us realize there's a whole big world out there ahead of us. Maybe we'll be together. But if we're not, we're okay with it."

Michael Papport added his two cents, "Coach, I shouldn't be on that basketball court. I couldn't even hit the rim. You worked with me. My teammates worked with me. And more importantly, you showed us that there is more to life than a basketball. You've provided us tools to succeed in life."

Devin stood. "What we're saying, Coach, is we'll miss you if you leave, but we also want you to spread your wings like you told us we could do. You may be in your thirties, but you're still not an old man. Believe me, Mrs. Cason will always be there for you."

They all laughed.

"What?"

Brody glanced down at the floor. "She loves kissing you. And she'll never give that up."

They all laughed at an embarrassed Myles. "You've said your piece. Here's my piece. Don't let Ashton come onto our court and beat us. No one beats River Valley on its home court."

The boys ran out of the locker room and poured it on in the second half racing away to a 90-65 victory to keep the record unblemished.

Myles watched as the team celebrated the victory. Brielle raced past him, stopped, and gave him a big hug. "Good job, Dad."

Willow slid her arm into her husband's. "Wow, way to turn it around."

"It was the kids. Nothing to do with me."

"Oh?"

He turned to Willow. "Do you really love kissing me?"

"Oh, you mean like this?" she said reaching up and planting a solid kiss on his lips. "You bet, any chance I can. Why?"

"The boys said something in the locker room about you loving to kiss me no matter where I am."

"No question about that."

The two turned toward Sadie and Kyrie. "Well girls, what did you think?" Myles asked.

"Not bad," Sadie said.

"Good," Kyrie tried to say.

Sadie turned quickly toward her. "What did you say, Kyrie?"

"Good."

Tears streamed down Sadie's eyes. "Oh my gosh, she hasn't talked in six months at least. Those are her first words."

Sadie lifted the girl up and held her tight.

When Walter Crocket came over to talk to Myles, Kyrie quickly buried her head into her sister's shoulder. "Coach, excellent job. Heading out. See you on Monday."

"Nice to see you, Willow." He walked out.

Myles peered at Sadie. "Is she okay?"

"The man scares her."

"She knows him or has seen him?"

"I think so," Sadie said.

Both turned at Olivia who came running over to them. "Mom, Dad, there's going to be a basketball party tonight at Devin's house. Can we go?"

"Sure. Be home by eleven," he said.

Olivia turned to Sadie. "Would you like to join us?"

"No, I have to watch over Kyrie."

"Go."

Sadie glanced at Kyrie. "Did you say, go?"

She nodded.

"Will you be okay with Myles and Willow?"

She nodded and lifted her hands out toward Willow. Willow lifted her up, and the little girl snuggled into her.

"Wow, that's never happened. Not even with our mother."

"Go, Sadie. Enjoy yourself," Myles said. He handed her his phone. "If you're worried and just want to call to check on her, do it. Willow's number is on speed dial."

"Thank you," she said.

Willow touched her arm. "Your life is going to be better. Kyrie's is also. I'll make sure of that."

Myles looked at the others. "Monopoly anybody?"

Hours later, they were playing their third Monopoly game when the door opened.

"Wow that was fun," Brielle said.

"I bet," Olivia said putting her hands on her hips. "You know Devin kissed Brielle on the cheek before we left."

Brielle blushed. "Olivia, you said you wouldn't tell."

Sadie grinned. "Olivia, I think the Brody boy may have kissed you on the lips."

This time Olivia blushed. "You tattletale."

The three girls laughed and started to run upstairs.

"Brielle?" Myles said.

"Dad, none of us did anything inappropriate. I promise."

"I wasn't worried about that. Did you have fun?"

"Of course, we did. And we made sure Sadie did also. Elroy thinks she's kind of cute."

"He does not," Sadie said her face turning red. "Now who's the tattletale."

The three ran upstairs.

Myles gazed over at Willow. "Teenagers." She shrugged.

Ricardo said, "Yuk. I'm in no hurry to kiss a girl. Of course, unless it's Brielle. She's beautiful."

"But too old for you, little brother," Natasha said.

Tabitha smiled.

"What, Tabitha?" Natasha said.

"I know you like that Micah boy."

"I do not," she said blushing. "Oh, okay, he may be kind of cute."

Myles intervened. "Enough kissing talk. Let's return to the game."

Willow smiled. "What game? It's over and you've lost. Again." She climbed off her chair. "And for what it's worth, I enjoy kissing the boys' basketball coach. He's kind of cute."

After everyone was upstairs, Myles and Willow sat down on the couch. Willow snuggled into Myles' chest with her legs stretched out on the couch. "What a day."

"Yeah. Lots of stuff."

"I really liked the house, sweetheart. But I don't know."

"What don't you know about it? There's plenty of room for our budding family."

"That's just it. They're not our family. The sheriff and I have sent out requests around the country to see if these kids have any relatives out there. It's only been a couple of days, but nothing has come back. And I can't send them through the foster-care program. Especially Kyrie."

"There's something more on your mind?"

"Yes, there is, but I don't know how to manage it. I know you're proud of what I've accomplished. I'm also proud of who you've become. The problem is I see so much more in you, and I feel like I'm holding you back."

"Why would you say that?"

"Your mind was not in the game tonight. You were in Sweden, Libya, wherever. But not in River Valley. I don't want that to be the case."

"You're about to be a judge. I can't take that away from you."

"I'm your wife. That is first. My mother had wonderful opportunities, and she took advantage of them at the expense of her children. I promised myself that I would never do that to the ones I love. And I won't. I would give it all up to raise my family."

"That's a lot to ask of you."

"I'm okay with it. Anyone else, no. You, yes. Besides, I want to be the woman who's riding on the passenger side of the car." She reached up and kissed him, then slid back down into her original position. "All the warrants have been served, and it sounds like everybody is in custody including the Halters and Sloan in D.C. The president isn't a happy camper."

"I can imagine. That was quick."

"Dear, the sheriff has a wide array of contacts around the country. It's almost like he pulls them out of his hip pocket."

"Leaves two issues. The kids and Walter."

"We'll see what happens with the inquiries. I'm thinking the Hunters have relatives somewhere. Sadie and Kyrie don't. You wouldn't have a problem adopting them?"

"No, I'd be okay. If I do take that job in Washington, that's not fair to the kids."

"You let me worry about the children. It's what I've always wanted to do—raise our children. I'll love them as much as I do you. And I'm deeply in love with you."

"I'll think about it. Walter is another story. He was in our house today. Or someone was."

Willow jumped up. "What?"

"Left me a note saying, 'it's just begun.'"

"You sure it's him?"

"Makes sense, especially after what happened with Kyrie tonight. Cain said the answers are in the book."

"Well then tomorrow I'm going to scrutinize every page."

"I can help."

Nope, you have children duty."

"And what does that mean?"

"You figure it out. I'm reading a book." She climbed off the couch. "Good night, love. And this house is perfect for our family. It's our house, and we haven't even touched the bedroom on this floor."

~

Willow slipped into pajamas and crawled in next to Brielle.

Brielle spoke. "Are you okay?"

It spooked Willow. "Sorry, thought you'd be sleeping."

"Just thinking about what Devin said."

Willow sat up and laid against the front of the bed. "What did Devin have to say?"

"He talked about my dad and his feelings."

Brielle took a deep breath. "Mom, I think Dad wants to take that job with the president but won't because of your accomplishments."

"He kind of said that to me tonight also. I've tried to explain to him that I'll be right by his side."

Brielle sat up. "You mean you'd give up everything you've accomplished to do that? That's not fair to you."

"I'd do it because I'm so in love with your father. He makes me feel so special. I'm on Cloud nine when I'm around him."

Brielle slid back down. "You're kind of weird that way."

They both laughed.

Willow spoke once more. "It's not as much about me as it is about you and Olivia. You have a world that's awaiting you. You have something wonderful going on here. A boyfriend. Friends. A basketball team. An education."

"I can have that anywhere. But Libya. Come on. There's so much desert there we'll shrivel up there, and our beautiful bodies will go poof."

"Poof?" Willow laughed.

"Yeah, poof."

The two stared at the ceiling. Brielle turned toward Willow. "I do want my father to take this opportunity. But he won't because he doesn't want to end up like our family."

"What do you mean?"

"The Halters were so splintered. Ronald screwed around all the time. Cadence said she loved him, but she never did. Henry was an asshole. Harper was the only one who was nice. Maybe it's only because she's ten. Now look at them. Their lives have been destroyed because of the choices they've made."

"You think that'll happen with us?"

Brielle paused before she answered. "Yes."

"It won't. I won't let it. I've seen all that you've seen and more. There was something different about your father from the first time I saw his gorgeous blue eyes in that gym. It's hard to explain but my heart raced, and I had such a tough time breathing. That's never happened to me. I stopped wearing makeup. I haven't even thought about another man since Myles showed up. That's the new me."

"Are you sure?"

"Positive. That life is past. It is for you and Olivia also. You'll have a wonderful life ahead of you. Your dad and I will also. Even if I'm not a judge or a country prosecuting attorney, it doesn't mean I can't help Myles. I'll be right there with him."

"And Sadie and Kyrie? And the Hunter children?"

"What?"

"Oh, yes. Sadie has already said she wants to stay with us. Olivia and I agree it will happen."

"There's no guarantee."

"The two girls will be traveling with us to Libya."

"You know, your father has a chance to go to Sweden."

"He can be kind of dense at times."

"I still love him."

"We can all tell."

Chapter 21

After breakfast, the group went in different directions. Brielle and Olivia decided to go downtown with friends. Myles decided to take the others to Chamberlain for a trip to the Akta Lakota Museum & Cultural Center.

"Are you ready, Kyrie?" Sadie asked.

Kyrie sat by Willow.

"You want to stay with Willow?"

She nodded.

"You sure you'll be okay?"

She nodded again.

"I'll watch her, Sadie."

"Thank you, Mrs. Cason."

"Go enjoy yourself."

Willow and Kyrie sat on the couch. Kyrie lay on Willow's lap while she read the book to find out about Walter Crocket. She had read for about thirty minutes when she peered down to see Kyrie fast asleep snuggled into her. She reached over and grabbed a blanket to cover her up, then continued reading. Halfway through the book, she found her first reference of Walter. It was a vague discussion about cancer. That would make sense because Walter did have cancer. Willow continued reading until…

She stopped and tried to control her breathing.

Walter was Austin's and Cynthia's father. He blamed Myles for the killing of his son. Why hadn't anyone figured this out? The book was incredibly detailed. Why would Cynthia do this? Or was she the one who wrote the book? It made no sense.

She jumped when her cell phone rang. "Hi, Sheriff."

"Are you busy?"

"Not really. Just reading this book that everyone's been

talking about. I've found what I'm looking for."

"Great news. I've found the Hunters' relatives. They live in Chicago and they're flying out here today to get their grandchildren."

"Are you sure they're legitimate?"

"Everything adds up. I'll stop by after lunch if that's okay?"

"Sounds good."

~

Myles arrived at the museum just past ten-thirty.

"A museum?" Ricardo asked.

"Education and cultural experience, young man. *Akta Lakota* means to honor the people. This museum was built to honor and preserve the culture of the Lakota people and the students here at St. Joseph's Indian School."

Myles and the kids walked into the facility.

"What do we have here?" a young Native American woman asked.

Ricardo spoke up. "An education and cultural experience."

She smiled. "Let me show you some things. First, this is 'Lakota Buffalo Days,' a thirty-six-foot diorama by artist, Tom Phillips. It gives a view of life on the prairie from the Missouri River to the Black Hills."

"Wow, this is cool," Tabitha said.

"We also have interactive displays that feature the symbolism of animals which is important in the Lakota belief system. Our audio and visual observation area transports you back into the realities of a daily experience." She walked with the group to another area. "This is our collectors' gallery. In it are original sculptures, paintings, and traditional crafts. The gift shop features jewelry, star quilts, dolls, books, cards, baskets, pottery, moccasins, and other items."

They walked outside. "This is our Medicine Wheel Garden. It is a sacred symbol to the Plains tribe. It represents the knowledge of the universe. Each color and line signify an essential element in the circle of life."

Natasha peered up at Myles. "This is so cool. Thank you for bringing us here."

The young lady smiled once more. "If you have any questions, please ask me."

"Thank you," Myles said. "We'll just look around."

After spending an hour or more looking at all the different items, they headed into the gift shop. The two Hunter girls spent time together at the jewelry section. Ricardo found a five-inch eagle he thought was cool. "Can I have this?"

"If that's what you want."

He nodded. The two girls came running out with turquoise rings. "Can we have these?"

"Sure."

Myles turned to Sadie. "See anything you like?"

"I don't have any money, Mr. Cason."

"My treat."

"I couldn't."

"It's okay. If there's something you want, please get it."

She shrugged. "Well, I like to read."

"The book section is wonderful."

Sadie hurried toward the direction of his pointing finger. She found a book and brought it to him. "This sounds interesting. It's about the myths and legends of the Sioux."

"Okay, if that's what you want," Myles smiled.

Sadie glanced at Myles. "Did you buy anything for Willow?"

"Nope. She should have come with us if she wanted something. Same with Brielle and Olivia. I did find this little bracelet for Kyrie. Do you think she'll like it?"

"She'll love it."

After he paid for everything, they headed to the car. Once inside, Myles turned to the kids in the back. "We've already been here so they were able to purchase what they wanted. Buckle up. Anybody hungry?"

"Yes," they all said.

"Al's Oasis it is."

~

Willow glanced up at the clock. It was almost one. She shook Kyrie. "Are you hungry?"

She nodded. Willow headed to the kitchen when she heard the door open. "Hello."

Walter stepped in.

"Myles is not here."

Kyrie hid behind her and pointed. "It's him."

"What, honey?"

Walter spoke. "I hoped she wouldn't remember."

"Remember what? Walter, what is happening here?"

"Willow, you are a lovely woman, but Zachary needed to take care of you before you figured it out."

"Figured out what?" she said backing up a few steps, her hand shielding Kyrie.

"Myles killed my son."

"You know he didn't. It was the same group he's been chasing down for all these years."

"Willow, you were there. You were only sixteen, but you saw him brutally murder my son."

"I wasn't there. I didn't know Myles before that night in the gym. You're insane."

"Maybe. Maybe that's what cancer does to a person."

"What do you want?"

"Several things. I want that damned book Brielle stole, then I'm going to take care of the two of you. Once that's completed Myles is the only thing left."

"Why is this book so important?"

"It has all my secrets. I didn't know Cynthia had written them down. If I'd known none of this would have had to happen. You would have lived. But for sure, Myles would still have to die."

"It's over. Your group is all under arrest and won't get out of prison for a long time, if ever."

"Unfortunate situation. They were careless. Now I don't have to worry about killing them like I did Hunter's wife and that stupid principal."

"You killed them?"

"Of course, I did. I would have killed the two hit men also, but your husband reached them too soon."

"And the F.B.I. is involved with you also?"

"Throckmorton is just as greedy as the next man."

"It's over. Can't you see? You may kill the both of us, but Myles already knows."

"How could he?" Crocket's eyes opened wide.

"The bombings. And the fact that so many personal things were known about him. You and I are the only ones who know his secrets."

"That's also unfortunate. But no matter, your life is about to end. Now give me the damn book!"

"Why would you even come near Brielle if you hated Myles so much?"

"That's Cadence's idea. And a brilliant one. Got me close to Brielle. And she's loved her father since she was old enough to know the difference. Cadence and Ronald couldn't change that because of you. The lies you told her about her father. The little bitch found the book and didn't tell anyone."

"What did you mean when you wrote Myles a note saying, 'the games have just begun'?"

Crocket snarled, "I wrote no note. I have no idea what you're talking about." He turned at the sound of the door opening. Willow grabbed a lamp and threw it at him. "Run. It's Crocket." She lifted Kyrie up and dashed toward the door.

Brielle stepped in and stopped in the doorway when she saw the man. "What's happening, Walter?"

Olivia grabbed Brielle's hand. "We have to run. Now."

The duo scrambled out of the house. Brielle dialed the sheriff. "Sheriff, Walter's here to kill Mom."

"I'm almost there."

Willow picked up the little girl in her arms and raced toward the river. Searching for a place to hide, she ducked with the little girl behind a brush.

"I will find you. There's nowhere to go," came a roar behind her.

Through the bushes, she saw Crocket walking close by along the riverbank, a rifle hanging over his shoulder. At that moment, Kyrie sneezed. He stopped, cocked his rifle, aimed and shot into the bush. He missed. Willow jumped, lifted the little girl up, and headed onto the river and stepped onto the ice. She had a challenging time keeping her footing but managed to reach a hill further up the river. She pushed Kyrie up toward the bank, then crawled up after her.

"Run, Kyrie. Run. I'm right behind you."

The little girl ran as fast as she could. Willow came flying behind her. Walter finally made it up the bank, his footsteps close behind. "Faster, Kyrie," she breathed

Kyrie slipped and fell. Willow dove down beside her, rolled

out of the bank, and covered her up. Walter inched over toward Willow and pulled out a pistol. He aimed the pistol at her.

"You don't have to do this."

"Yes, I do," he said as he stepped closer. He hesitated for a moment. "It's sad having to kill a creature as beautiful as you."

The weapon clicked. Kyrie screamed. "No, don't hurt my mother."

The scream startled Walter. Willow took advantage of the split-second hesitation, reached out, and kicked him as hard as she could between the legs. He buckled over. She jumped up, lifted Kyrie into her arms, and ran as fast as she could toward the house. She circled around to the front and ran into the sheriff.

"It's okay, Willow."

She tried to catch her breath. "He's coming." Walter scrambled around the hedge. "Far enough, Walter. It's over."

Walter took a deep breath and lifted his pistol to fire. The sheriff drilled him in the chest twice, killing him instantly. Brielle ran over to Willow and hugged her. Tears streamed from her eyes, and she hiccupped.

"You're okay?" the sheriff said.

"Yeah, Kyrie saved our lives."

Kyrie's chin jutted at them. "I wasn't going to let him kill my mother."

"I'm not your mother, sweetie."

"I hope you will be," she said snuggling into her.

Olivia and Brielle bear-hugged the two of them. "I didn't know you could sprint that fast," Brielle said.

Despite the situation, they all had to laugh.

Brielle glanced at the sheriff who checked the body to make sure Crocket was dead. "Does that mean it's over?"

"I think so," Willow said.

"Does it mean we can head to Libya?"

Willow's head tilted at the question. "That's up to your father. Right now, anybody else hungry for pizza?"

Chapter 22

Myles arrived with the others back at the house around three-thirty. Willow smiled. “Did you enjoy yourself, sweetheart?” she asked.

Just then, Ricardo ran over to her and jumped onto the couch.

“Whoa, young man, watch it. You’re going to hurt yourself jumping on the couch like that,” Willow said.

“Sorry.”

“Now tell me what happened?”

“We saw a museum with art and all kinds of things. This is what I got.” He showed her his eagle.

“That looks cool.”

“It is.”

Tabitha plopped down on the other side of her. “We both bought turquoise rings.”

“How exciting!” Willow winked at Sadie. “Your sister is upstairs with the girls. She hasn’t stopped talking for the last two hours.”

Sadie’s eyes lit up. “What?” She scampered up the stairs. The other three chased after her. Myles dropped down next to his wife.

“Please hold me,” she asked as she slid over to him. She peered up into his eyes. “Walter is dead. The sheriff killed him.”

“What? How?”

“Things are going to be okay.”

Myles peered into her eyes. “Are you sure you’re okay?”

“Kyrie saved my life. She screamed, and it startled Walter who trained a gun on us. It allowed us to escape around the house where Jack was waiting. He shot twice and killed him instantly.”

Myles slapped his forehead and took a deep breath. “I should have been here.”

"You can't protect me all the time. In my heart you're always there. That protects me."

Myles sat up. "I can't take the job with the president."

Willow's eyes darted up to him. "Why can't you?"

He gazed into her hazel eyes. "I've almost got you killed twice this month. My past life will haunt you forever."

Willow seized his hands and kissed each knuckle. "We'll be okay."

Myles gently pulled his hands away. "I can't. If anything happened to you, it would kill me."

"Aren't you being a little too dramatic? I can run fast when I'm in trouble. And I am able to use any kind of weapon." Willow said, a shaky smile on his face.

Myles climbed off the couch. "I have some things I need to do at school for this week."

Willow gazed at his back. She could see he was hurting. "Always remember, I love you and no one else."

~

Myles strode down the road toward the school. He needed some air and time and space to think about everything. Willow was right. He couldn't always protect her. She didn't realize how devastating it would be if she died because of him. Eventually, he would have to tell her. The people he couldn't save.

It took him thirty minutes to reach the school. There were a couple of cars parked outside. One was Miss Roberts'. The other one he didn't know. He walked into the school. Quiet except for a noise coming out of Miss Roberts' classroom.

Myles stopped and heard moaning. He shook his head. Like Brielle said, that woman was piece of work. He opened his door, turned on his light, and sat behind his desk. The next couple of hours were spent grading papers.

The cell phone buzzed around six. "Bother," he said to himself. He picked it up. "Are you coming home for supper?"

"No, go ahead."

"Really, Myles. That's not like you."

"Not really hungry right now."

"Are you sure?"

"Yeah, Willow, I'm sure. I'll grab something when I get home." Myles clicked off the cell phone and gazed up at a figure standing in the doorway. “Hi, Myles, Willow said you would be here.”

“Hey, Jack. Thank you for saving Willow and Kyrie. What’s up?”

“The three kids’ grandparents are in town. I dropped them off at your house with the kids. Willow wanted to make sure they were suitable for the children.”

“That’s Willow.”

“Wow. I’m known you ten years at least, and this is the first time I’ve ever seen you sulking,” he said sitting on top of one of the desks. “What’s wrong?”

Myles stared at the sheriff. “I couldn’t protect Willow. And I sure and the hell wouldn’t be able to protect her in another country. We’re better off here. She’ll be a wonderful judge. And Brielle has found a boy she likes.”

“Take a ride with me?”

“I can’t.”

“You can. Even if I have to arrest you and put you in the back of the car.”

Myles smiled. “If you put it that way.”

The two drove south down a back road.

After minutes of silence, the sheriff said, “Everything you said is true. You won’t be able to protect Willow in a foreign country, and she will be a wonderful judge here. Brielle does have a boyfriend. And someday you two will have children and you’ll spoil them just like all parents do.”

The two pulled into a graveyard.

“A cemetery?”

“Not just any graveyard. A special graveyard.”

The two ambled around family monuments and nameless stones covered with moss. He stopped in front of one gravestone. “This man died two years ago. For several years all he wanted was to see his grandson come back from Afghanistan. He was able to see him just before he died.”

They walked to another gravesite. “This woman was heartbroken for the longest time because she thought her daughter would never come home. The girl returned three weeks before her mother’s death. She got to see her and her granddaughter for the first time.”

The two walked to three more gravesites. The same story. At the final gravesite, Jack knelt and brushed away the snow. "My father. He died a year or so ago."

"I'm so sorry I wasn't here."

"I didn't know where you were. He was a sheriff. Many times, he thought about giving it all up. Just like I have. He also told me that if we don't do it, no one will, or the wrong people will. That's what keeps me going."

Myles stood quietly as the sheriff said prayers over his father's grave. After a tearful amen, he turned toward Myles. "The graves I've showed you are pertinent to you."

"What are you talking about?"

"Every one of them was able to see their loved ones because you helped them come home. One you freed from Afghanistan. Another from a mountain home. It goes on and on. If you don't join the president, someone else will. Maybe it will work out; probably it won't.

"As for your wife, don't you dare worry about her. She used a damn letter opener to fend off Hunter. She would have found a way to kill the son of a bitch. And Crocket? She kicked him in the midsection to escape with the little girl. She protected that little one. That's who she is. Willow, like you, needs a purpose. You're her purpose. She'll do anything for you and her children."

"You mean well, but she's a judge. A bonafide judge. What an accomplishment! Someday—maybe not today—but someday she'll blame me for taking her away from that job."

Jack took a deep breath. "You are a bonehead. Everyone around town who knows her knows she could give a damn about being the judge. She's thrilled. But you know what's she more thrilled about is having your child. Willow told my wife a couple of times after she first met you, she'd have a hard time saying no because she thought you were so hot."

"My wife asked her why she didn't. The first words out of her mouth were, 'because I love him. I've never loved anyone. I don't want to be that girl anymore. No matter where life takes us, I will be with him.'"

"My wife asked her, 'you know what he does?'"

Willow nodded. "I have a good idea he works for the government."

"'That means he'll go places I may not like.' These are Willow's exact words. And this was in October when she first met you. 'I would give up everything I've worked for, and that includes being a judge, if it means Myles and I could spend the rest of our lives together.' And this girl had only seen you from a distance."

"I don't know what to say."

"You do. As long as I've known you, you've never been afraid to take on a challenge. This will be your biggest challenge, but that lovely woman will be right there with you. She'll protect your family and be there for you. That's what a woman in love does. Believe me I know; Molly has been doing it for me over the past twenty-five years. She can tell you about the many nights she stayed up all night waiting for me to come home or brought me a batch of chicken soup when I was running late. Willow is that woman for you. Not very many men can say they have a woman like that. Treasure her." The sheriff smiled at him.

"What?"

"In a way she's like you; she likes living on the edge."

Myles had to laugh. "Thank you. I needed that."

"What are friends for? And Myles, you've been my best friend. You've done a wonderful job as a teacher and a basketball coach here, but as a best friend, I'm telling you to take that woman and your family, explore this world, help others. That's who you are."

Myles sighed. "We have some high school girls."

"Haven't you heard a word I said? Willow will take care of your family. I'm an old John Wayne fan. In one of his movies, Maureen O'Hara needed milk for her baby. And when John Wayne was out fighting Comanches, she walked several miles to get a bottle of milk for their child. That's what Willow would do if she had to."

Myles glanced at Jack. "That sounds like her."

"She would do anything she could for her family. Now for the second time in the last ten minutes, quit your pouting, take that woman and your family, and explore this world. Send me postcards of wherever you go. I'll collect them and give them to you when you come back." The sheriff slapped him on the back. "I'll drop you off at your house. It's almost eleven."

The next morning Myles opened his eyes to a pair of eyes

staring at him. "Where did you go?"

"I needed to do some work, Kyrie."

"Everyone worried. Should have called."

"I'll remember that. Are you the first one up? We should wake everyone up for school."

Kyrie nodded. She ran over and shook Willow who had been sleeping on the floor next to Kyrie and Sadie.

"What's up, sweetie?"

"School."

"Right." Willow rested her eyes on Myles. She took a deep breath. "Are you okay?"

"Yes. I'm better."

"I'm glad. Let's get the kids off to school. I have to go to work."

"Okay."

She turned to shake Sadie. "Come on, Sadie, time to get ready for school."

"School?"

"Yes, you and Kyrie and the three Hunters are going to school with Brielle and Olivia."

Sadie bolted to her feet, hands on hips, and glared over at Myles. "Don't ever be like my father!" She spun around, took Kyrie's hand, and started up the stairs.

"What was that about, Willow?"

She frowned. "No one in this house knew where you were. If you're going to be an asshole, at least let someone know you're okay." Willow hurried upstairs. Myles slapped himself across the head.

"Did that hurt?" Brielle asked.

"No, I'm okay."

"Too bad."

"You too?"

"Yes, me too. I thought my father would never disappoint me. Last night you did. You left a woman who loves you and didn't have the decency to let her know you were safe." Brielle started to head out the door.

"Don't you need a ride?"

"No, Mom is taking us to school. Remember, Dad, you told me one time maybe I should have stayed with my mother. Last night I actually thought about it." She hurried out the door.

Myles went upstairs to get dressed. Willow had just finished putting on her suit. She turned toward Myles. "Please, don't ever do that again!" Willow hurried to the door but stopped in the doorway. "Always remember you're the man I love and the one I will spend the rest of my life with. But whatever this is, it can't continue."

Chapter 23

Myles headed toward the courthouse for Willow's swearing-in ceremony. He walked into her office. "Is Willow in, or has she already gone upstairs?"

"Yes, she is, Mr. Cason. Go on in." The woman smiled.

Myles walked back and knocked on the door. Willow looked up. "Myles." She smiled. "What's up?"

"Aren't you supposed to be sworn in today?"

"Please close the door?" She came around her desk, took his hand, and sat down on one of the chairs around the table. "I couldn't do it. At least not until you and I straighten things out."

"What's there to straighten out? You're going to make a wonderful judge."

"Sweetheart, I don't care about being a judge. I care about you. I care about us. That's the only thing I care about. You just left me last night. No word whatsoever. Not even the courtesy of calling me to let me know you were okay."

"I was with the sheriff. He took me to a graveyard."

"To a graveyard?"

"Yep."

"I don't have time to talk to you about it now. I should have told you the ceremony had been cancelled. I really don't know if it will ever happen."

"I understand," he said standing up. "I'll let you return to your work. I've got practice."

"Okay, I'll see you later."

He started to walk out the door but turned as she had back at the house. "This morning, Brielle told me I was a disappointment. I never wanted to disappoint either one of you. I've disappointed too many people in my life. And here I let down the two people I love the most in the world. I'm sorry."

~

Myles made it back in time for the boys' basketball practice. The boys weren't out from the locker room yet.

"Dad?"

He turned around to Brielle's voice. She ran over to him and hugged him. "What's that about?"

"I'm sorry about this morning."

"No need to be. You were right to be upset at me for the way I treated Willow."

"You aren't a disappointment to me. You never will be. You are my father, and I'll always love you. But Willow feels pain also. She needs you to talk to her. Quit shutting her out. Willow will always be there for you. Please, talk to her."

"I promise."

"Good." She reached up and kissed Myles on the cheek.

The boys went through their drills. Myles stood along the bench, looked up, and saw Willow standing against the bleachers. He walked over to her.

"Looking pretty good, Coach." She smiled.

"They continue to improve each day."

"Why wouldn't they? Look who's coaching them."

"I should go back to doing my job."

"Myles."

He turned.

"You'll never disappoint me." Willow spun around and walked out of the gym. Myles watched as she left the gym, then went back to coaching the team. An hour later practice was over. He was walking out of the school when his cell phone rang.

"Hi."

"Hi, sweetheart. I'm outside in the parking lot." Click.

He headed toward the parking lot. She sat on the front hood of her car. "What is this?"

"I wanted to be here to pick you up when you were done with school."

"Okay, why?"

"I wanted to take you for a ride. Hop in."

He climbed into the car. "You don't have any plans to off me, do you?"

She laughed. "You are such a goofball. How could I ever off the man of my dreams. Now let's go to Chamberlain."

"Where are the girls and Ricardo?"

"Don't worry. They can take care of themselves. Just enjoy the ride. You said you wanted to be driven around by me. I'm doing it."

"I didn't literally mean it."

"I know you didn't."

Thirty minutes later Willow drove onto I-90, then turned into the first rest area which overlooked the Missouri River. She shut the car off, went to the back of the car, and returned with a blanket and a cooler. "Join me." She grabbed his hand and the two walked down a trail. After spreading the blanket on the rocks and sitting on it, she crooked a finger toward him. "Have a seat." She opened the cooler. "The girls packed roast beef sandwiches for us, some chips, and of course, our patented lemonade. Your supper."

The two sat quietly and enjoyed the meal. Willow broke the silence. "This is the first time I've ever brought anyone to this spot. I would come here when I needed to think about things. And it was often."

She peered up at him. "I came here as soon as I could the day after I looked into your gorgeous blue eyes. All I wanted was to make love with you. It would have never happened. Because you're not like any man I've ever met. And I would never want you to think I was a slut or anything like that." Willow took another bite out of her sandwich. "After I met you, I would sit here and just stare out at the river. I hoped that there would be a sign to tell me what to do. Should I try for you or just let you go? Several times I decided to let you go, but my heart couldn't. I didn't want to be with anyone but you. I still don't want to be with anyone but you."

"Even after the way I acted?"

"Yes, dear, even after that. I wasn't mad at you. I just was hurt you didn't think enough about the two of us that you wouldn't at least tell me where you were. After all we've gone through, I just needed to know you were okay."

"I'm sorry. I should have called you."

Willow took a deep breath. "The reason I brought you up here is to tell you something I've wanted to say to you for a long time. Remember the night you called me around midnight?"

Myles nodded.

"I was sitting here at midnight, half asleep staring out into the river. I asked God for guidance on where to go with you. Then unexpectedly you called me. My first thought was you wanted to meet me at some hotel halfway between our two towns. I would have made love with you in a heartbeat. And it would have been making love, not jumping into the sack and a minute or two later, getting dressed and leaving. Never again will I do that. That's how much I love you. My sister needed help. You were there for her when no one else was." Willow took Myles' hand and peered into his eyes. "That's where I'll always be. There, when no one else will be. I want to be a judge, but I want to be your wife more."

"I can't even protect you. How can I protect our family?"

She turned his chin softly toward her. "You won't be doing it by yourself. I'll be with you. And there is no way anyone is going to split us apart. I guarantee that. I've been a selfish bitch for thirty-three years of my life. But I'm spending the rest of my life with you. That's all I want out of my life—Libya, Sweden, Spain, Russia—It won't matter. I'll learn how to speak the language. I'll teach the girls how to speak the language. I'll show them how to interact with youth from another country. I'll make sure we don't disrespect our hosts. But if we stay here, I'll be just as happy." Willow drank some of her lemonade. "All I ask from you is always to be honest with me. And I'm tired of hearing you do it to protect me. I don't need you to protect me; I need you to be honest with me."

She took another slurp of her drink. "So, why don't you really want to take the president's job?"

Myles took a swig of his drink. "Because of you, the girls. I would be devastated if anything happened to you."

Willow scrunched up her face. "So, what you're saying is if I was injured after a bomb blew up in River Valley, you'd be devastated? Oh wait. That happened in River Valley, South Dakota. You can't predict what our life is going to become. I want to live life with you anywhere and everywhere. I don't just want to exist through life. But we can do that whether we stay here in South Dakota or travel the world for the president."

Myles laughed. "The sheriff gave me a history lesson, or should I say—movie lesson—when we stood in the graveyard."

"Why were you in the graveyard?"

"He showed me these gravesites where people died happy because they were able to see their family member one last time. And that's all they wanted to do. I helped them by bringing them home. Anyway, he discussed an old John Wayne movie where Maureen O'Hara needed milk for her baby. While John Wayne was out fighting the Comanche, she walked several miles to get a bottle of milk of their child."

"*McClintock.* One of John Wayne's best movies. I would travel across the Libyan Desert to do that."

"That's about what the sheriff said. He told me to quit pouting, take that woman and our family, and explore this world. 'Send me postcards of wherever you go. I'll collect them and give them to you when you come back.' he said."

Willow stared into Myles' eyes. "You haven't told me the real reason why you won't take this job."

"I just did."

"No, Myles Hunter Cason. That's the reason you want to give. It's not the real reason. Please tell me the real reason."

Myles blew out some air. "Five years ago, I made my way through China. There were three of us. We were almost to our destination. Hong Kong. Just like that we were surrounded by a Chinese guard and captured. I found out later Halter turned us in. That's why I've been after him. I was there to bring those two home. They never made it home, and it was my fault. My fault. I couldn't do anything. To this day, I think about those two. I think about the others I couldn't bring back safely or couldn't help. Or those I've seen die in front of me."

"Who were they?"

"Married American scientists."

"Did you do everything you could?"

"It didn't matter. I couldn't get them out. And now you're asking me to do this with a person I love more than anything in this world. I can't do it."

Willow framed his cheeks and gently kissed his lips. "You've never asked me what I wanted. I want you in my life. That's it. I want you in my life. I don't care where we are." Jumping up off the blanket, she grabbed his hand, pulled him toward her, and kissed him passionately on the lips. “It’s your choice where we go with our life. I’ve told you how I’ve felt. Let’s go home. As much as I would enjoy it, I really can’t make love with you here. If caught, it would be kind of bad for a person who could be a district judge to have to go to court for indecent exposure.”

Chapter 24

The week had gone by fast. Saturday the boys and girls would host Rosewood in a basketball doubleheader. Myles and Willow became guardians for Sadie and Kyrie. It was a formality because no one else wanted the two girls. Willow also put in the paperwork to adopt the girls. They both were in school on Tuesday. Kyrie continued to talk and started to come out of her shell. The three older girls made sure one of them was always with her.

The Hunters were also still living with them. Their grandparents believed it was better for them to stay in South Dakota away from all the criminal activities happening in the Chicago area they'd lived in. All five of the children were enrolled in the River Valley School District.

Friday after practice, Myles leaned back in the bleachers staring at the ceiling. The cell phone rang.

"Hey, sweetheart, daydreaming again?"

He gave her a wistful look. "You could say that. Sitting in the bleachers thinking about tomorrow. First time I've had any connection to Rosewood in several months."

"Brielle has been kind of feeling down today. Of course, Olivia tried to cheer her up. Said they would finally have a win because Rosewood was even worse than they were last year."

Myles had to laugh. "She probably has a point there."

He returned to his thoughts, and the silence was deafening. "Okay, Myles Hunter Cason, you've been going on like this for too long. The most you've done all week is kiss me. For Pete's sake I've thrown my body at you, walked around naked in our bedroom, and still nothing. This must stop. You're making me feel old. Like I don't have anything worth admiring anymore."

"Okay, you've done none of those things."

"Well, would you want me to?"

"Let's spend the night in Chamberlain."

She straightened. "Are you serious?"

"I could handle going away with you for one night. Escaping it all and just sitting all night on your favorite spot. That is, if it's okay with you?"

"Of course, it is, sweetheart. I'll ask Jack and Molly to watch the girls. Give me about thirty minutes and I'll pick you up. I'll make sure Brielle has your car keys."

Myles shut his phone off and turned when Jacie Tuthill came walking toward him. "Hey, Myles, you like to sit here and think also. Sorry I interrupted your thoughts."

"No, you might as well join me."

Jacie sat next to him. "Wow, I've never seen you so down before."

When Myles didn't say anything, Jacie spoke up, "Jack told me you have an opportunity to take over some sort of task force and are having a tough time determining whether or not to do it."

"I thought sheriffs were supposed to keep their mouths closed."

Jacie laughed. "Something like that. I'm sure you've heard the same ole story—Willow will follow you anywhere because she loves you so much. She is being a fool for turning down the judgeship. And why would anyone want to stay with a murderer?"

Myles laughed. "Yep, I've heard those and more."

Jacie sighed. "I remember a story about a man five years ago who tried to save two American scientists from China. Thought he failed. This man never failed. My brother and his wife now are scientists at a large facility on the West Coast. They told everyone they wouldn't have been alive if it wasn't for a man called 'The Wolf.' Never knew who he really was. But we both know."

Myles head snapped up. "They're alive?"

"Yes, they are. And you helped rescue them out of there."

"What? How?"

Jacie smiled. "The Wolf has the support of a lot of powerful people in a lot of powerful places. Just your name helped them escape. You saved my brother's life just like you saved many people's lives here in River Valley in the past few months. Myles, this is your destiny. You bring a lot of good to the world. That's who you are. And Willow understands that. Hell, the sheriff understands it. Sure, you could stay here and coach boys' basketball and football, but eventually the fire within you will die because you'll realized you've made a mistake. You don't belong here. The world is yours for the taking. Willow figured that out a long time ago. Everyone else has also. You're just the only one who hasn't."

Jacie took a deep breath. "I'm a woman, and I know that you're probably worried about putting your family in harm's way. You live in River Valley, South Dakota. How has that worked? I lost my whole family. A bomb almost killed Willow. Think about it. If you weren't married to Willow, you would have jumped at the opportunity. Willow is not your ordinary woman. Don't you ever think that. That woman used a letter opener and stabbed a man who was twice as big as she was."

Myles stared at her.

"One last thing, Myles. Do you know who dug up all the dirt on every one of these criminals you are about to put behind bars? It wasn't the county sheriff, the circuit judge, or even the F.B.I. It was the woman you married. I've known her family all my life. The Reynolds, the Jacksons, the Halters. They are the scum of the earth. She has fought for you because that woman loves you. Hell, *I* want you to take this job."

"You do?"

She smiled. "Yep, because I'm going with you. I'm going to help Willow protect you and your family."

"And why would you do that?"

She hesitated. "Because you've risked your life to save those I've loved and others' loved ones. There are at least six or seven people in a graveyard down the road whom you allowed one last chance to see their family members. No one else gave a damn."

She stood up. "Thanks for listening. Myles, no one gives a damn. But someone needs to."

Several moments later Willow came waltzing into the gym. "Dear, are you ready for a night in Chamberlain?"

Myles laughed. "Sounds good."

She threw the keys at him. "What's this for?" he said.

"You're driving. I'm sliding right next to you and snuggling into you all the way to Chamberlain."

Once they were en route due north toward Chamberlain, Willow slid over next to him and put her arms around him. "I've always wanted to do this."

"Doesn't it hurt sitting on a console?"

"Don't feel a thing because I have my arms around the man I love. Now do you want to tell me what this week has been all about?"

"I'm trying to wrap my head around all that is happening."

"Why has it been so difficult for you, dear? You get married and poof, you're a different man?"

"We have a family."

"Correct. But that doesn't mean you stop being the man I love. The person who makes my heart pitter-patter all the time. The one who has wise answers for the girls. The man who makes those stupid goofball zingers that come out of nowhere. That's who I married. The man I married took down a group of highly sophisticated criminals. The man I married helped me with my issues. The man I married helped Olivia and Brielle and a group of teens straighten out their lives. That's who you are. And just because we're married doesn't mean you have to stop being that person."

"Easier said than done."

"Yes, it is easy, sweetheart. You're not being who you are. Just be you, and you'll be fine. You are the man I'm deeply in love with. There's no way I would drop doing my nails and toes just like that if I didn't love you."

Myles laughed.

"I'm just kidding about doing my nails and toes. Hell, I threw that stuff away. The point is after tonight there will be no more of this sulking around, feeling sorry for yourself, not sure what you want to do, or any of that. You want to take the president's job? Then do it. If you don't want to take the president's job, then don't!"

Myles pulled over to the side of the road. "What are you doing?" she sat up and looked around.

He started kissing her, then unbuttoning her shirt, and caressing her breasts.

"What are you doing?"

His eyes drilled into hers. "What do you think I'm doing?"

"Right here? Right now?"

"Why not? I've always wanted to do this with you."

Willow kissed him. "I have a better idea. How about my favorite spot?"

"What about...?"

She put her fingers to his lips. "I told you I only care about you."

The next morning Willow rolled over and kissed Myles on the lips. "We had better get dressed and leave before others get the same idea."

They both quickly dressed and were walking down the path when they ran into the sheriff and one of his deputies. Upon seeing them, both roared with laughter.

"What's so funny?" Myles asked.

The sheriff feigned covering his eyes. "Willow, maybe you could button your pants?"

She glanced down and quickly pivoted. "Oops."

The sheriff smirked at the deputy. "Isn't this indecent exposure?"

Willow grimaced. "Sheriff, I'd hate to contradict you, but you have no evidence of indecent exposure. You may have seen my pants unbuttoned, but there was no skin, so you have a weak case at best."

The sheriff rolled his eyes and sighed dramatically. "Oh, Willow. What has become of you?"

"What do you mean, sheriff?"

"This is not the woman who we've all come to know and love."

She grinned. "So sue me, Sheriff. For some reason I love this husband of mine with all my heart."

"Everyone knows you two love each other."

The four of them headed to the rest area. "How did you know we were here?" Myles asked.

"Believe it or not, another couple called it in because you had taken their make-out spot."

Myles guffawed. "What? You're joking."

"Nope, every Saturday morning when the weather's appropriate, they come here and make out for a couple hours starting at exactly four in the morning."

Everyone laughed. Willow took Myles' hand. "We have them beat, sweetheart. We've been there since midnight. Oops!"

More laughter. The deputy glanced at the two. "Tell me, Willow, what was it like making out on top of the Missouri River?"

Willow blushed. "I don't know. I was on top of Myles. Oh my God. I actually just said that out loud?"

The sheriff waggled his eyebrows at the deputy. "Arrest her for stupidity."

The deputy pulled out his cuffs and started to put them on Willow. "George, I was joking."

Myles rolled his eyes. "Well, Sheriff, since the two of you are here, let's have breakfast at Al's Oasis. Our treat."

"Sounds good. Too much excitement so early in the morning."

~

Willow smirked at Myles once they were in their own car. "Now wasn't that fun?"

"If you say so."

She twisted her hair into a messy bun on top of her head.

He winked at her. "I don't know what got into me, sweetheart. I've never done anything like that in my life. You're corrupting me."

"Me. How?"

"You're just so damn gorgeous."

"No, dear. You're the one who is gorgeous. And I will also say damn attractive under the moonlight." She kissed him on the cheek.

"Aw, you love me. You already knew that on our evening next to the fire."

Willow gazed up at him. "That's the Myles I married. Don't change that person."

"I'm sorry about the way I've been acting."

"I'm sure all of this is hard for you. Me, I enjoy doing this stuff with you because you're the love of my life." Willow reached over and kissed him on the cheek. "You had to admit it was romantic last night."

"Yes, it was. And you're right. I would have never done anything like that unless it was with the woman I loved."

"It's about time you felt that way. I've felt that since the first day I set eyes on you."

The two joined the sheriff and his deputy at Al's Oasis. They all ordered eggs, pancakes, and toast. While they were waiting, the sheriff provided an update on what was happening with everyone in the criminal case.

"They've all been arrested and are sitting in cells in Sioux Falls. All have been arraigned. Judge Townsend did not allow bail because of the terrorist designation. There are questions about federal jurisdiction that are being dealt with. However, Mrs. Jackson was set free. It was found she knew nothing about anything that happened."

"Wow," Myles said. "Married all those years and not a clue about her husband."

"Her lawyer proved she had nothing to do with it."

"Now Cadence's testimony was interesting. She said that Myles was part of everything from the start. He left after he killed Austin Gold seventeen years ago. An attorney disputed the information. To make a long story short, it was proven that you had nothing to do with any of it. Neither had Willow."

"Why was Willow's name even brought up?" Myles asked.

"Because she's a Konnor. And all Konnors are evil, I guess."

Willow didn't say anything but nibbled on a piece of toast. Finally, she spoke. "I'm just glad it is all coming to a close."

The deputy finally spoke, "Now that's it's over, when do you become the new district judge?" he asked.

Willow glanced over at Myles who was spreading jam on a piece of toast. The deputy continued. "Judge Townsend said he has to go out and look for another judge. That's too bad. You'd make a great judge."

Willow sighed. "I just haven't decided yet."

"What's there to decide? Who would turn down a lucrative job like that? Especially since your husband is a schoolteacher."

"Deputy!" the sheriff said.

"I'm just saying what the people in the community are saying."

"Yeah, and they all have big mouths," Willow said.

Myles and Willow drove back to River Valley. Not one word was said the whole thirty-minute trip. Once the car pulled into the driveway, Willow turned in her seat toward Myles. "I'm tired of all of this. I'll tell Judge Townsend I'll take over as district judge. Because you asked me to." She started to open the door. "I know you're worried about what may happen to me. Something has already happened. I fell in love with you and gave you my heart. Everything will be fine." She crawled out of the car and walked into the house without a glance back.

~

Brielle was sitting on the couch reading when Willow entered. "How'd it go?"

"Last night was great. This morning, not so great."

"The worldwide trip again."

"You got it."

"Maybe it's simply better to take the job as the judge and let him be a basketball coach and teacher. He can't get it out of his head that we'll be just fine traveling around the world."

"I did. I'm tired of people telling me that I could do better than Myles because he's a schoolteacher."

Brielle climbed off the couch and put her arms around Willow. "What have you told us?"

"Don't worry about what others think."

"Dad has said the same thing. You've done so much for us and for my dad. Why don't you tell him what you've done for me, for Jasmine over the years?"

"I can't. Your mother asked me not to. She did it to protect him."

"Everybody is always trying to protect everyone. This is getting old. And it's bogus. My Father. You. Me. We'll all be fine."

Willow took a deep breath. "Where are the others?"

"They're helping prepare for the girls basketball game."

"There is that. How about we grab some lunch and head down to the gym?"

"Let's go have tacos."

"Tacos. Where do they have tacos?"

"Where have you been? They have a new taco place that just opened south of town. I hear it's surprisingly good."

Chapter 25

Sadie, Kyrie, Natasha, Tabitha, and Ricardo were sitting on the bleachers when Myles walked into the gym. Kyrie saw him and ran over to him. "Dad, you made it. Are you okay?"

He had to admit he liked being called Dad since Myles and Willow had become guardians of her and her sister, Sadie, earlier in the week. She called Willow, Mother. "I'm doing good. Kind of nervous."

"You're funny. Olivia and Brielle are nervous too."

He lifted her up and carried her over to the others. "Good afternoon, everyone."

Sadie smiled. "How was your romantic evening?"

"Started off well. Ended badly."

"How'd you blow it this time?" Olivia asked.

"Same ole, same ole."

Sadie smirked. "Maybe you should try to be nicer to Willow."

"Sadie," Kyrie said, her arms crossed over her chest.

"It's okay, Kyrie," Myles said. "She's right. All of this has gotten out of hand. I'll fix it."

"I hope so," Sadie said. "Don't turn out like my father. He was a jerk. And a killer."

A tall, graying lady walked toward them. "Myles, is that you?"

"Mom! What are you doing here?" He smiled broadly.

"Come on, my son and granddaughter are here on the same day. No way I would miss it."

"Who do we have here?" Abigail Bolton asked.

"This is Sadie, and this is Kyrie. And here are Natasha, Tabitha, and Ricardo. We're guardians of the children. Kids, this is my mother."

"Nice to meet you," Olivia said, thrusting out her hand.

Myles hadn't moved but just stared at the woman in front of him. Olivia turned back to the children. "Come on, girls, join me in the locker room. There are some things we need to do. Ricardo, stay right here near Myles."

They left. Myles and his mother continued to stare at each other. "Aren't you going to give your mother a hug?"

"I can't believe it, Mom. After all these years, I finally get to hold you."

"It has been almost eighteen years. What are you still doing here?"

"What do you mean?"

"Come on. You should be running around helping your father's cousin."

"It's just not that simple, Mom."

"It sure is. Especially when you have all those talents and are married to Willow. I wanted to come so bad to your wedding, but it sounds like it was a good thing I didn't."

"Yeah, it is a good thing."

"Here, sit down by me, son. Join us. Ricardo, is it?"

Ricardo nodded.

"How did you get here?" Myles asked.

"Mrs. Jackson brought me to watch her daughter play. And to see my granddaughter play. Where is Brielle? I haven't seen her in forever."

"She'll be here soon."

"You look so much like your father. It's unbelievable. He would have been happy with what you've become. He wouldn't have been happy you didn't help his cousin out."

"Mom, I couldn't protect Willow or Brielle if I left. My family is growing, and I enjoy it here."

His mother looked around. "Let me tell you about the woman you married. She is not your average woman. She was the one who helped Brielle and Jasmine. That woman did everything she could to make sure they knew about you. She would bring Brielle to me so I could hold my granddaughter. It was always in a secret place because of our families. But she always made sure Brielle got to see me. When Brielle was twelve, Willow helped her find out about you. And while Willow was helping Brielle dig into your past, she started taking an interest in your case. Being an attorney, she dug into the background and facts about your case. It was Willow who did more than you'll ever realize to help you, son. Willow had never met you."

"Why did you stay with him?"

"Where would I go, Myles?"

"Anywhere."

"It was better I stayed because at least I could see my granddaughter and daughter at times. Jasmine was born on a fling I had after your father died in Vietnam in a humanitarian situation. He and others were bringing supplies into the country to help those in need. Your father died in a crash. The Vietnamese were nice enough to return his body. If you know your history, you know others who perished during the war weren't as fortunate."

She took a deep breath. "Before your father died, he asked his cousin who was a congressman in Minnesota at the time if he ever became president to start a task force to help other countries in need. Your father thought the task force should be humanitarian—helping them with economic development—something other than fighting. After Johnston became President, he worked to pull this task force together. His first candidate to run the task force has always been you. But he's been telling me you're balking because you're afraid something will happen to Willow. Son, I've seen Willow's strength. Don't you worry one bit about her. She'll take care of herself, and she'll take care of your children."

They turned at the voice. "Grandma, is that you?" Brielle ran over to her. "Oh my, it is you. You came to watch me play?"

"I wouldn't miss it for the world."

She glanced up at Willow. "My, Willow, you have become so beautiful."

Willow bent down and hugged her. "Grandma Bolton, it's so great to see you again." Willow went over and took Myles' hand. Ricardo jumped up, and she grabbed his hand also.

Mrs. Bolton said, "I've been trying to talk some sense into Myles. I just finished telling him he's an idiot because he hasn't taken the job as the task force commander."

"Grandma Bolton, Myles is not an idiot. That's over with. I've taken the job as the judge. It'll be okay because the most important thing is I love this man."

"I know that, sweetheart," she said. "You loved him before

you even saw him."

"Now how would you know that?"

"Come on. You were kind of a jetsetter. But for the past five years, the only man you ever dated was that Reynolds clown. If you can call that dating."

Willow blushed. "Myles, can I talk to you?"

Myles' mother nodded at Willow. "Go ahead, I want to hold my granddaughter."

Willow took his hand and pulled him away from them. "Are you okay, sweetheart?"

Myles took a deep breath. "I'm sorry for everything that has happened this week."

"Don't be. It'll all work out. I promise you. I was just worried about you and what the deputy said."

He smiled at her. "I'll get used to it."

She reached up and gave him a lusty kiss. "Like I've told you before, those are the lips of the man I love. And will always love. We'll get through this. Go spend time with your mother."

"No, dear. You're part of our family. We'll spend time together with her."

Willow smiled at him. "You bet."

"It sounds like you spent a lot of time with her over the past few years."

"Yeah, about that. She asked me not to say anything."

"I figured as much."

The two joined Myles' mother. Fifteen minutes later Casey and Joanna came in with their respective girlfriend and boyfriend, along with Mason Roe. Mason was another Rosewood student. His girlfriend Joni, had been Brielle's best friend in Rosewood.

"Wow, look at this," Casey said. "I knew my big brother, Myles, would become a superstar once he got here." Casey smiled. "You wouldn't believe how pissed off the superintendent is at Rosewood. He had thought about firing the activities director because you were winning out here. "His exact words. We could be unbeaten right now instead of two losses. Number three will come later today."

"Don't be too sure. Rosewood will rise for this game because of what happened to me back in Rosewood. I'm sure glad you brought Mother here."

"She insisted," Joanna said. "She was bound and determined."

They all turned when Mrs. Jackson walked in. "Myles, Willow, can I talk to the both of you."

"Sure. What is it?" Myles asked.

Once they were away, she handed Myles some papers. "Here is everything you need to make sure my husband and all the others never get out of prison. I've been such a fool. So many people have told me how stupid I was not to know what was happening. The money was all I cared about, so I didn't think much or even care to know what was happening. I'm sorry Myles, Willow, for everything that has happened over the years." She took a deep breath. "One other thing, Willow. Your mother and father asked me to tell you they were deeply sorry for everything that happened in your and Olivia's lives. They hope you forgive them and visit them in prison."

Willow's lips tightened. "I can't speak for Olivia, but I'll have nothing to do with any of them ever again. I've moved forward. And I'm happy with my life and the person whom I married."

Mrs. Jackson laughed. "Kind of what I told them, but I said I would pass it along."

Joanna ran over to them. "Come on, y'all, the game is about ready to begin. Willow, Mom wants you to sit with us if possible."

"Sure." She smiled.

"I have things to take care of before the next game," Myles stood.

Willow took his face and gazed into his eyes. "You're my man. Always remember that."

Myles turned toward Ricardo. "Are you ready?"

Ricardo smiled and took his hand. "You bet."

~

The girls' game started. River Valley jumped out to a quick lead and never relinquished it with a score of 87-53. Brielle scored a game high of thirty points and Olivia added twenty-two points. The girls raced over to the bleachers where Willow sat. "Mother, we did it," Brielle said hugging Willow.

Mrs. Jackson and Abigail Bolton stared in wonderment at Brielle.

"What? Willow is my mother. And will always be my mother." Olivia's eyes landed on Heather and Casey. "Oh wow,"

Brielle said. "You were here? It's so great to see you. Sorry we had to thrash your basketball team."

Casey laughed. "I'm sure you're not. Good performance, you two."

Joanna hugged Olivia and glanced over at Brielle. "You have your father's talents in you, Brielle."

"Thanks. Wait until you see the boys play."

They all turned as the boys team came running out onto the court. Heather turned to Brielle. "Who's the boyfriend?"

"Devin Bush. He's number twenty-five."

Heather nodded. "Wow, he's handsome. That number twelve is handsome also."

Olivia smiled. "That's Brody. My boyfriend."

"No wonder you two don't want to come back to Rosewood," Joni said walking up to the girls.

"Joni, you're here also?" Brielle said, hugging the girl who, along with Heather, had been her best friend in Rosewood.

"Car problems. But I get to see the hot boys."

Mason blushed. Heather smiled and kissed her boyfriend on the cheek. "Not as hot as you."

Everyone laughed.

"Come on, let's get some food before the boys' game," Olivia said. "There may be some fireworks tonight."

"What do you mean?"

"Jaden and Henry can't stand Myles. I'm sure they'll make it difficult for his team," Olivia said.

Sure enough, the teams weren't even a few moments into the game when Jaden knocked Devin to the floor with a screen. No foul was called. Devin jumped up and played. By the end of the half, River Valley trailed 42-35.

~

Myles scanned the boys' faces. "This has been another tough week for you. Your coach has been pouting like a big baby because of a decision he has to make. Everyone has told me it's not rocket science I should take the job and travel around the world. My disposition has impacted all of you."

"No, it hasn't, Coach," Devin said. "We know you'll do the right thing and take the government job."

Brody added. "We want you to take the job, but we'll miss

you so badly."

Myles was so proud of these boys. "That's appreciated. I'm not sure if I'll do anything but keep right on coaching you."

Elroy shook his head at Myles. "Coach, we *wan*t you to take the job."

"Why?" Myles asked.

"If a boy from a small South Dakota town can do something as awesome as you will do, it gives all of us hope that we can do something awesome also."

He ruffled Elroy's hair. "You can do something special. Don't ever forget that."

Micah stared at Myles. "Coach, *you*'ve seemed to have forgotten that."

Myles took a deep breath. "Okay, guys, remember what we've talked about. No one will beat us on our home court. And tonight, I'm staying right here. Because like you said, 'you need me.' More importantly, I need you."

The two teams went at it in the second half. Elroy Hubbard took control from his point guard position. He dished out fourteen assists and added twenty-two points as the Eagles rolled to a twenty-five-point win to keep their record unblemished.

Myles sat on the bench watching all the excitement. He looked up as his mother sat down behind him. "Way to go, son. Those kids responded to whatever you had to say to them in the locker room."

"Not really, Mom. Did you or Dad ever think I was special?"

"Of course, we did. You have a gift many men don't have. You think through solutions, know what to say to help others, and most important, you are willing to sacrifice for the people God puts in your path. That's why the president wants you to take this job. I know you're hesitant about it. That's understandable because of all the things you've had to go through. Your father used to balk whenever I pushed him to help others. Even though he was killed in Vietnam, I never regret telling him to do what he does. From what I understand, you're even more gifted than your father."

"Why do you say that?"

"You have a couple of things he didn't have. First, you have the respect of many around the world. You've been to so many places, and the nationals know you and remember your fairness in dealing with them. Second, you have Willow."

"What does Willow have to do with it?"

"Willow has everything to do with it. She pushes you to be the best you can be. I did that for your father, but like I said, he balked. She told me the reason she never got married was because she hadn't found the man she could trust to be who they were. Just looking at her today, I see the woman she's wanted to be. And it's because of you, son. She'll push you and be there for you so you can be the man you should be. You do a fantastic job coaching basketball. But there is so much more to you than coaching. Willow knows that. Quit worrying about what you can't control. Follow your instincts, take Willow's hand and heart, and find out about our world. Not many have that opportunity. You do."

He stared at his mother and pointed at the boys on the court. "*This* is what I want to do. I want to be a social studies teacher and basketball coach. And watch Willow be an incredible judge. More importantly, I refuse to be an absentee father."

Abigail Bolton sighed.

Myles continued. "How would you like to spend some time with us?"

"You mean it?"

"Yes, we'll take you back to Rosewood whenever you're ready."

"I'd love to. Are you sure it's okay with Willow?"

"Why don't you ask her?"

"Ask me what?" Willow walked over and put her arms around Myles.

"Myles asked me to stay with you all."

"We'd love it. And Grandma Bolton, you can stay as long as you want. Because we're not going anywhere."

Chapter 26

Saturday evening, Willow made up the bed for Myles' mother with Sadie's help.

"Well, thank you, Sadie."

"You're welcome. Are you okay?"

"Yes. Why do you ask?"

"You and Myles haven't seemed to be seeing eye-to-eye this week."

"It's been rough for him."

"One of the reasons I hoped you would take Kyrie and me in is because I could see the family you had. And I wanted to be part of that family. Now, I don't see it."

"What do you mean?"

"When you two are out of sync, the whole family is out of sync. Myles is the person who brings us all together. But he's not doing it. He's conflicted about you, about your job, and his job. He doesn't want to be a basketball coach. He wants to take this job and travel around the world. You see it. Everyone sees it."

"You're right, honey. He does. I can't force him to take the job."

"You have to convince him. Kyrie and I came from a fractured family. Everyone in this house has gone through it. We know what that's like. It sucks."

The two finished putting together Myles' mother's bed. "Thanks, Sadie."

"You're welcome."

"Not just thanks for helping with the bed. Thanks for your insight."

"You're welcome. This is a perfect situation for all of us here. Don't let it end."

Willow walked downstairs and flopped down next to Myles who was talking with his mother on the couch. "Grandma Bolton, your bed is ready."

"Thank you, Willow. Myles and I have been talking about things we should have discussed when he was growing up. He missed all of that."

Willow said, "Sometimes things don't always go as planned."

Abigail Bolton yawned. "I'm tired."

"I'll show you your room," Willow said.

"Thank you. Where does everyone sleep?"

"Brielle and Olivia are sleeping in Brielle's bedroom. The Hunter trio is in Olivia's room. And we're taking the couch." Willow helped Grandma Bolton upstairs to her bedroom. She came down several minutes later. "Would you like some lemonade, Myles?"

"Thanks."

She brought each of them a glass then climbed up on a chair across from Myles and pulled her legs up to her chest. "Whenever I look into your eyes, I see the man I love. I also see a confused husband."

"You'd be right."

Neither said anything for a moment. "Did you really not get into the dating scene for the past five years?"

Willow took a deep breath. "I was tired of what was happening in my life. Felt it was going nowhere. I saw a way to help your mother and particularly Brielle, so I dug into everything about her father I could find. Interesting to find that at eighteen you happened to be in Israel and visited the Wailing Wall. How cool is that?"

"It was. How did you know?"

"I'm an attorney. I have ways of finding information that others don't. Anyway, I continued to dream about finding a man who would or could take me places I'd never been. I knew that someday I would be a judge. That would have been great, but it wasn't everything I wanted. Especially after I met you in October."

She took a sip of her lemonade. "I wanted to be more than just an attorney or a judge. I wanted to have influence. I wanted to spread my wings. So, I'm being a little selfish when I say I wished you'd become head of the presidential task force. I don't want to end up like most people who just stumble through life. I want us to be part of life.

"You've had a lot of people tell you what you should and shouldn't do. I'm sure your mother had plenty to say. The girls have told me how they feel. I will never push you to make the decision I want. But one thing Sadie said to me earlier bothered me. She talked about us being fractured. And, Myles, right now we are a fractured family. We both know what that's like. No matter what you believe, you've always been the person who holds us together. I can't, so, you must. If you don't, we'll end up being no different than the families we grew up in. I don't want that to happen to our family."

Willow climbed off her chair and walked over toward Myles. She kissed him on the cheek. "I do love you, Myles. The decision you make will impact our family more than you can ever imagine. I know that's a lot of burden to put upon you. You've always been my strength and you're the girls' strength."

She climbed onto the couch and snuggled into Myles' arms. "I really enjoy this. But we need to find our own bedroom. Good night." Willow could feel Myles staring at her. "What's wrong?" she asked looking over her shoulder at him.

"I'm not sure anymore. I thought I had things all together upstairs, but I don't know if I do. I was holding you in The Depot after the explosion, and all I could see was you never being in my life again. It was too much for me to deal with. Deep in my heart, I know I should take this job with the president. I've caused so much pain in everyone's life. So much disappointment. And I don't want to do those things to you, ever. I can deal with hearing people say I'm just a social studies teacher, and my wife is a judge, and I'm a disappointment to her. The hard part for me would be my wife thinking the same thing."

"I would never think that."

She snuggled into him. "This is all I need, Myles. For you to hold me tight. We'll give each other strength. You'll never disappoint me or cause me pain. You can't because I'm so deeply in love with you. And it'll always be that way. No matter where we are."

~

Grandma Bolton came down the stairs peering over at the girls sitting on the floor and staring at the couch. She started to say something when Brielle held her finger to her lips. The old woman sat on a chair and joined them in the stare.

"Isn't this sweet?" Olivia said. "I've always said that Willow loved Myles with everything she has."

"You would be right," Grandma Bolton said. "Willow loved him when she and Brielle started finding out things about him. She just didn't realize it."

Sadie glanced over at Brielle. "Do you think they made out on the couch?"

Brielle shook her head. "Willow would never do that with us in the house."

"I agree," Olivia said. "My sister has always said when those two make love with each other, it'll always be special and their own."

Kyrie frowned up at Brielle. "Then why did she ask you about the best places to park?"

Brielle smiled. "You heard that?"

"Oh yes, I don't talk much, but I listen a lot."

"Someday you'll have to ask her," Sadie said.

Kyrie jumped up and shook Willow. Her eyes opened, and she smiled at her. "Why did you ask Brielle and Olivia about the best places to park?"

"What?" Willow's eyes popped open. "That's really not something you should be talking about. You're a bit too young."

Myles still hadn't moved.

Grandma leaded forward. "Willow, I don't know what you did to my son last night, but I can't remember him ever sleeping that soundly."

Willow smiled. "All he did was hold me tight. I needed it. He needed it. We'll be okay."

"Will we go to Libya or wherever?" Kyrie asked.

Willow smiled at her. "Someday. Right now, we're staying here in River Valley."

~

Throughout the day, the family played different board games. It was around three when the doorbell rang.

Willow opened the door and stood aside for the man to enter. "Mr. Swanson, please join us. Can we get you anything to drink?"

"That would be great, Mrs. Cason. What do you have?"

"Water, lemonade, sodas."

"Lemonade would be fine." He turned to the three at the table. "What do we have here?"

Kyrie spoke up. "We're playing Monopoly. And Dad lost again."

"Then it's a good thing he can teach." Mr. Swanson turned when Willow came out.

"What can we do for you, sir?"

"I hoped you two might have a minute to talk."

"Sure," Myles said.

Brielle climbed off her chair. "Girls, Ricardo, let's go upstairs and let them talk."

Once they were gone, Mr. Swanson looked at the two. "This is going to be a tough conversation. First, Myles, the school board is not firing you or anything of that magnitude. It's our superintendent search. The board has decided to hire Mr. Horn. The problem is Mr. Horn wants guarantees that you and your wife will still be part of the school district."

Willow and Myles stared at him. "What's this all about?" Myles asked.

Mr. Swanson swallowed. "There has been some chatter around the community that you've been offered a job with the U.S. Government. That concerned Mr. Horn."

"Why would that matter?" Willow asked.

"Mr. Horn has been very thorough about his research before coming to this community. He's talked to every family member of the boys' basketball team, and they have nothing but high praise for you. For both of you. He's talked to the Native American community down on the south end of town. They are interested in starting racial impact discussions. However, they won't start them unless Myles is part of the program."

"Mr. Swanson, that is not fair to Myles. The superintendent is basically putting a choke hold on him."

"It's not fair. But all three of us know he's the best candidate."

Myles rubbed his face. "So, what you're saying, Patrick, is unless I agree to stay in River Valley, this man will not become the superintendent. Are you sure you want someone like him? In a way he's extorting the community."

"You could say that."

"And the school board is allowing that?"

"We really don't have a choice."

"Yes, you do. Choose the other candidate or wait for a better one. That's not fair to my family, and you know that. They've all wanted to travel around the world with me. I won't be blackmailed into anything. We've all struggled enough throughout our lives."

When Swanson didn't answer, Myles took a deep breath and spoke once more, "Would you mind I take a trip up north to talk to him and see exactly where he's coming from?"

Mr. Swanson's eyes popped up. "That would be wonderful."

Willow eyed the school board president. "You know all of this is highly irregular."

"It may be. But it's been a long time since this community has been able to do some positive things like it has over the past few months. We want to continue forward not progress backward. The students are excited about going to school. The boys' basketball team has brought some excitement to the community. I'm sure the girls' team will be there soon. A wonderful atmosphere we want to continue."

"I'll take some time on Monday and Tuesday to run up and talk to him."

"Thank you. Maybe hearing firsthand from you would be beneficial for the community. That means you're staying—"

Willow interrupted, "He never said that."

~

The next morning as Myles drove Willow to the courthouse, the car was uncomfortably silent. Finally, Willow spoke up. "What do you think of this Mr. Horn situation?"

Myles responded, "It's the school board president trying to find out if we're staying."

"Why would he lie?"

"He didn't lie. Let's just say he stretched the truth. Mr. Horn probably asked a simple question, and it spooked the school board."

"I hope it's that simple. Anyway, I need to hurry. Busy couple of days. Again, thanks for coming with me. Be safe." She reached over and took his head into her hands. "I love you deeply, sweetheart. Drive safely to North Dakota. Watch out for buffalo."

"I love you also."

Chapter 27

Harriet smiled as Willow walked in. "Judge Townsend would like to talk to you as soon as you have a moment."

"I'll head up there now." Willow started the climb up the stairs to the third floor. She stopped by to say hi to the clerks as she always made a point to do.

"The judge is waiting for you, Willow."

"Thanks."

Willow knocked on the door. "Come on in, Willow," he said.

"How did you know it was me?"

"Saw you as I came out of the men's room."

"Got ya. What can I do for you, sir?"

"What have you decided about taking over as district judge?"

"I believe I'm going to take it. But I want to talk to Myles once more tonight and let you know in the morning."

"Okay then. On today's court docket, I see there are several cases related to meth usage and sales. Did you know this was happening in the area?"

"Every once in a while, meth comes up. But recently it has been increasing. Mostly high school kids."

"I see three of these kids are Native American youth. Is there something happening with them specifically?"

"I can't really say. I don't know any of the names appearing today. I'll have a talk with Sheriff Watkins and see what he has to say."

"Great. Now about the country prosecuting attorney situation. My understanding is you have talked to Gabrielle Drayton about the position. I've worked with her many times in East River. She'll be a wonderful addition. I know you haven't made your final decision, but I'd advise you to invite her up here this week if possible. It looks like the caseloads are getting heavy. I want to acclimate her to what's happening here."

"I'll talk to her tonight." Willow worked through the misdemeanor cases in the morning. She took a break for lunch and headed down to the school to have lunch with the girls. On the way in, Principal Newcombe stopped her.

"Hi, Willow. How are things going?"

"Good. Yourself, Alexandria?"

"Busy. You can relate to that. Have you heard from Myles?"

"No, I don't expect him to reach Washburn until early this afternoon. He left right after he dropped me off. Anything I can do?"

"Yeah, can you teach social studies?"

Willow laughed. "I can oversee his government class later this afternoon."

"Would you do that?"

"Sure. I can talk to the kids about the court system."

"Wonderful, the class is the second to the last period of the day. And if you're really nice, I'll let you handle his psychology class the last period of the day."

"Sure, I can do that. I'm going to go join the girls for lunch."

"It's nice you take an interest in the girls. I wish more parents would come and join their kids for lunch."

"Not many have the opportunity to join them because of work schedules."

"True. Again, thanks."

Willow hurried toward the lunchroom and grabbed a salad. She scanned the area for the girls. Their table was full. She looked for another place to sit and saw a couple of young girls sitting by themselves. "Can I join you two?"

"Sure. You'd be the first who'd want to sit with us," the older girl said.

"I'm Willow Cason." She stuck out her hand.

"The basketball coach's wife?"

Willow smiled. "Yes, ma'am."

"Did we say something funny?"

"No. No. Usually it's the other way around. They know me as a county prosecutor before they would Myles as a social studies teacher and coach."

The young lady nodded. “High school students see your husband as something more important to them than a prosecutor. He cares about us. Lawyers just want to put us away.”

Willow shrugged. “I understand.”

The older girl took a bite of her lunch. “My name is Sonya, and this is my younger sister, Jonie. I’m a junior. She’s a ninth grader.”

“Nice to meet you. I usually sit with my husband, but he’s not here today.”

“We know. We see you two every day. It’s so cool the way you intermingle with your husband and the girls. I wish our parents would do the same thing with us.”

“I’m sorry. Sometimes parents get so busy.”

“Ma’am, you’re always busy. You’re the county prosecutor. But you are everywhere with your husband and still have time to be at your daughter’s and husband’s basketball games.”

Willow nibbled on her salad. Once she finished, she commented, “Our children are our priority.”

“I’m glad to hear that. Clovis was telling me you needed help at the county attorney’s office,” Sonya said.

“Yes, I do. What are your plans?”

“I’d like to be an attorney someday. I know it’ll take time.”

“Well, I’ll talk to the principal. If it works out, you can join me for a couple of hours in the courtroom.”

“I would love to. Thank you.”

They all looked up when they heard Brielle’s voice. “Mom, I didn’t see you come in.”

“Been enjoying lunch with Sonya and Jonie. They are a wonderful couple of girls.”

“Can I sit with you?”

“Sure,” Sonya said.

A few moments later, a few other kids came over and joined them. Willow jumped up. “I’m sorry, but I have to get back to the courthouse. I’m going to be handling a couple of classes for Myles this afternoon. Government and psychology.”

Brielle jumped up and gave her mother a hug. “See you soon. Is Dad okay?”

“Haven’t heard from him. I’m sure he’s okay.”

Willow hurried back to the office. She still hadn’t heard from

Myles but she realized he wouldn't arrive until before three. After finishing her court work, she told the ladies goodbye, and headed to class. Her first class was government. She scanned Myles' desk for notes or lesson plans. Nothing.

She looked in his drawers and pulled out a piece of paper. On it he had a made of list of pros and cons. At the top of the pro list was her name in bold letters. With a smile she read the con list and noticed the one listed first: *Couldn't save them.*

Willow stuck the list back in the drawer when the first students came in. Then more came spilling in with different reactions to her presence.

"Nice ass," a voice said as she wrote on the board. Willow whipped around.

One of the Native American boys spoke, "Show some respect, Nathaniel. Especially to Mrs. Cason."

Willow looked at the list of students she recovered from the podium. "Randall, is it?"

"Yes, ma'am."

"Thank you. I'll take over now."

She turned to the class. "Nathaniel's comment is a terrific way to start today's government class. Or I should say an unethical way to start the class. Sexual harassment is a grave concern in South Dakota and in other states. For some workplaces it means automatic termination. In class here it means providing an understanding of just what sexual harassment means. From a county prosecutor's point of view, which I am, or even a judge's point of view—either way it doesn't go over very well. More importantly, if my husband heard anyone say something like that...well, you can ask a man who's serving time in the state penitentiary right now what happens when you try to harass a young woman."

Willow sat on the side of the desk. "Be truthful to me, Nathaniel, why did you say I had a nice ass? Is it because I'm a woman?"

Nathaniel hesitated. Willow stared at him. "I want to know. Please tell me."

He looked at his feet. Willow climbed off the desk. "My guess is he said it because of my looks. Now if I was some chubby, checkered women, my guess is it wouldn't have come out that way. It may have been derogatory. So now not only are we dealing with sexual harassment; we're also dealing with the looks of a woman."

Willow took a deep breath. "Women don't have to put up with derogatory comments about their personalities or their bodies. And a woman sure doesn't have to have sexual intercourse if they don't wish to. In fact, in a court of law, that is considered rape. And it's just not for women. If a man chooses not to have sexual intercourse, it is also considered rape."

She studied their rapt faces. "We could discuss the issue more, but today I'm going to talk to you about my work in the county court system."

After the bell rang, Nathaniel stopped by the desk. "I'm so sorry, Mrs. Cason."

"Forget it, Nathaniel. Always think before you act or speak."

Nathaniel scooted out of the classroom. Several minutes later the next class came in for psychology. Olivia stopped in front of her desk. "Some of the kids said you were teaching last period and put one of the boys in his place."

"Wow, it didn't take long for that to spread. I told them not to say anything."

"They didn't say who it was. Just someone had said something about your ass."

"I hear that all the time. I'm so used to it. But not from high school kids. How do you deal with it?'

"I don't have to worry about it."

"Why?"

"Come on, big sister. They're afraid of Myles. They just didn't know you were Myles' wife. Everyone knows now."

"Ugh. High school."

They both turned to Brielle's voice. "Wow, Mother is actually teaching class. This should be interesting."

"What have you been talking about in here?"

"Psychology." Brielle grinned.

Olivia added, "Cognitive theory."

"You've got to be kidding me."

"Nope," Brielle said.

The rest of the students came in. "Mrs. Cason," several of them said.

"I'm sure many of you are shocked my husband isn't here today. I have a surprise for you. You're going to tell me what you know." They all looked at her confused. She smiled. "We're going to break up into four teams and play Pictionary."

"What?" a couple of kids said.

"Yes, Pictionary. I have a list of words related to cognitive theory. You're going to draw them on the blackboard, and the team who gets the most answers correct is the winner for the day." Willow divided the students into four teams. "Let the games begin."

After class, she headed toward the entrance. Principal Newcombe stopped her. "How'd it go?"

"Not too bad. Decided to play Pictionary in psychology class because I know little about cognitive theory. I used terms associated with the theory, and they had to draw it on the board. It was comical at times. I could tell they took something from it."

"Did a boy make a sexual harassment comment toward you?"

Willow sighed. "I never took it as that. He made a stupid comment."

Principal Newcombe studied her. "Since you don't have an issue with it, I won't press it."

"Thanks, Alexandria. I need to hurry to the courthouse."

"Again, thanks for your help."

"You're welcome."

The cell phone rang as Willow was halfway to the courthouse. "Sweetheart, you're alive."

"Yep, just arrived. It's cold up here. I've been invited to supper with the Horn family this evening. He was surprised I was here but was glad we had a chance to sit down and chat. Mr. Horn has a couple of concerns he wanted to address with me about the school district. I shouldn't be the one answering his questions. The school board should."

"Maybe he trusts you to give an accurate description of what's happening?"

"I've only been here three months. Four months."

"Ask me what I did today?"

"What did you do today?"

"I was the teacher in your two last period classes."

"Wow. You're a talented woman. I hit the jackpot when you

said yes."

"No, dear. *I* did. I'll tell you all about it. Will you please call me later?"

"I will. Love you."

Chapter 28

Myles rang the doorbell at Garrett Horn's house in a small community outside of Washburn, North Dakota where Horn was the superintendent in the Groveton School District. A young boy answered the door.

"Good evening, sir," Myles said. "Is your father home?"

"Are you the man who is supposed to dine with us tonight?"

"Yes, sir. I'm Myles Cason."

"My name is Adam Horn. And you don't have to call me sir. You can call me Adam."

"Okay. Adam."

They both turned at Garrett's voice. "Come on in, Myles. Nice to see you again," he said shaking his hand. "You've met my son, Adam. This is my wife, Lydia, and our second son, Elijah. And this is our home."

"Nice to meet you, ma'am. A lovely home you have."

"Thank you, sir," Lydia said.

"Please call me Myles."

"Okay, Myles. You're just in time. Supper is being served. Please join us."

Myles followed them into the dining room where a long oak table was covered with steaming platters of food, salad, and Jell-O.

"Mom makes the best beef stew in the world," Elijah said. "I'm the youngest. I'm eight. Adam is the oldest. He's ten. My father is forty-three. And mother is—"

Lydia intervened. "Sweetheart, I don't think Myles is concerned about our age."

"Oh, I thought he may be."

"Thanks for the info, Elijah. I'm actually thirty-five and my wife is thirty-three."

"You have a wife?" Adam asked.

"Sure do. Best thing that ever happened to me. Here, I'll show you a picture of her." He handed her picture to Adam who passed it around to his brother and mother.

"Wow, she's beautiful," Adam said. "But not as beautiful as my mother."

This put a smile on Lydia's face. Myles noticed it. "I would say not. I hope Willow is as beautiful when she turns forty-two."

"How did you know?" Elijah asked.

"I just guessed."

"Well, you'd be right," Lydia smiled. "And thank you for the compliment. Let's eat."

The Horns said grace before they started eating. Lydia dished beef stew onto the boys' plates. "Myles, please hand me your plate?"

She gave him two heaping ladles of stew. He took a bite. "Wow, this is wonderful. Can I have the recipe to give to Willow?"

"Surely."

Once supper was completed, Lydia sent the boys off to do their homework. She started to clean off the table. "May I help? I do it a lot at home because Willow's busy."

"Thank you, Myles. I can handle it. What does your wife do?"

"She's a county attorney. But she has been asked to be the judge in our district."

"What an honor! When does she start?"

"She hasn't said she'd take it yet."

"And why not?"

"Lydia, don't be a Budinski."

"I'm sorry, dear. I didn't mean anything by it, Myles."

"None taken. Let's just say her husband is having a tough time adjusting to everything."

"I see," Lydia said. "Sometimes men can't handle a woman making something out of herself."

"Lydia," Garrett said sternly.

Myles laughed. "It's okay, Mr. Horn. I'm ecstatic for my wife. It's just I have an opportunity, and it makes it difficult for the both of us. But we'll figure it out."

Garrett stood. "Myles, how about you join me in the den?"

"Would love to. Mrs. Horn, the meal was wonderful. Thank

you."

Once in the den, Garrett glanced up at Myles. "I'm sorry about that."

"Don't be, sir. She's right. I want her to take the job, but the president wants me to run a task force that works in other countries to help with economic development, relief for typhoons and hurricanes, etc."

"Sound interesting. How did this all come about? And why were you chosen?"

"My father is the president's cousin. He was killed in Vietnam, and one of his last wishes was for his cousin to start this task force if he should become president. He did, and he wants me to run it because he believes I'm the man who could do it."

"I don't know much about it except for what you've told me, but I believe you could do the job."

"Thanks."

"I'm sure your wife becoming judge makes it difficult for you. Why would a judge marry a lowly schoolteacher?"

Myles laughed. "Heard that and many other things."

Garrett grinned. "Same here. My wife is the president of the local bank. And she does an excellent job. She hears all the time about teachers who get three months off during the year. 'What kind of job is that? And you're married to that man?'"

"It sounds like you don't have that man's ego that everyone talks about."

He laughed. "Nope. Neither do you. Despite what people say, I believe we have a high calling helping students make something out of their lives."

They turned as Lydia brought them out glasses of cranberry juice. "Thank you, ma'am," Myles said.

"Thanks, dear." He turned to Myles. "I'm not sure why you're here."

"I'm kind of apprehensive about this conversation that we're about to have."

"What do you mean?"

"This is probably a conversation the school board members should have. They're excited about you coming to the school district if that is what you choose to do. The school board president stopped by our house yesterday and asked what my plans were for the future and—"

Garrett laughed. "I asked a simple question as to what your plans were in the future. He did seem concerned that would be a deal breaker if you weren't part of the program. Myles, I never meant it as to whether I would take the job or not. But it does bring up a concern to me. Is the man being truthful or finding ways to manipulate what he wants?"

This time Myles laughed. "That's the furthest thing from his mind. The River Valley School District's former principal was involved with some shady dealings with high rollers in the past. The school district is starting to rebound, and he just wants to continue that trend."

Garrett rubbed his jaw. "The bombing devastated the community. At least thirteen killed. Sad all the way around. The community is rebounding."

"It is. Now that we have that question settled, you said you had a couple of concerns you would like to address."

"I was really intrigued about your question on race relations. Could you elaborate on it?"

"In the lunchroom one day I had three members of the same family sitting at our table. One parent in jail, the other dead. The children had nowhere to go, so we kept them until their relatives could be found. A couple of boys came by and made racial comments. My daughter, Brielle, stepped in and a Native American boy knocked the boy down who made the comments and was ready to punch him when I intervened. The boy who intervened and the high school principal both mentioned they had talked to the previous superintendent about starting a race-relation group. The principal asked if Willow and I would head that up."

"And?"

"It's still in the works."

Garrett took off his glasses. "Interesting. Another thought I had was test scores. Looking at the test scores in the school district, it seems that many of our students score below the statewide goals. Do you know why that is?"

"I can't answer that. Principal Tuthill told me the same thing when he hired me. I've made efforts to convince the students to be more involved in their education. I've found it helps when you build a relationship with them."

"I've seen that firsthand."

Myles looked confused.

"The boys basketball game we attended in Bluffton. You and I both know Devin Bush could have found a way to get the final shot. But you made it a point to give Michael Papport the ball."

"Why would you travel all the way to the southeast corner of South Dakota to watch a basketball game?"

He smiled. "I have colleagues who graduated from the school and attended USD. They invited me down. Personally, I had hoped you would beat them. You did it to help the boy."

"More importantly, for those group of kids who come to every game to cheer Michael on even if he didn't play a minute. He and those kids were on Cloud nine for a week."

"I can imagine. Well, I'll be candid with you. I'm not sure if I'm going to take the job. There still are some things I must work out in my mind, But I do know one thing. You'll never be just a teacher or a coach. You're more than that. And that's what school districts need. Those boys on that basketball team rally around you because you provide them hope. And that's what a teacher can do for students. Provide them hope that there is something better for them after high school. I'm sure Michael Papport will continue to work hard to be something because you gave him a chance. That's what you seem to do. Give those kids chances. I'll never tell you what to do with your future, but if you think being a teacher is just another job, you're nuts. Not everyone can connect with students. Especially students in today's world. You're one of the few that I've seen who can really do that and make it mean something."

"Willow has said that also. She's just afraid it won't be enough."

"Maybe. Maybe not. You and your wife will have a wonderful life no matter what direction life takes you. Just realize that you have done some good for these kids. And at that age, they need guidance. Many parents provide guidance, but someone else's voice will help them realize what their parents have been saying all along. Other times those kids have only the teacher."

Myles took a deep breath. "Thanks for everything tonight. I realize one thing after our conversation. You have a decision to make also, and you would help River Valley immensely if you come there. And at this time, they need that leadership that isn't being provided. The principals try their hardest, but it's just not enough."

"I haven't had a dinner where I've learned as much as I did tonight."

Myles made his way to the small bed and breakfast in town. It was close to ten when he finally was settled. He called Willow.

"Hey, sweetheart, how'd it go?"

"Enlightening. The guy has questions about the school district, but if he does decide to take it, he'll be good for the kids."

"Oh. What was it with the school board president?"

"Blown out of proportion. Garrett asked what our plans were out of curiosity. And the school board members took it to mean if we weren't there, he probably wouldn't come."

"Wow. It doesn't surprise me. I see it all the time in the courtroom."

"About that. You told me I should take the task-force job. You should really take the judgeship. You're a natural."

"You mean you'll be okay playing second fiddle?"

Myles laughed. "For you, yeah."

"Sweetheart, you'll never be that. You have so many gifts. I never really realized that until I taught your two classes today. In psychology, you helping the kids understand cognitive psychology. Cognitive psychology? I had to look up the definition to know what it meant. So, all I did was let them play Pictionary using words dealing with cognitive psychology. Some of the drawings were very interesting."

"What?" Myles laughed. "I've lost them now."

Willow laughed. "Think that's bad? I got picked up by a high school boy in your government class."

"Nathaniel."

"How did you know?"

"He's always trying to pick up girls in class. They're smart enough to realize he's a lot of hot air."

"Yeah, he said I had a nice ass. I used it to discuss sexual harassment in the workplace. Your principal was concerned about it."

"I take it you weren't."

"Very inappropriate, Myles, but I don't want to ruin a boy's life just because he made one stupid comment. Besides, I've heard that comment so many times. The only one I ever care about is when you say it. But Principal Newcombe was concerned even after I told the kids this stays in the classroom. She's going to let it slide because I didn't press it." Willow stopped for a moment.

"Lemonade?"

"Yep, surprisingly good. But I'm also sitting here on the couch with your t-shirt on—nothing else."

"Wow."

"I know. And I'm sorry. No, I'm not really. Anyway, back to Nathaniel. The boy stopped by tonight to apologize. He talked to the principal about what he had done. The two had a talk. He actually suggested he would stop by and apologize. After he was gone, Olivia and Brielle said he probably got dumped on by the students in the school. No one can do or say anything to our daughters. And that now includes their mother. Some kind of code to protect the women in your family. I have no clue what that's about."

"Micah told me the same thing. He said I had given him a chance. And many of the kids an opportunity." Myles took a deep breath. "It's funny. Mr. Horn was at the Bluffton game and mentioned Michael making that final shot when he knew Devin could get open. Figured me out."

"Yeah, you care about those kids. That's what makes you a wonderful teacher. But your mother believes you're a natural to help the president."

"Do you believe that? Honestly?"

"Yes, I do. And I'll be fine with it. All I've ever wanted to be is your wife and the mother of our children. I love you sweetheart. Always remember that."

"You always say that."

"And I always will because you are my everything. My dream."

"I love you too, sweetheart. And I always will. Good night."

"Good night. Please drive safe."

"I'm leaving as soon as I wake up so hopefully should be home sometime after lunch."

Chapter 29

Myles watched the boys warm up for their home game against Cloverview. The school was about thirty miles south of River Valley about ten miles west from the Missouri River. The game would signify the end of the first round of opponents. If they won, the team would be 10-0 and in first place in the Wider Dakota Conference. River Valley was also rated fourth in the state ratings.

Myles turned to Mr. Swanson's voice. "I don't know how you did it, but Garrett Horn has accepted the position as superintendent this afternoon. He starts July 1. Just have some details to work out."

"That's good news."

Willow touched Myles' arm as Swanson hurried to speak with another teacher. "Seems excited."

"Yeah, Mr. Horn accepted the position."

"Good. The school district will be fine. And you?"

He lifted her up into his arms and kissed her. Once he sat her back down, Willow tried to catch her breath. "What was that all about?"

"You never gave up on me. My parents, Cadence, many have given up on me."

"No way would I ever give up on you, dear. I've told you many times you're the man I love." She turned to the woman sitting next to her. "I'd like you to meet the new county prosecutor. Gabrielle Drayton, this is my husband, Myles."

"Wow, you're right, Willow. He's gorgeous."

"Nice to meet you, ma'am," Myles said shaking her hand. "I'd better get ready for the game."

Willow reached over and kissed him. "Good luck, Coach."

"Thanks."

River Valley raced to a 15-3 lead after the first quarter. They continued the onslaught and won the game, 89-60. Devin finished with forty-four points and Elroy chipped in with twenty and had thirteen assists.

In the locker room, Myles paced in front of the boys. “Wonderful first half of the season. You guys have worked hard throughout it. I’m proud of every one of you. Game ball goes to Elroy. Son, you’re the first River Valley basketball player to ever have a double-double in points and assists.”

Everyone clapped. “Thanks Coach. One thing.”

“Yeah.”

“Do you mind if I ask Sadie to the dance tonight?”

Myles frowned at him. “As long as you’re kind to her.”

“I will. Thank you.”

He perused the room. “Guys, it’s been tough for you the last few weeks. Wondering whether your coach is going to go or stay. The bombing. Just everyday life. I wanted to tell you I’m proud of you.”

The boys beamed.

“Go enjoy yourselves. You earned it. No practice until Thursday.” Myles walked out of the locker room. Willow and the girls were waiting for him.

“Good job, Coach,” Sadie said.

“Thanks. Darndest thing happened in there. Elroy asked me if he could go out with you, Sadie.”

She smiled. “He did? What did you say?”

“What was I supposed to say?”

“Hopefully, yes.”

“I said yes.”

She reached up and kissed him on the cheek. “Thank you. I have to find Brielle and Olivia.”

“Why’s that?”

“Come on, Dad, I can’t be a disappointment on my first date.”

“Right.” Myles shook his head as Willow covered her mouth. Kyrie glanced up at the two of them.

“Thank goodness I’m only seven.”

Natasha looked crushed. “Did Micah ask about me?”

“No, he didn’t.”

“Oh.”

Myles grinned. “I told him you’d be at the dance. Maybe you would be interested in dancing with him.”

Natasha smiled, reached up, and kissed him on the cheek. “Thanks.” She turned and raced toward Sadie.

Once she left, Willow burst out laughing. “I’m sorry, sweetheart. Everyone has to ask your permission to date in this school.”

“I guess so.”

Willow glanced down at Kyrie and Tabitha. “What do you think? Should we ask your dad if he’ll escort us to the dance?”

Ricardo held out his hand. "I will for sure."

Kyrie smiled and glanced up at Myles. “Well, Dad?”

He reached down and picked her up. “Come on. I’ll be with the two prettiest girls in the whole school district.”

~

Later that evening, Myles and Willow relaxed on the couch. “The girls had a wonderful night. Even Kyrie was excited to dance with her father.”

“Yeah, they had fun. It’s probably the right thing to do.”

“What’s that? Dance with them?”

“No stay here and remain a teacher and a coach.”

Willow probed his eyes. “Are you sure about that?”

“Why do you ask?”

Willow took a deep breath. “Myles Hunter Cason. You’re doing this for me. And I love you for it. But when I taught those two classes, I realized something more.” She snuggled into Myles before she spoke once more. “I walked by other classrooms. For one the teachers didn’t have the command of their students in the classroom like you have. Even when Nathaniel said my ass was nice, one of the students jumped down his throat. If he wouldn’t have, the others would have. They came there expecting to learn something. In my case, they got to learn how to draw.”

Willow sat up and ran to her bag and pulled out her cell phone. “I took some photos of their creations.”

“What is that?”

“The term ‘cognitive behavior.’ And here is patterns of thinking. And finally, depression. The kids caught on quickly.”

“It shows depression. Patterns of thinking looks like a computer diagram.”

"It was so cute how hard these kids worked to persuade their peers to find the right word. The point is they were receptive to my different teaching style."

"I thought about what you said about Mr. Horn and Michael Papport. He's right. Devin kept himself open all night long. You allowed another boy to be the hero for the evening. You did that with Joshua Tuthill. God rest his soul. And Devin and Brody, along with Micah and others. Honey, you're helping these kids find out who they are. That's why here is where you belong. Where *we* belong. You can help kids in the classroom. Hopefully, I can help poor souls on the bench as a judge. If it's okay with you, I'll have Judge Townsend swear me in on Friday."

"All right with me."

"You and I will always talk about everything. That's what we've done and that's who we'll always be. I'll never make a decision that will impact both of us and our family without consulting you first. And that's what I'm doing. You do the same thing."

"Yeah, you're right. Go for it, girl."

She reached up and kissed him on the lips. She moved his hand down toward her breasts. "It's okay with me if you unfasten these buttons and reach underneath my shirt." Willow buried her head in Myles' chest when the light came on.

"Sorry, Mom, Dad. I came down for a drink of water," Brielle said. She stopped and gazed at the two. "Wow, it sure didn't last very long for you to change your mind, Mom."

"What? Why are you blaming me?"

Brielle and Myles laughed. "So, it was you, Mother?" Brielle said vanishing into the kitchen.

Willow buried her head into Myles' chest. "I'm not in the mood."

Myles lifted her up and kissed her passionately.

"Whoa."

Myles turned to Brielle. "Please turn off the lights when you go to bed."

"Sure thing, Father. Good night."

~

The next morning Willow strolled into her office. "Good morning, ladies."

"Good morning, Willow. How are you feeling today?"

"Wonderful." She smiled. "Harriet, could you join me in my office for a moment?"

"Sure thing."

The two walked back toward her office. Once inside, Willow closed the door.

"Have a seat, Harriet."

"Yes, ma'am."

Willow sat across from her. "Myles and I have decided to stay here in River Valley. Meaning I'll become the next district judge."

"Congratulations. I'm so happy for you and so proud of you."

Willow was stunned. "You are?"

"You've done so much for us here in this courthouse. In this office. I couldn't be prouder of anyone in the position you're in."

"Thank you. What it also means is I want you to join me upstairs. You've always been here for me during the good times and especially during the tough times. I would have never made it through without your ear and advice. Especially with Myles. You told me to go for him. And it's the best advice you've ever given me. Thank you. Now, I'm asking you to continue down our journey. It would mean your own office and a pay raise. Something you've deserved for a long time."

The older lady appeared to be stunned. "I don't know what to say."

"At least think about it."

"Of course, I'll take the job. Thank you for considering me."

"There is no question I would consider you, Harriet. Thank you for being there with me."

Willow made her way up to Judge Townsend. She knocked on the door. He answered it.

"Willow, please join me."

"Thank you, sir."

"What can I do for you?"

"Myles and I have talked about it. We're staying in River Valley. I'd like to accept the job if it's still available."

"It's always been yours. I was just waiting for you to say yes."

"Thank you, sir. I'm bringing Harriet up here with me."

"Harriet?"

"Yes, sir. She's been with me since I started. She'll be a

wonderful addition."

"So be it. When do you want to get started?"

"Friday, if possible."

"We'll make it work. I'm so happy for you. And you'll do fine. I'll set everything up. You'll be sworn in first and you'll then swear in Gabrielle right after."

"Thank you."

Chapter 30

Friday morning, Willow glanced up as Myles came out of the bathroom after taking a shower. He plopped down on the couch next to her.

"Good morning, dear."

"Good morning."

She winked at him. "Maybe you could take this blanket off of me and we could fool around a bit before we go our separate ways."

"Nope, don't have time." He laughed at the pouty look she gave him.

"Very rarely do you turn me down. But that was a direct hit."

Myles took Willow into his arms. "I would love to spend time making love with you, but we both have several things to do this morning."

"For instance?"

"I have classes to teach. You have to go to Kyrie's classroom for her show and tell."

"Shoot." Willow jumped off the couch and headed toward the bathroom.

~

Myles was eating lunch with Brielle, Olivia, Sadie, and Natasha when Willow came in with her salad. She sat down next to Myles and kissed him on the forehead.

"How'd the show and tell go with Kyrie?" Brielle asked.

"I was a hit."

"Why would you say that?"

"They asked me so many more questions than the others."

Myles glanced at her between bites of his sandwich. "I see."

While they were eating, several students stopped to chat.

Many congratulated Willow on becoming a judge.

After the kids left, Willow turned toward the girls. "What's this all about?"

"Come on, Mom. You're a hit in the school."

Olivia added, "You've swept way past Myles in popularity."

Everyone laughed. Mrs. Newcombe walked by. "Myles, can I talk to you?"

"Sure, ma'am."

He kissed Willow. "See you later."

Once he was gone, Willow glanced at the girls. "I wonder what that was about."

"Who knows?" Brielle said. "Seems those two have been talking a lot today. She actually called him out of the classroom this morning."

Willow glanced at her clock. "I should go back to work. See you three later."

"You bet," Olivia said.

~

Willow dashed into her office. "How was lunch, Willow?" Harriet asked.

"The salad was good."

"What is it about you and the salad at the school?"

"It's not the salad. It's just being there with Myles and the girls."

"I know, dear. Those girls love you."

Willow picked up her cell phone. She glanced at Harriet. "Excuse me."

She headed toward her office. "What is it, dear?"

"Can you stop by my classroom at three?"

"Sure."

Willow worked for another hour before she wrapped everything up and headed out of her office. The office was empty, which was surprising. She over to the school and slipped into Myles' classroom. He was sitting at his desk and looked up when she walked in. "I'm here," she said sliding into a chair near the desk. "Have I been sentenced to detention with the handsome social studies teacher?"

Myles laughed. "I have something special for you."

"Well, what is it?"

Myles handed her a wrapped item. She sat on the corner of his desk, unwrapped the item, and held a desk set engraved with the words, "Judge Willow Cason."

She wiped away a tear. "This is so special, sweetheart. Thank you." She leaned over and kissed him on the lips.

Myles stood up and took her hand. "Ready to head home?"

"No practice tonight?

He didn't say anything. The two walked past the gym. "What's going on in there?"

"I don't know. Let's check it out."

The two walked inside the gym. The gym erupted when the two strolled in. Willow peered up at a stage where Judge Townsend was standing. Her eyes darted to Myles who smiled at her.

"Willow, please join us. Or should I say, soon to be Judge Willow Cason," Judge Townsend said.

Myles put his arms around Willow and escorted her up to the stage. Once she was there, he ducked out of the way.

Willow frowned. "What is this all about?"

"Your husband, the school principal, and members of the boys' and girls' basketball team wanted to participate in your swearing-in ceremony. There wasn't going to be enough space in the courtroom, so Myles and Alexandria talked me into having the ceremony here in front of…it looks like the whole town."

"I don't know what to say."

"Nothing right now. You can say all you want after I swear you in as the district court judge."

"Please, Your Honor. I want my family up here with me."

Judge Townsend smiled. "You heard the judge."

After she was sworn in, Willow swore in Gabrielle Dayton as the country prosecutor.

Judge Townsend grabbed the microphone. "I hear there's a party at the Cason's. Is that correct, Myles?"

"Yes sir."

Myles and Willow held hands all the way to the house.

"Why are we walking, sweetheart?"

"Just because."

"That was a monumental moment for me today. A judge and with my whole family around? I couldn't ever imagine anything like this."

"I'm so proud of you."

"Thank you."

The two strolled to the house in less than ten minutes. Standing outside of the house were Devin and Brody, along with a couple of the players from the girls' basketball team.

"What do we have here?" Willow asked.

Devin spoke up, "Ma'am, Coach asked us to wait for you."

Willow peered up at Myles. He smiled, lifted her up into his arms, and carried her toward the door. Brody and Devin opened the door for the two as he carried her over the threshold.

"What's this about?" Willow asked.

"I never did get to carry you over the threshold after our wedding. Thought tonight would be perfect."

She kissed him gently on the lips. "I love you, goofball."

Once he carried her into the house, everyone congratulated her. Myles set Willow down. Brielle was the first one over to her. "Mom, we're so proud of you. Tonight, is specifically for you. Enjoy."

Willow wiped a tear away glancing at all the people there. "Wow! This is a lot of people."

Olivia hugged her sister. "Big sister, I'm also proud of you. You and Myles have shown everyone in this room that there is hope to become whatever you dream. You're a judge. And that's spectacular."

Sadie and Kyrie handed Willow a gift. "What's this?" Willow asked.

"Open it, Mom," Kyrie said.

Tears streamed down her eyes. "This is beautiful." The medallion read, "Thank you for coming into our lives, Sadie and Kyrie."

Willow placed it around her neck. "It'll never leave my neck."

Kyrie grinned. "Maybe when you take a shower, you can take it off."

"I'll do that."

Sadie stood in the background as Willow hugged Kyrie. Once Kyrie ran over to Myles, Willow turned toward Sadie. "Thank you so much," she said hugging Sadie.

Sadie grinned. "We're not fractured anymore."

"No, we're not, sweetheart."

"I'm glad. Kyrie and I need you both."

"You'll always have the both of us."

Sadie hugged her once more. "Go enjoy yourself, Mom."

Willow saw Myles talking to School Board President Swanson. She turned at Nathaniel's voice. "Mrs. Cason, well done."

"Thanks, Nathaniel. Thank you for coming."

"Least I could do. You helped me a lot this week. Made me think about where my life was heading. I thank you for that."

Devin and Brody joined the two. "We're so glad you are staying here in River Valley," Brody said. "I sure would miss Olivia."

Willow smiled. "She'd miss you also. Thanks for taking care of my family. All of you."

Devin grinned. "Even Nathaniel can attest that without you and Myles, we'd still be a messed-up group of kids. You've given us hope."

The boys joined the girls. Garrett and Lydia Horn joined Willow. "Congratulations. What an honor, Mrs. Cason."

"Thank you, Mr. Horn."

"This is my wife, Lydia."

"Ma'am," Willow acknowledged. "I'm so glad you two could make it tonight. I'm kind of surprised."

"Don't be," Mr. Horn said. "Myles asked the two of us to join you today."

Lydia smiled. "Mrs. Cason, I could tell when your husband visited you mean much more to him than any kind of job. And that includes working with the president."

Willow didn't know what to say.

Mr. Horn smiled. "Lydia always says what's on her mind."

"Thank God, there is someone else like that in the world." The three laughed. Willow spoke up. "I'm sorry about what transpired between the school board, Myles, and yourself. Myles just wanted to make sure you understood where he was coming from."

"Believe me, Mrs. Cason, Myles Cason is a wonderful person. Saw that firsthand at a basketball game. He made a hero out of boy who probably wouldn't have a chance before."

"He did that, sir. He did it more for those kids who support

Michael Papport every game. Even if he doesn't play a minute, they're up there cheering him on. Now they're cheering the team on."

"I could see that. Since you're a judge, that must mean you're staying in River Valley?"

"Yes. At least for the time being. Myles has been struggling. He doesn't realize I could care less about being a judge. I just care about him."

Lydia clasped her husband's arm. "He realizes that, Mrs. Cason. I could tell that right away when we met. You mean more than you realize to him."

"Everything will be okay," Willow said.

"It will. My husband is excited about this opportunity. More than any other assignment he's ever had."

Willow glanced over at Mr. Horn.

"The lady is correct. I'm excited to get started."

Willow took a deep breath. "This community needs a person like you."

Chapter 31

Willow took off her clothes and slipped into Myles' shirt and crawled on the couch. Myles wrapped his arm around her and gently stroked her hair. "What's on your mind? You've been awful quiet this evening."

She smiled up at him. "Just thinking about everything. Let's fix up our bedroom. I really want to have a place of our own again. Now that everything in our lives is settled, let's finish making this a home and prepare for our children."

"Consider it done. Anything else?"

Willow hesitated and took a deep breath. "Myles, I'm going to be a judge. It's always been my dream. But now it's here, I don't want to fail."

"Why would you think you'd fail?"

Myles adjusted on the couch. She climbed into his lap. "I felt that way the first time I stepped onto the basketball court. Joshua Tuthill was a real asshole. Testing me the first time he met me."

"How did you manage it?"

"I remembered who I was. And where I came from. High school kids are nothing compared to what I've seen and dealt with in my life. Willow, you know what you're doing. You have a good head on your shoulders." He took a deep breath. "Why did you fall in love with me?"

Willow gathered her thoughts. "Lots of reasons. The way you looked at me with your blue eyes. They are so warm, so soothing. I needed to see those eyes in my life. You've always made me feel important even if I didn't feel that way. And your strength. Oh, are you strong. Stronger than any man, or for that matter, any person I've ever met."

Myles kissed her on the forehead. "What I love about you is

your compassion for people and your passion for life. You didn't have to drive two hours at midnight to help your little sister. You did it."

"She's my sister," she said.

"Your father or mother or brother didn't care about her. You didn't have to either. The relationship you have with Brielle. She told me once you cared about how she felt. You treated her like your own daughter."

"She's your daughter, but I care for her as if she were my own blood relative."

Myles wrapped his arms around Willow. "You're more than a mother to her. You're a person she trusts to protect her. And you realize that has never happened in her life before you showed up in it. When you sit on that bench, you'll know exactly what to do. You have a heart and will use it for the benefit of a criminal or a victim. I'm not worried whatsoever about how you handle yourself."

"What about what people have to say?"

Myles laughed. "You saw the sign in the Bluffton High School gym about me being a murderer. That was a common theme for me over the years. Everywhere I went. Especially in a Communist country or any country who hates America. Please don't worry about me. You do your job. Like I said earlier. I'll try to keep my kids out of your courtroom."

Willow sat up and kissed him gently on the lips. "You don't know how much it means to me for you to talk to me the way you do. You're so calming. I'm deeply in love with you and always will be."

The two turned when the doorbell rang. Myles opened the door. Randall Two Flaggs stood there, tears flowing down his cheeks.

"What happened?" Myles asked.

"I didn't know who to turn to. I need your help. My sister, Monique, is missing."

THE END

Other books by this author

Freedom Flight

Fight for Survival

Road to Hell

A New Life Begins

Relentless

Missing

Targeted

Author Bio: My wife, Susan and I have two sons, Justin (Kayla) and Jeremy and a grandson, Aiden. Born and raised in South Dakota. I enjoy spending time with family, traveling and putt-putt. I recently retired as managing editor of a small-town Iowa newspaper. I am a former Marine Corps veteran, getting my start in the publishing business in 1981 working for several years on base newspapers. I spent time running my own freelance business. I love writing. I enjoy reading anything and everything. I also love the history of our country and enjoy reading western books, mysteries, and adventure novels, and watching mystery, adventure, and western movies.

Made in the USA
Monee, IL
03 March 2024